Of all the shabby, chicken-wire-between-
the-glass offices in New York City,
she walked into mine . . .

She sat on the couch, her long, shapely legs
stretched out over two cushions, her bare stockinged
feet resting on the edge. *Man alive, what a dame!* Tom
popped open a soda and handed it to her. He pressed
another can against his temple. *She might be beautiful, but she was high-maintenance for sure. He could spot
that one a mile away . . .*

Riley had an incredible physique under his bad clothes.
Marla was used to seeing great bodies, and his
biceps filled up his short-sleeved shirt just as well as
those on her personal trainer. *Not to mention his big,
strong shoulders . . .*

*And the dark wavy hair, not bad. But she'd have to
shoot his barber . . .*

"*Risky Business* is no risk at all,
just surefire fire from the first page to the last.
Love and laughter at its very best!"
Jill Barnett

SUZANNE MACPHERSON

Risky Business

AVON BOOKS
An Imprint of HarperCollinsPublishers

AVON BOOKS
An Imprint of HarperCollins*Publishers*
10 East 53rd Street
New York, New York 10022-5299

Copyright © 2002 by Suzanne Macpherson
ISBN: 0-380-82103-6
www.avonromance.com

First Avon Books paperback printing: December 2002

Avon Trademark Reg. U.S. Pat. Off. and in Other Countries, Marca Registrada, Hecho en U.S.A.
HarperCollins® is a registered trademark of HarperCollins Publishers Inc.

Printed in the U.S.A.

10 9 8 7 6 5 4 3 2 1

With love to James,
the most patient husband on the planet.

THE BIG EASY COMMISSION

Of all the shabby, chicken-wire-between-the-glass offices in all of Manhattan, she walked into mine.

Her thick blond hair swooped over one eye like Veronica Lake. She was all in black, with a quilted satin baseball jacket over her minidress. Her gams were up to there. Man, I mean she was a pin-up queen, outta this world. The rest of her was put together like a factory special—custom-built all around, chassis you could get crazy for, almost six feet of her, I figured. You just don't see a dame like this one every day.

She didn't say a word, just parked herself on my ugly brown couch. As she moved I saw her shiner—a real whopper of a green and yellow bruise around her eye. It could've been a great eye, but it was swollen shut. Her other eye was definitely blue. That blue so pale it spooks you out to look at it.

Why was she here? Why my place? Probably because . . . I covered her district. She must have had death on her mind. I put down my trombone, straightened my tie, got out a notebook, stuck the end of a Bic in my mouth, and pushed my reading glasses back up my nose. They scraped at my skin. Damn glasses, the tape was getting dry.

"Mr. Riley?" she said.

"You can call me Tom."

"Mr. Riley, I need your help."

She was in trouble. I sat up taller and lowered my voice a notch. "Are you in some kind of trouble, Miss . . . ?"

"Meyers. Marla Meyers. No, I'm not in trouble. I need some insurance."

"Oh." I felt disappointed. "I suppose you'd like a term policy? I'd suggest the whole life insurance. It's a better investment in the long run. 'Course, if you're short on cash, the term'll take you a ways. We can always convert it later."

She stared at me with her one good eye until I was finished.

"No, no. Not that kind. My agency sent me here so you could insure my face."

"Looks like it's a little late." I stated the obvious.

"What are you, a comedian?" She leaned back, ran her fingers through her hair, then twisted a hank of it. Nervous type, I guess.

"So what happened?" I hid my irritation at her comment, marveling at her amazing hair all the while. Lady Godiva.

"I had a run-in with a dummy. They seem to think I'm accident-prone."

I took the Bic outta my mouth. "I hope the dummy took the worst of it, otherwise my cousin knows some guys that can make a dummy like that remember it's not nice to hit a lady. Just what line of work are you in, Miss Meyers?"

"A dress dummy, Mr. Riley. I'm a model. Heard of me?"

"Can't say that I have, Miss Meyers. But I'm out a wife at the moment, so the glossies don't hit the house much anymore." I threw that in so she'd know I was single, even though the edge in her voice was less than becoming.

"Oh, I can't imagine why a woman would let *you* go. Well, the deal is, if I smack up my face, everyone loses money. They want some insurance for that. Three million, to be exact. Can you help me?"

I sat up straighter. That was one hefty policy. I ignored her tart remark about my marital status. She shifted toward me, probably interested now that the fact I was single was sinking in. She put her elbows on her knees and leaned her chin in her hands. Too bad she was such a mess; she coulda been a dish.

"We call that a special rider policy. I'll explain the details to you. Who's payin'?" I shuffled in my lower desk drawer for some forms.

"As an act of good faith, I've decided to pay for it myself. It's just to cover their portion of my pay—their commission, you see." She shifted back, and the short black skirt shifted with her. I'd kiss the man who invented Spandex full on the lips if I ever met him. Still, models were a bit on the dumb side for my taste. Didn't keep me from getting uncomfortable in the shorts, though.

"Well, I'll try and keep the payments reasonable, but that's big numbers you're talkin'."

She rolled her eye at me. I didn't see the joke.

"Mr. Riley, I make a million dollars a year," she said. "It's their fear I might not be able to fulfill a contract, which might get them in trouble, see? I know they're being unreasonable, and the amount is probably out of line, but that's the story."

I got more uncomfortable. Rich and gorgeous. So she was a klutz. So what? I noticed her black velvet, open-toe, mile-high heels. Do-me shoes.

"I have a one-thirty appointment, Mr. Riley. Can we rush this along?"

"Well, then, I'll draw up the papers. I'll need—" The phone rang. I couldn't afford a secretary. The home office was running me on the cheap: Granite Insurance, *The Boulder*, my ass. I picked up the phone, put my hand over the receiver, and did my best touchy-feely tone. " 'Scuse me a moment, Miss Meyers." I leaned back in my wooden swivel office chair and put my back to her. "Tom Riley here."

"Where's my check, Tom?" A deep, nasal, Brooklynese accent made my ears hurt. "Ya know you're supposed to have that check here on the first of every month. *Well*, Tom?"

I lost all my warm feelings and felt my heart plunge into my guts. Ouch. Doris. "Yes; absolutely. I was planning on having that delivered to you this afternoon, sir. As you know, I've never failed to do that."

"*Sir*? What, do you actually have a client there? Well, don't blow this, Thomas Riley. I'll expect you to '*deliver it*' in person by four o'clock, otherwise I'll be talking to my lawyer."

"Yes, starting up a new office has been rough, but I think the client base is there, Mr. Billings."

"Sure, sure, more of your games. See you at four." The phone went dead.

"Thank you for your confidence in me, Mr. Billings, I won't let you down," I said to the buzzing receiver. How I could have ever married that woman was a mystery, a total unsolvable mystery. But then I remembered the reason—Max.

I spun in my chair, just in time to see the back end of Miss Meyers slide out the door. That woman must be the queen of her StairMaster, to have such a fabulous backside.

Her card fluttered on my desk as the plug-in fan rotated its direction. Whew, that was a relief; didn't want to lose *this* woman's number.

My heart slowed down a little from its moment of panic. I mopped my brow with an old YMCA towel I kept on the file cabinet. Even in winter this crappy office was stuffy. She had written on the back: *Call me at 3:15 P.M.—555-5151.*

As long as I got the thing written today, that worked. Impatient dame, wasn't she? I shoved my horn rims up again and pulled the baloney sandwich outta my drawer. Lunch is served. I winced. Nothin' worse than baloney with no mustard.

I scrounged in my pocket for two quarters for the Coke machine down the hall. At least I could wash it down with an ice-cold one. Subway token and lint. Shit. I picked up my thirty-pound free weight and did curls with my left while I stuffed the baloney sandwich down my face with the right. Dry. I checked my calendar. Yep, full moon last night, and a blue moon at that. Two full moons in one month—anything could happen.

Suddenly I remembered my "petty cash" stash. I jumped outta my chair and checked the file cabinet under *M* for *maybe*. The old tin box in the bottom of the drawer popped open easy, but it only had a dollar's worth of quarters rattling around in there. Boy, *petty* was right. But petty was enough to wet my whistle. I headed for the soda machine . . . a man with a mission.

Chapter One

HER PROBLEM WITH STAIRS

What a strange man. Marla laughed once, but it hurt too much to laugh again. Her hand went up protectively to her painful eye. It was her own fault for not giving herself more time to do this task, but she sure couldn't wait around while he chatted on the phone. She had to make that one-thirty hosiery ad call. Mr. Riley would have to wait. He could get the paperwork together and get back to her.

Her time with him had been productive in one way—she'd definitely have to put Mr. Riley in her next book. The poor man looked like he was living out some crazy fantasy of being a private detective.

She recalled the scene. His door had those black letters painted on it: THOMAS RILEY—GRANITE INSURANCE. The office must have been decorated once, in the 1940s: black phone, old wooden desk, the metal desk lamp, a curvy sofa with wood and metal claw foot legs. Those claws had a glass ball in each of them. Too bad the moths had won the war with the upholstery.

She *did* like the poster of Hawaii, all dog-eared and dusty. He didn't reek of whiskey or anything, but the place smelled like baloney. Maybe he was living in his office. There was a six-month stack of *New York Times* issues in the corner. No socks drying on the radiator, though.

Then there was the plant. An angel-wing begonia, if she wasn't mistaken. She'd killed a few in her time, and his was huge and well cared for. It just didn't match up with the rest of the picture, that Mr. Riley would baby his begonia. Very odd. The rest of him was so . . . not cared for.

Actually, he had an incredible physique under his bad clothes. She was used to seeing great bodies, and his biceps filled up his short-sleeved shirt just as well as those on her personal trainer, Lars. Not to mention his big strong shoulders.

And the dark wavy hair, not bad, but she'd have to shoot his barber. Her mind whirled with book ideas. Maybe that would be the crime for her next story.

The moon-phase calendar, though. Now, what was that about? Maybe Tommy boy was superstitious.

Marla punched the down button, but nothing lit up. The elevator must be out of order. Geez, it had worked on the way up. She shuddered to think of that: the plunging elevator. That could be the method of death. Her next novel was taking shape, all right.

Great. She and her face had to make it down fourteen flights of stairs. Oh well, Rita was always bugging her about getting some definition in her calves.

She'd better get her Tom Riley details down on paper before they vanished. Marla dug for her notebook and pen in the black leather Chanel tote she had slung on her shoulder as she balanced down the stairs. In the middle of that, her heel caught in the loose stair runner and snapped right off—and down she went.

How predictable, she thought as the last dozen years of her life flashed before her. The floor loomed up quickly. She did a yoga miracle move to keep herself upright and grabbed the rail for all she was worth, bending painfully into the rough stair top.

Her bag flew down the stairs to the landing, scattered six gold tubes of lipstick, three compacts of various types, a brush, a comb, her wallet, her writing notebook, the five black Uniball pens she kept in the bottom, a pair of tennis shoes, and various unmentionable feminine products.

Slumped on the stair, she rubbed her twisted, skinned knee. Maybe Rita was right about her being accident-prone. She'd been a bit of a klutz ever since her body shot up to nearly six feet. She didn't mind being tall, but she'd expected to outgrow gawky.

"Oh God. Miss Meyers! Are you all right?" She turned to watch the insurance guy take two stairs at a time behind her. He got to her, sat down on the same stair, and "steadied" her holding her upper arm, almost tipping her over again.

"I'm fine. Fine. Your *building* should have insurance."

"That's a liability issue. There's probably some kind of coverage if you want to file a claim."

"I'm kidding. I'm not the suing kind. A girl like me can't go around blaming people for her inability to stay upright."

"Now, I think you're being too hard on yourself, there. Here, let me help you up." He stood up beside her.

She gratefully accepted his offer. He extended a big hard-muscled arm to hang on to. My, my, my. Rising, she grabbed on to him and balanced herself with the banister.

She mustered a smile as he stared in her face for

a moment, then switched to look at all her strewn things.

"You stay right here, I'll get your stuff. Hang on." Mr. Riley seemed to make some kind of decision based on her supposed stability, and it wasn't the one she wanted.

She cringed as he started down the stairs. "No. No, please don't!" She gestured toward him, not wanting her feminine pads in his grasp, but underestimated her twisted knee. A pain shot up her leg, and it collapsed underneath her. Before she could utter a gasp, she felt herself falling.

In slow motion, Marla saw Tom Riley turn just in time, take one leap up, and catch her full in his arms. He managed to stay on his feet too. She looked up into his shocked face and saw the most intense chocolate brown eyes she'd ever seen staring back at her from behind quarter-inch-thick glasses. That dark, sexy kind of chocolate. Yum.

"Thanks."

"How about you just stay put, and we'll get back to my office? We can take a look at that knee."

She looked down to see her stocking torn and blood seeping from a scrape. Her leg still hurt like hell too. Damn, there went the one-thirty hosiery commercial. She'd have to call them. Considering her options, she might as well accept a ride from Riley.

She took a deep breath. "Normally I'd decline, but I think I twisted something. So, it sounds like a plan, Mr. Riley. Bend me down, and I'll grab my wallet. I saw a Coke machine in the hall. This calls for some caramel-colored, sugar-shot caffeine. Can I buy you one?"

"I was just on my way to the soda machine anyhow, it's on me. I'll do the grabbing, you hold on tight." Tom bent his knees, and she sensed him feel, then snag something, and scoop up what turned out to be her wallet.

"Can you get that black notebook too? Everything else is expendable." Tom got the notebook without dumping her over. Marla hung on to his neck for dear life and was impressed with his moves. Very impressed.

She leaned against his chest as he climbed up the stairs, the various items clutched in his hands pressed smack up against her rear. It felt nice to have a man be her hero for a change, even one with a poly-blend shirt and a bad haircut.

Most of the men she knew had boyfriends, or were so vain they only wanted her as a trophy— or worse, for her money.

Tom Riley reminded her of the country boys from her hometown in Indiana. He had that solid feel: strong arms, strong jawline, but that natural bronze complexion of the Mediterranean instead of pale and Dutch.

He shifted her weight and his warm arm across her backside created a minor heat wave, a feeling so buried in her it was like creaking an old rusty gate open. She leaned into him. Her head swam dizzy for a minute as she attempted to recover herself. He looked at her funny and kept climbing stairs. The heat between their bodies was enough to melt the snow off winter wheat.

His glasses slid down his nose and she automatically reached up with her index finger to push them back. Their eyes met briefly. She noticed he smelled like Ivory soap, and some other scent. Like a . . . man. She breathed him in. It had been a long time since she'd encountered that essence.

"Thanks," he said. They turned into the doorway, causing her legs to whack into the wall.

"Sorry, sorry."

"I'm okay," she lied. Ouch. Damn, what was she, the bruise magnet of Manhattan? She breathed in through her teeth, then let out a big sigh.

She really was awfully prone to bumps. It wasn't just in the city either. Back home there had been the chicken-coop slip on a broken egg, the ice incident when she tried to skate the duck pond, and too many others to count. Thinking about all of it made her start missing the open spaces in Indiana.

Of course, she didn't miss her stepmother's ranting refrain: *You'll never amount to anything, Marla. Go on ahead, that city will eat you alive.* Funny how Marla wasn't burning in hell as the woman had predicted, hadn't become a prostitute, and wasn't dead in a gutter. Though any of those would have been better than staying home with Ivy.

It was some consolation that all of Ivy's venom was reserved for her, not for her dad. She'd never seen Ivy take on her dad. It was like she had a split personality. Daytime with Marla, Ivy was evil. Nighttime with Walt, she got all domesticated. Reverse vampire.

It must have come as something of a shock when two years ago Dad asked Ivy for a divorce. It did Marla's heart good to know her dad finally woke up. It also did her heart good that she finally told him the truth about Ivy when she went to visit that Christmas. It surely must have facilitated the divorce, but somehow that fact wasn't weighing on her at all.

What she couldn't fathom was the institution of marriage. It seemed to be all screwed up in Marla's head. She kept trying to remember her counselor's advice—just because her dad had made a bad choice didn't mean all choices were bad.

Now that Ivy was gone, she should really go back and visit more. Her dad had sounded funny on the phone last time they spoke. He had some hired help on the farm, but he must be lonely in the empty house at the end of the day.

However, in the ten years she'd been in New York and the eight years she'd been modeling, she'd only managed one serious relationship. Derek Stiles. Talk about bad choices. Just bad. What a bad taste a man can leave on your lips. She could still feel her insides cave in and ache at the thought of it; funny, after two years you'd think it wouldn't hurt anymore.

She just hated being taken for a ride like that, then dumped for this year's nineteen-year-old supermodel as soon as the fateful words *prenuptial agreement* came out of her mouth. Fast as falling down a flight of stairs, she was out on her can. Bastard.

Why were some men such good actors? Derek had said all the things a woman wants to hear, first to get her in bed, and then even to the point of getting engaged. She'd been so wrapped up in the fictional life he'd woven in her head she didn't see who he really was. Smooth as twenty-year-old scotch going down. But the hangover was hell.

She'd take reality over fantasy anytime. It was lucky her current work left little time for a social life. Girls who stayed up to party until three looked like the undead at their nine A.M. photo shoot. She knew it was her clean life and consistency that had helped to finally launch her into the big leagues, and now that she was there . . . well, no fancy-talking New York man—especially a strange insurance man, for heaven's sake—was going to get her all upset again and distract her.

Mr. Riley opened his office door with a reach for the doorknob underneath her that shifted her weight back against him. Her skirt was doing a very fine shimmy up her legs. His hand slid a little on her stockinged thigh.

She felt a flush roll over her, starting from his touch, proceeding up the rest of her body, then straight up to her cheeks and on to her scalp. What in the heck brought all this . . . this *feeling* on in her? Boy, she must have twisted more than her knee, to be lusting after the insurance man a few minutes back. Sometimes hashing over her Derek pain gave her a great way to refocus. Current goal: Get out of Thomas Riley's clutches.

Tom deposited her gently on his couch and dropped the wallet and notebook on the coffee table. Her skirt had done a crawl up her thighs that had him in a hot sweat. He wasn't sure whether to grab it and pull it down while he carried her, or just let it ride . . . so to speak.

Lucky boy. Here he was with one of the city's top models in his arms. She really did feel like an ordinary woman after all, a very sexy, curvaceous

ordinary woman. Holding her against him was
the most pleasure he could remember in . . . well,
a long time.

Tom tried to think about something else. Although she wasn't the thinnest model he'd seen,
Marla Meyers still needed a meal. She weighed
about as much as his neurotic boyhood Irish set-
ter. He'd have to take her to his sister Rosalee's for
a good old Irish-Italian dinner. Tom tried to picture Marla at the Riley family table with all the
nieces and nephews and meddling aunts and sisters. What a laugh. She was probably used to the
fancy china and good silverware crowd.

Grabbing a clean but graying handkerchief out
of his back pocket, he wet it with the last drops out
of the water cooler. "I'll be right back with those
sodas and the rest of your stuff. Here, put this on
your knee and elevate it."

He handed her the cloth and strode out of the
room toward the soda machine. A cold soda
would have to replace the cold shower he needed.

What made her fly down the stairs anyhow?
Man, this dame was an accident waiting to happen. If he was half the insurance man he should
be, he'd call her a preexisting disaster and refuse
to write it up. But his commission off a three-
million-dollar policy was going to be sweeter than
honey on a hound dog, as his Irish grandma used
to say. His Italian grandma used to say something

else more fitting to the Bronx, with hand gestures for emphasis.

He went back to the stairs and stuffed all her things in the black tote bag. For a model, she traveled light. But he could tell expensive leather when he saw it. Mighty smooth. Like a three-million-dollar policy.

After all, rich girls didn't have to set up monthly premiums, Tom mused as he climbed back up the stairs and headed toward the soda dispenser. She'd probably pay the annual up front.

He shot two quarters in the machine, punched the button, and pulled a Coke out of the bin. Then two more quarters and hit the button one more time for himself. Amazingly, the machine worked for the first time in eight months. Congratulations, Tom, you old dog, he thought. This is your lucky day.

Man alive, if he got that money he could quit sweating the first of every month, use his commission as a nest egg, and draw off of it when he needed to.

He'd love to give Doris more money. He'd give her twice as much as the divorce agreement if he had it. He was glad she was using it to keep Max's life decent. He could eat dry baloney and buy his clothes at the Goodwill, but his kid should have a good life. Soccer camp, trumpet lessons, new shoes—that all cost money. He walked back to his office door.

She was still on the couch, her long, shapely legs stretched out over two whole cushions, her bare stockinged feet resting on the edge of the end. Man alive, what a dame. She was just finishing a call on her cell phone. When she put it back in her jacket pocket, he popped open one soda can and handed it to her. The other one he pressed against his temple. Cool down, boy.

"Got a glass?"

"Nope." She may be beautiful, but she was high maintenance for sure. He could spot that one a mile away. Just like Doris. He took a long, cool draw on the soda. It was *real* good.

She took a sip and smiled: a real toothpaste commercial smile. It was the first time she had flashed it full at him that day. Kind of made his stomach twist up funny, like when Sheila Warner used to smile at him in sixth-grade math. Even with her braces, Sheila was the hottest girl he'd ever never kissed. Until now.

"Let's look at that knee." He sat on the coffee table and waited for her to take the cloth off. She removed it; the bleeding had stopped. It was just a minor scrape.

"Can you walk on it?"

She slipped off the couch and tested her legs. Great legs they were too.

"Pretty good. I'll make it. Thanks, Riley. I've been a little clumsy in my life, but I'm not usually *this* accident-prone."

"That's not what your agency thinks, is it?"

"I've just had a run of bad luck. They're being paranoid." She pulled out her black leather Keds, tied them on, then put the rest of her things back in her bag.

He seriously doubted that, but hey, the worst that could happen was the old Granite boulder would lose a few chips, pay up . . . and fire him. What the heck.

"I believe you, sweetheart . . . uh, Miss Meyers," Tom corrected his Bogartism and made his move. "Let's get the thing written up right now." He got to the desk, swept a handful of trash into his right top drawer, and rolled her form in his IBM Selectric typewriter.

"Wow, I didn't know they still made those things." She plopped back down in his client chair.

"The home office hasn't sent me any equipment yet," he lied. "Amazingly enough, I remember how to type." He glanced up as she rolled her eyes. Ignoring her, Tom went full focus on his task, pushing his glasses back in place. He pecked at the keys and shot off questions to her like rubber bullets.

"Age?"

"Twenty-eight."

"That's on the upside for a model, isn't it?"

"Is that on the form?" she said coolly, and removed a long strand of hair from her cheek.

Tom smiled and refocused. "Married?"

"No."

"Boyfriend?" he said quickly.

She stared at him with a wry look.

"Girlfriend?"

"None of the above. Keep yourself on track, Riley."

"How long have you lived in Manhattan?"

"Ten years. I don't see the relevance in that."

"Any diseases?" Tom continued.

"Has anyone ever told you your bedside manner tends to slip now and then?" Marla said.

"Yep." Tom gave her his best smile and kept the questions flying. In twenty minutes the form was signed, sealed, and delivered in his stack. Her check for the first year's premium went directly into his wallet, close and personal-like where he could keep an eye on it.

"That ought to do it. Thank you, Miss Meyers. It's been a pleasure." He picked up the soda can on his left and swigged some down. Later he would buy himself a nice corned beef and an ice-cold beer at Jay's Grill to celebrate. "Can I get you a cab?" he offered.

A sudden wave of panic washed over him.

Doris. He jerked his left wrist up to check the time, flipping a splash of soda clear across the coffee table and straight onto her well-endowed, Wonder Bra bosom. She let out a loud gasp and stood stock-still.

Shit! It was three o'clock. Were those real? Holy shit. Tom grabbed his handkerchief off the coffee table and attempted to blot her . . . cleavage.

"See what I mean? Stuff just happens to me." Marla snatched the cloth out of his hand and mopped at the soda spot. "The cab would be great."

"I'll share it with you. I'm late for an appointment. Sorry about that stain." Tom grabbed his gray suit jacket and her black tote and all but dragged her out the door. Hell had no wrath like Doris kept waiting.

He was too focused on the thought of Doris wringing his neck to worry about the fact that he'd just flung soda all over a supermodel.

Then again, she must think him a complete idiot. And here he was kind of liking her now that she turned out to have a few brains. He probably should have gotten a separate cab for her, just to avoid the inevitable part where she might turn on him for ruining her designer clothes and sue him for the cleaning bill.

On the other hand, he could keep an eye on her awhile longer. She was pretty easy on the eyes.

After he got through taking Doris's crap and playing some catch with Max, he'd return to the office and get the paperwork sent to Granite. Too bad he'd had to hock his fax machine to pay his phone bill. It was scrape up a buck and hit the all-night Kinko's to send to the home office. Just the fax, ma'am. Bob Hayes was going to kill him when he got this policy.

The midmorning light stung his eyes as he lifted his throbbing head off the desk. He reached over and pulled down the blind. Man, he'd made it to Doris's yesterday with one minute to spare. Doris really had a bark, and it was just as bad as her bite.

You'd think since the divorce was *her* idea she'd be a little easier to get along with. Tom could never quite figure what got Doris's panties in a bunch. Guess she was just cranky. Despite her inability to get along with Tom, she seemed to be doing all right with Max, and that was all that mattered.

At any rate, it was all worth it to hang out with his boy and tuck him in for the night.

Memories of the rest of the evening came back to him through a fog. Faxing forms, making deposits. He did remember he managed to stuff a great corned beef sandwich down his face, washed down with four beers. It would have been only two beers if his buddy Pete hadn't shown up. Tom wasn't much of a drinker, so four beers were enough to rattle his body into a mini-hangover.

At least he'd gotten Marla Meyers's check to First Federal last night. Once that was cashed, the home office couldn't say jack. Well, they could, but a deal was a deal. Tom folded his arms and put his head back down on the desk. Someday he was going to quit selling insurance. A little hole in the universe would open up and allow him to slip between financial obligations and leap into some other line of work. Preferably something *out* of the city.

He'd taken over the Fulton Street office with hopes his commission quota would rise. Instead he found himself locked in an overterritoried district with his father's old clients back in Queens dying off. In the old days new members of the clients' families would stay with the same agent and firm. These days people were surfing the Internet for insurance—plus Granite Insurance was a dinosaur. Faxing was their newest skill. Tom pulled on his earlobe and yawned.

The phone rang like gunshot next to his head. He grabbed it quick before it went off again. God, he hated morning, and no coffee yet.

"Tom Riley here."

"Bob Hayes here. What the hell is this De-Per policy? Three million on some woman's face? Riley, you really stuck your neck out here, and I'm gonna chop it off. Rip this thing up. No face is worth that, and you violated about ten procedural directives on top of it."

"Bob, Bob. Relax. If you read the report I sent you, you'll see this is just an assurance to her agency. She's a very successful model. Our exposure is minimal here. She has an investment in keeping her face intact too. Besides, I deposited her check in the transfer account yesterday, so it's too late."

Tom picked a pencil out of the orange juice can Max had covered with paper and drawn stars and rockets on. He sharpened it as he talked, in a tiny blue sharpener.

"Which means you'll be getting me my portion in twenty-four hours, right, Bob? That's a helluva premium there, pal. The big boys will buy you a martini for lunch on this one."

"It'll be the first premium we've seen here in a while, Riley. How the hell did we let you take the downtown territory anyway? Don't answer that; I did it because you used to be one of the best when you worked with your dad, who must be rolling in his grave. Now, *there* was an insurance man. Now that you're on your own, you're a loose cannon. We don't like loose cannons here, Riley. And Riley, we don't drink martinis in Minnesota. We stay sober."

Tom cringed and the blood rose up to his eyebrows. Damn them. Sure, his dad was one of those natural-born salesman. If Tom had had his way he'd be making police detective in some 'burb. Not trying to fill his dad's shoes. God love his dad, but this job was about as boring as they came.

He kept his voice as level as possible. "Well, buy your wife a new hat on your bonus, Bob. You didn't do me any favors giving me the old Fulton office. Maybe you should have told me you had two other offices opening in the city this year."

"The client base is out there. Just turn on some of that Riley charm like your dad used to." Bob waxed nostalgic.

"That was 1965, Bob. It's a new world out here now." He gave up with a teeth-grinding sigh of exasperation. "I have a client coming at eleven-thirty. Gotta run," Tom lied, flipping a pencil between his fingers as he worked to keep his voice calm.

"Not so fast, Riley. We had a morning meeting on this, and the board has a job for you. We want you to devote some special attention to this client. So get rid of your eleven-thirty, because you are going to be spending all your time looking after the insured face of Miss Meyers."

"What? What the hell are you talking about? I have an office to run here."

"You wrote it, you deal with it. We want you with this girl every waking hour. That's her hours, not yours. Did you just get up, man? You sound like hell."

He felt like hell too. He'd had one hour with his head on the desk and had that stale beer and sweat smell on him. They must be kidding about this.

"You gotta be kidding. This lady runs in the big leagues. I own one suit, and I don't think she likes me or it. She isn't going to let me near her."

"According to her agency, she can't work without this policy. According to us, we won't issue it unless she agrees to have you as a watchdog. You could hire her a bodyguard, but it'll be coming out of your own expenses if you do. Bottom line, Riley: We're gonna hold your commission check until you agree to this. And get your fax machine on-line. These calls cost money. We don't like spending money here in Minnesota."

His check! His beloved check that would get his office equipment out of hock, pay his child support for the next three months, and some rent on his cockroach-ridden apartment. Not the check, anything but that. Those cheap bastards. Trying to run a New York office on Minnesota's idea of capital was bad enough. His nerves jumped like a bird taking a ride in the cat's mouth. The pencil he was flipping snapped in half.

"Okay, Bob, you've got my nuts. Quit twisten'

'em. I'll be her shadow. I'll keep her face un-scratched. Consider it a deal. Now transfer my check, Bob. I'm gonna need it."

"Good. Now, the company is willing to toss in an extra bonus after three months. Two grand."

"Three months? Thirty days."

A long silence followed that had Tom's stomach twisting.

"All right, thirty days. I'm a reasonable man. I'll expect a report every week. However, Riley, if she does get hurt during this interim period, we're go-ing to expect your commission to be returned."

Tom smacked his hand to his forehead, giving himself a worse headache. They'd have to find him in an obscure village of Barbados if it came to that. "So long, Bob." Tom slammed the heavy black phone down on its rocker and bolted out of his chair. Coffee. He needed coffee.

"Hi, you've reached the voice-mail service for Marla Meyers. Please leave a message, and Ms. Meyers will return your call as soon as possible."

Tom figured it couldn't be her home number scribbled on the back of her card; that would make him . . . lucky.

"Tom Riley here, Granite Insurance. We need to talk about your policy. And you left your shoes in my office." Tom left his message and hung up.

Her high heels were sitting on his desk, next to

his brand new beloved cup of extra-large take-out java. Tall, black Helmut Lang's, he read the inside label. He toyed with them, picked the broken one up, and bent the shoe back and forth. So rich girls wore out their shoes, too. How did this thing even hold together anyway? There was an obvious separation between the heel and the base. Tom got lost in the aerodynamic properties of her high heels. Fifteen minutes later his phone rang.

"Tom Riley."

"Mr. Riley. Marla Myers."

He got nervous. How was he going to tell her about this unusual turn of events exactly? Better just jump right in there.

"Miss Meyers, my company has assigned me to . . . in essence, guard their policy interests. I'm going to have to . . . uh . . . be your shadow. Yes, that's it, be your shadow and make sure you don't hurt your face for thirty days. Then they will consider you an acceptable risk and we can . . . uh . . . relax."

There was a long silence on the other end.

"So, basically you're telling me they won't insure me without this?"

"That's right." Tom slumped over his desk and held the black receiver away from his ear, waiting for the scream.

"Mr. Riley, what do you think my chances are with another company?"

"Zero. I'm probably the only agent on the planet that would have written this up, Miss Meyers. I don't know what that makes me, but that's my opinion. You asked for it."

"Well, then, there's nothing to be done about it because I can't work without it, and I have to work. We'll set up a schedule. I'm assuming when I'm home you'll be off duty? Or are you planning on moving in here?" Her voice was a little caustic, but even-toned.

Tom was surprised. She was no Doris. Actually, her voice was very low and sexy, even when she was mad. He brought the velvety suede high heel he'd been holding up to his face and scratched his day-old beard against the softness. A really bad and wicked fantasy rolled through his entire body. Mmmmm.

"Riley, you aren't planning on moving in with me, are you?" the sexy velvet voice said.

"Yes, fine. I mean, no. . . . I'll try laying off when you're home, if you promise not to slip in the bathtub or anything." He heard a snort-laugh from her end of the phone. So the dish had a sense of humor after all.

"I'll do my very best if it will give me a few hours of privacy."

"Great. Then I'll meet you tomorrow and just get the kinks worked out. I'm sorry about this, Miss Meyers."

"Not as sorry as I am, Riley. Just try and keep out of my way. I run at a fast pace. I'll see you at eight in the morning at Rita Ray's downtown agency. I've got a major runway show tomorrow and two photo shoots this week."

"Eight?"

"Yes, we get to sleep in tomorrow. Be there on time so I can smooth this over with Rita. Are we clear?"

"Eight. Downtown. Clear. Thanks." He had been reduced to talking in single syllables by the end of the conversation.

"Good. Thirty days isn't forever. I'll see you tomorrow then. Good-bye, now, Mr. Riley."

"G'bye."

She hung up. He put the heavy black receiver back on the cradle. This was a pain in the ass. *She* was a pain in the ass. Probably had a Day-Timer that told her when to pee. She was going to drive him completely crazy. On the other hand, tailing a gorgeous babe like Marla Meyers wasn't all bad. Then there was the money. The lovely money. Damn, he forgot to tell her about the shoes. Oh well, he'd bring them along.

While he'd been talking to her, he had absentmindedly bent back the loose heel. Several small nails had popped out of position. It looked funny, like she must have had the heel fixed once before. Boy, they did a crappy job. He'd have to talk to her about her shoe repairs. The Shoe Doctor was his man. Miracle Joe had saved him buying shoes for three years now.

Tom set down the shoe and took a long drag off his coffee. Eight. Eight in the ever-lovin', snot-nosed morning. He could just shoot himself instead: It would be just as painful, but a quicker death.

Marla punched the off button on her portable phone and laid it back down on the marble kitchen countertop. She ran her fingers up her temples and into her long blonde tresses in a combined gesture of headache and annoying hair. Her life was like a well-oiled machine, and Tom Riley was a piece of gravel in the gears. This was going to be thirty days of hell. Thank God Fashion Week was over and the bulk of the runway shows down to a trickle.

Now, this had to have a positive side. Marla tried hard to turn things around in her head, but the only possible benefit besides the obvious one of getting the insurance company off her case was that she would have time to study this guy and use him in a book. Better than nothing.

She went to work in the kitchen, creating herself a salad with teriyaki chicken strips, sesame seeds, and six different veggies. *Murder Takes a Cruise*. She ran title ideas around in her head as she tossed her special raspberry-flavored oil and balsamic vinegar dressing into the salad. Maybe she could cast him as a news reporter: *Murder on the News.* Her mind kept going back to Riley.

Murder Takes a Snooze was more like it. Considering his boring profession, his lack of ambition, his style oblivion, and his obvious lack of manners, Tom Riley was going to bore her to death. A slow, painful, thirty-day death.

And when would she find time to finish her next Mike Mason mystery, for pity's sake? She poured a tall glass of iced tea out of the pitcher she'd made up that morning and dropped two ice cubes in. She'd only sketched out a basic plot outline at this point.

On that thought, she plunked herself on a chair in front of the dining room table and booted up the laptop. She'd better start stealing minutes where she could.

Balancing her salad on one side and the keyboard on the other, she hunted up her work-in-progress and fingered in a few phrases between bites.

I peered down the black, silent elevator shaft. What a way to go. It wasn't so much the bottom as the moments in between the twelfth floor and the darkness at the end of the ride. Sure, it would only be about five seconds if you used that old acceleration free-fall thirty-two-feet-per-second formula. Still, I'd hate to know it was coming. Quick, with no warning. That was what I wanted in a death.

I straightened up and took a hard look around. I got that feeling like I wasn't alone. That shiver-down-the-back-of-your-neck feeling. I checked the reflection in the hotel hall mirror and caught sight of a black-haired woman in a red coat. There was something oddly familiar about her.

I moved fast, but she had a head start. The stairwell door handle was cold, so she must be in one of the suites. Have to do a room-to-room search for that, and the St. Regis Hotel wouldn't be too pleased. It'd take an hour just to shake down the right suits to ask.

I turned back toward the elevators to think on that and spotted a single long-stem red rose on the carpet. It had a thin black ribbon around it, tied in a bow. So the lady left a calling card. Something about that setup was nagging me. Like I'd read it or seen it before. I decided to hunt up the hotel manager after all.

Marla rolled her head from side to side and noticed her neck was getting stiff. Laptops weren't the best choice for ergonomics, but once she started in, she'd learned not to move to the big computer and break her train of thought. Where you start is where you be. She took a few bites of her salad. Now, Mike Mason, back to the lady in red.

Chapter Two

WE'RE NOT IN KANSAS ANYMORE

"Marla, darling! And how's our black-eyed beauty this morning?" Rita Ray swished over to her, then cupped Marla's chin and examined the offending eye. "It's not too bad. You can get away with it on the runway anyway. Anton can cover it up."

Marla gave Rita a real live hug. Rita's warmth was something Marla just needed to start the day with. "What's this you have on? Can I borrow it?" Marla took Rita's hand and turned her around like a dancer.

Rita took a spin in her blue, purple, and aqua silk ensemble. It made her aqua-blue eyes blossom and her soft platinum blonde hair even more elegant. Her tall, slim figure and well-pampered face defied her fifty years.

"Like it? It's from the new Givenchy line, which is part of the charity gig we are doing today along with three other designers at two o'clock, you know. Of course you know, darlin'. You've never been late in your life, have you?"

Rita's soft hint of southern accent betrayed her Texas roots. Marla's heart went soft on her with a twist of wishing she'd had a mother like Rita.

Maybe if she'd been a boy she wouldn't have this emotional weak spot. Maybe, with a son, Dad wouldn't have felt compelled to remarry. This was silly. Same old thoughts, same old answers. It was her stepmother's voice degrading her for not being the son her father surely must have wanted. Ridiculous.

She was a strong, beautiful woman and could make herself just as useful as a son would have been. Only in different ways.

Marla rubbed lightly on her right temple to sooth her nerves. She was very happy she could send portions of her income to the Centerville Mortgage and Loan for all the farm funds her dad had taken out over the years. That was pretty useful.

If only she had gotten serious about this modeling thing sooner instead of going to college, trying to make money as a writer, and only working side jobs with the agency. Well, at least she could make up for that now and earn as much as possible. Plus her little pulp-fiction habit was starting to pick up at last. Finally the seemingly useless English degree was starting to pay for itself.

"Earth to Marla. Honey, you did get yourself checked out at the doctor, didn't you?" Rita said, peering in Marla's eyes intently.

"Yes, you great clucking mother hen. I'm fine. Take your feathers back to your office. I'm also the recipient of a watchdog that comes with that policy you made me get. He should be here . . . seen a geeky guy in bad clothes?"

"I'm truly sorry about that, Marla, honey, but in case you didn't notice, you've moved up in the last five years and we could really take it in the teeth if you weren't able to meet a contract. I swear we'd have to turn into an escort service if you missed two months of work. The overhead here is giving me the vapors." Rita fanned herself dramatically.

"Also maybe it's not the best idea for anyone to know about him keeping an eye on you. How about we pass him off as an old friend or something? You understand, don't you, dear?" Rita said.

"I truly do, Rita, and I'll try very hard to keep from letting you down. I think this was all a fluke. I'll think of something creative to disguise Mr. Riley's true purpose." Marla took Rita's hand and patted it. "Anyway, I'm going to have my eyes checked next week. Maybe I just need glasses."

Rita patted Marla's hand in return. "Of course, you'd look great in glasses. Or just think, we could do violet contact lenses and dye your hair black"—Marla looked at Rita as her Texas mouth went on rambling—"turn you into Elizabeth Taylor, except you have a foot up on her, and eighty pounds down. Well, we'll keep you the million ways you are, I guess. That Veronica Lake look is always in demand."

"Good, Rita, because I like me this way." Marla gave Rita a peck on the cheek.

"Eeeek!" Rita hissed. "Who is *that*? I better call security." Marla turned around, then cringed at the sight of Thomas Riley.

"Don't bother. He's the new escort, courtesy of Granite Insurance, like I was saying." The two women turned to observe the tall, shadowy figure that slunk through the reception room's glass doors. He seemed to have spotted the coffee urn in the corner, and his whole body leaned toward the scent of java. His legs followed. "Is he Colombo?" Rita looked shocked.

"He thinks he is." Marla smirked, then raised her voice. "Thomas Riley, please come over here."

An audible groan came from under the rumpled gray felt fedora hat. The tan trench-coated figure turned and came toward her, without a sty-rofoam cup in his hand.

"Miss Meyers."

"Rita Ray, this is Thomas Riley. He has been assigned to watch over me for thirty days so Granite Insurance will rest assured I am an acceptable risk."

"Oh, I see. How do you do, Mr. Riley?" Rita gingerly held out her hand, fingers extended, for him to shake. He looked at it and sighed.

"I'm not a morning person, Ms. Ray." He ran his hand over his unshaven chin, tried to straighten his body out, failed, and slumped back into his coat.

"That's for damn sure. Well, sugar, call me Rita." Rita's eyes lifted to a girl across the room, and she gestured to her. "Francine, will you please get Mr. Riley here a great big ol' cup of coffee, please? Regular or black, Mr. Riley?"

"Black."

"Black, Francine.

Rita lowered her voice. "Mr. Riley, we appreciate you lookin' after our star. Let's make you comfortable while everybody gets here. We have some hair and makeup basics to do for the next two hours, then we'll take a limo over to the hotel and put on the finishing touches. I suppose you'll want to be next to Marla all the time, won't you, darlin'? Doesn't every man?"

* * *

Tom took the hot black coffee offered him from a stunning redheaded girl. He sipped it slowly as Rita rattled on about something. He heard, "Call me Rita," something about a limo, and not much more. The redhead put her arm through his free one, which would have been real exciting if he'd been awake. She led him down a hallway into a large room that looked like a giant beauty parlor. Red planted him in a swiveling barber chair. He leaned back and took a good drag off the coffee.

The thaw started somewhere around his hands and crept up to his mouth, then his eyes. The rest would come slower, he knew from experience. He took out his glasses and rummaged for his book.

Marla had come in, shed her coat, and sat in a swivel chair by a bank of mirrors. She didn't have any makeup on at all, and her hair was pulled back in a ponytail. Suddenly she reminded him of his kid sister Kathleen. But then he was still in a partial REM state and lost in his thoughts.

"MAMA MIA! What in the name of all that is holy is Rita expecting from me?"

A voice not unlike Doris's made Tom's nerves jump like a reflex test at his centennial check-up. The voice had on purple velvet pants and a blouse with huge peasant sleeves sporting lace-edged ruffled cuffs.

"His bones are great, yes, but I have three other

girls today. I wasn't aware I would be performing a resurrection!" The ruffled cuffs fluttered in the air. Tom felt seasick watching the motion. He drank more coffee.

"Anton, it's okay, this is my . . ."—Marla's voice lowered—"bodyguard. Sort of. He's from the insurance company. He's here to keep an eye on my face for thirty days."

Marla was a head above Anton in height, and Tom felt a smile crack on his mouth watching her look down at the semi-hysterical man and pat him on the shoulder. Anton bore a striking resemblance to Louis XIV, in hair and attire anyway. He had an Italian accent with a touch of Bronx under it.

"Oh. Well, thank the stars above. Let's hope he does his job, Marla, my little *bambini*, I tire of making your bruises disappear." Anton crossed one arm, placing one hand under his chin like Jack Benny. He eyed Tom, humming.

"But if we have time . . . he is quite a stunner under those clothes and behind that hideous eyewear."

Tom's eyebrows shot up his forehead. He wasn't that asleep anymore. He pushed his glasses back up his nose.

"Listen, buddy, I'm not that kind of guy."

"What kind, Mr. Riley? The kind that's gay? Or the kind that hides his light under a gray felt hat?"

Anton retorted, with a dashing smile on his face, looking Tom straight in the eye and waving his Jack Benny free-arm about.

"Got me there, Anton. I surrender. I'm hiding." Tom laughed and went back to the last half of his cup. Two more cups and he'd be in decent shape. He looked up to see that Marla was around a corner tying a smock on over what now seemed to be just her bra. He must have missed that part.

"I promise Mr. Riley will behave, Anton. Tom Riley, behave yourself or I'll have Anton make you into Mel Gibson in a tuxedo." Marla pulled her long golden locks out from the back of the smock with a sweeping gesture. Tom stared.

"He's already halfway there, Marla. You've lost your eye for a good-looking man. Tsk, tsk. At your age. Now sit it down, dear. We've got your hair, which takes us forever and a day. It's got to be tied up like a geisha today to go with the butterfly gown. Then, of course, you *are* the bride, my sweet." Marla sat as directed, and Anton whipped out a chrome sprayer, wetting down Marla's smooth, wavy locks.

Tom lost interest until a gaggle of tall, lanky girls entered the room and took up his air-space with their bird-like chatter. He'd compare them to munchkins, but they were all at least five-ten. They threw off their tops, which made him pay attention. A rainbow of brassieres, some full, some not, danced around for a few minutes, then disappeared under light blue tie-on coverings. Tom sighed. Fun over.

The crew itself had also entered the room, wearing uniform black turtlenecks. It was beginning to feel like a modern dance performance right in front of him. The black-clad men and women looked like they were getting their karate honors in hair. The blue girls found stations and were immediately set upon by the modernistic pit crew wielding their silver combs and black spray bottles.

Someone turned on a *Trainspotting* soundtrack disk, and the whole place jumped into the music's driving rhythms. The scent of hair spray started to drift through the room. It wasn't like the old kind his mom used—*Aqua Net*? Must be hair spray, the next generation. Aromatherapy that also glued your hair in place.

Tom set his empty coffee cup down on the floor, took out his old copy of *Murder Gets the Blues*, and settled back into the chair, trying to preserve what was left of his little reality in the face of this new, noisy one. He'd read it five times, but it was his favorite, and he couldn't afford a new release. Until today, he suddenly remembered. He'd have to check the bank account by phone and see if Granite had transferred the funds yet. Hot damn. Papa's rich.

Now, if he could be the one to figure out who the mysterious author was who wrote the detective character, well, life would be good. Mike Mason Mysteries by M. B. Kerlin. Who was this guy? Nobody knew. Inquiring mystery readers like him wanted to know.

Marla watched Tom in the mirror. Anton was right. There really *was* some movie star in there. She smiled to herself. But was it Mel Gibson or Buster Keaton? George Clooney or Jerry Lewis? While Anton toyed with her hair, Marla scribbled notes in her black notebook.

He wore a beat-up topcoat that must have been his father's. His shoes were dull as dirt. The coffee seemed to bring some color back into his sallow complexion, but the unshaved face was the face of a man with an angle.

What was Mr. O'Shay's angle? Money? Power? He seemed lacking in both. His eyelids were heavy and low—a hint of danger sulked there. The shadow of his hat brim hid his true expression.

Or perhaps it was his hands. His powerful grip on the cup and the way his upper arm flexed, revealing tensed muscles under the guise of ineffectiveness.

"He certainly is buff, isn't he?" Anton whispered in her left ear.

"Anton, you are the most observant person I know."

"I see all, tell nothing. I can enjoy the view anyway, can't I?"

"Yes, you can enjoy the view." Marla giggled. Anton was one of her best friends. He really did see all and tell nothing. He'd seen her through the few flighty relationships she'd had in the last eight years, plus the one big bad one. He always knew what to say. Not "Marla, you are suffering from a father complex that leaves you unable to commit to a man," like her therapist, but the Anton version:

"Honey, he was dirt under your feet, not worth a second thought. You are destined to find Prince Rainier just like Grace Kelly did, and live happily ever after, girlfriend, you are so *bella*," he'd say, mixing his Italian and Bronx phraseology. She really loved him for always taking her side.

"I love you, Anton."

"I love you too, Marla." He stopped backcombing her crown and gave her a big kiss on the cheek. "So *bella* you are."

"I'm only *bella* because you make me that way, hon, it's all your doing."

"I'm only working with what nature already gave you, darling. You are a goddess, but thank you for the compliment, lovey." Anton teared up a little and wiped his eyes on his voluminous sleeve.

"Sweetie, I have this problem," Marla started in.

"Is he about five-eleven, dark, and handsome?"

"No. Now, cut it out and listen. For some reason I've been dwelling on the past lately. You know, the usual: Ivy, then fast forward to Derek. Predictable losses of childhood and adult life. That sort of thing. It's not like me to muck around in the past. Is Mercury retrograde or something?"

"My personal theory is that your spirit knows it's time for a major shift in your life. It goes into reruns to clear up old unfinished business. You should meditate on each memory as it arises, put it in a mental pink balloon, and let it go. Arise— balloon, get it?" Anton grinned.

"Ha, ha. I get the idea, though. I just don't see any need for my life to change. Things are fine the way they are. And why do I have unfinished business when I paid someone seventy-five dollars an hour for three years to cure that?"

"Oh, yes, Cleopatra, queen of de-*nial*. It's about letting go. . . ." Anton made waving motions in the air and went on talking. "And as for change, when was the last time you went out on a date? That cancer benefit last summer?"

"Dates are overrated."

"Love, that silly thing. So overrated. By the way," he said softly, "he's reading one of your books."

Marla quickly positioned herself to see the book cover in the mirror: *Murder Gets the Blues*. One of her favorites. Anton was one of the few people who knew her secret identity. But then, he kept everyone's secrets. If Riley only knew who really wrote those mysteries. She smiled a big cat-ate-the-canary grin in the mirror.

"You are sooo bad, honey. Now bend over this way and I'll spray you up good. I think I might take a crack at that sow's ear over there. I have an instinct about him. Will you hold him down for me?" They both dissolved into a gale of uncontrolled laughter.

"Seriously, darling, I have a tingling in my crown chakra that's telling me Mr. Riley might be the man that finally steals our Marla's heart."

"Are you out of your mind? His office looks like a time bomb went off in it in 1945. He's got terrible taste, and besides, there's that New York thing. No offense, but I'd rather be burned at the stake than date another New Yorker, and you know I'm too busy, and well, I just don't like him that much!" Marla protested . . . a lot.

"Details, details." Anton gestured. "And no offense taken. You know, not all men are like Derek

Stiles, honey, and you are going to have to *get over it* sooner or later." He delivered this last portion like a revved-up evangelist.

"Which reminds me," Marla changed the subject, trying to keep her mind from going there, "Rita wants him known as an old friend of mine from out of town. She doesn't want the other girls to get wind of this insurance thing. I can count on you to keep quiet, right?"

"Always, dearest. Hmmm, ah, yes, an old friend that reeks of New York, just in town for the month so you can show him the city? I think you're going to have to get a better story. I'll work on that." The comb started flying around her like a hummingbird again. "Now back to the subject at hand. Despite your protests, I'll bet just about *anything* you and Thomas do the nasty before this thirty days is up."

She was an inch away from a shriek of laughter, but stifled herself and talked low. "That's a sucker bet if I ever heard one. Anything, you say?" Marla pondered that for a minute. "How about a photo shoot with your best buddy Robby Tildon? You *are* on intimate terms, after all." Marla would love to update her photos with Robert Tildon. He was perpetually booked, and charged an ungodly amount of money, but he was the best—as far as the rest of Manhattan was concerned. She brightened up at the prospect of her prize and got over the mention of Derek Stiles's name.

Anton looked wary for a minute, rubbed his forehead with his fingertips, apparently adjusting his chakra connection, and contemplated Tom again. Marla figured he realized the error of his rash offer. She smiled smugly at him in the mirror.

"It's a deal. If you lose, I get to be one of your bridesmaids," Anton said, and doubled his efforts on her hair as if nothing had occurred. Marla straightened herself up a bit, looked at Tom's reflection, and returned to her sureness. She'd never sleep with Tom Riley, not in thirty days, not in three hundred, and for damn sure she'd never marry him!

He may have biceps, he may have chocolate eyes, but his life was a disaster area, his manners were beyond bad, his IQ was probably in the teens. He'd left a wife and who knows how many children, or maybe he'd been thrown out.

He must buy his clothes at St. Vinnie's thrift shop, which wasn't a capital offense, of course, because that would make her shallow. It was his *taste* in ragbag clothes, or his lack thereof, and basically his personal habits. Like he should have shaved in the shower this morning. She had a short vision of Thomas naked in a tiny Manhattan-sized shower.

She actually did a tiny jump in the chair, it was such a surprising image.

Marla straightened up. Nobody messed with her self-control. She'd never surrender to a man like Riley. Nope, never.

She picked at her nails and ignored any contradictory body sensations. Anton smiled and wiggled his brows like he'd read her mind. Brat.

Tom had fallen asleep in the chair. He looked like a pile of clothing. His chin was on his chest, and little snorts occasionally emerged from under the hat. The girls who were finished had begun to gather around him, sitting at his feet. They were obviously scheming up something. Marla looked on with amusement. Some guard he was.

Anton stuck the last silk flower in her rolled-up hair and let her go over to rescue Tom. She caught the drift of some "make-over" plan right off and decided to have a little fun herself with *all* of them. The power of her stunning figure was sometimes a great amusement to her. Besides, she'd come up with a better way to explain Tom Riley to the troops.

"Tom, honey, wake up." She joggled his arm. With a start, he flung his arms open like a toy puppet.

"Who . . . wha?"

"Yeah, that and *when* and *where* will get you a news story," she said with a smile.

Tom's bleary eyes finally focused on six beautiful women staring up at him. In the center was Marla, leaning into his chair, a hand on each arm, with her ample cleavage about ten inches from his face. He must be dreaming. He closed them again, then opened them, and the women were all still there. One said something in Swedish, and two of them giggled. A beer commercial. He was in a beer commercial. Suddenly the room was very warm.

"Ladies, this is Thomas Riley, my . . . boyfriend." Anton let out an audible gasp from behind them, followed by a giggle. Tom sat up like a shot. What? What the hell was she talking about? Couldn't she have said *bodyguard* or something? Because he'd guard that body anytime.

"Sweetheart"—she straightened up and ruined his view—"this is Livia, Morgana, Gretchen, Sylvia, and Boots." Marla went around the circle pointing at heads.

"Boots?" Tom looked down.

Boots held her leg straight up. She had a pair of red, elaborately embroidered cowboy boots on.

"Oh." He took his coat and muffler off and let them fall in the chair seat.

"Come on, Tommy, our limo will be ready in about fifteen minutes," Marla fairly purred, and held her hand out to him.

Boyfriend, was it? Now, he was no dummy,

and a good cup of strong coffee combined with a short nap was a great combination for him. Not to mention waking up to Marla's must-be-real-to-jiggle-like-that breasts in his face. She also smelled real good. Sort of like an exotic flower. Her lips were full and lavish with a natural rose-colored tint.

His body aroused, his mind fully awake now, he made his move. Rising from the chair and taking her hand, he pulled her into him, tipped his hat aside with his finger, angled in for the plant, and claimed her mouth for his own.

A big,
sexy,
long,
wet,
horny
kiss.

The really strange part was, she didn't stop him. As a matter of fact, after a very brief initial reaction, she melted in his arms as well as his mouth. And hers opened softly to let him in deeper.

MMMmmmmmm. Yes, sir, he was awake now! He smoothly moved his hands down her back until she suddenly let go and came up for air. She stared right into his insides with her wild forget-me-not blue eyes. He couldn't take his eyes off her.

* * *

Whatever Tom Riley wasn't, he was probably the best kisser she had ever encountered in her entire twenty-eight years. Even Matthew Sweeney, who kissed her eighty times in a row in the ninth grade, hadn't made her legs shake this bad. She brushed her hand across the side of her cheek where his beard had scraped her skin. Her lips felt like they were on fire.

He was a strikingly handsome man under that eight A.M. shadow. He had moody dark brown eyes that really penetrated you when he did his long, lingering look. There was something behind them too. He carried a wise soul, she decided. Too bad he was such an idiot in this life, and such a bad dresser!

She broke off her stare-down with Riley and glanced at Anton, who was making silent ha-has at her. She returned a look of utter disgust. Then gracefully extracted herself from Riley, took his arm, and maneuvered them both through the semicircle of women.

They made it to the doorway, where she was about to take him down a notch, when he stopped in his tracks. "My coat. I need my coat. It's *February* out there." She followed him back, holding his arm.

"I'll keep you warm," she said, still putting up

the facade, knowing they were being watched by the other girls, even though they were probably too far across the room to hear them now.

"Very amusing. A man gets attached to things, you know."

"Yes, I know. My dad has this green plaid shirt he won't throw away. It's a Sears special from the years when my mom was alive. I've sent him these gorgeous Ralph Laurens, but he still insists on wearing that shirt every Saturday. I'm amazed it's still in one piece."

"Your mom died when you were young?"

"I was seven."

"That's a tough break for a kid. Sorry to hear it."

"It's been over twenty years." An old place in her heart twisted, as usual.

"Even so . . ." Tom said.

Things were getting awkward. Finally, to her relief, Tom walked back over to the chair and grabbed his coat and muffle. Marla waited for him. Out in the hall she was refueling her plan to tell Mr. Riley which door would lead him directly to hell, but he stepped right in front of her and interrupted her speech planning.

"So what's with the boyfriend bit?" Tom asked.

"It was a spontaneous thing. I didn't get a chance to tell you. I had to come up with a cover story. Not everyone needs to know about this whole insurance policy bit. It's a little embarrassing. I can trust Anton and Rita to keep it quiet."

Marla had a sudden rush of memory. She'd gotten distracted. A small flare of anger made her scalp tingle where Anton had fastened her roots too tight. She planted her hand on her hips.

"And see here, Mr. Riley, I think we are going to have to get some ground rules straight. What was that kiss about?"

"I'm an opportunist. Besides, I assumed you wanted me to be believable in the role you cast upon me so spontaneously."

"So I see. Well, that will be the *last* opportunity you are given. Do I make myself clear?"

His eyelids lowered as he shot his reply back to her. "Look, Miss Meyers, we have thirty days to spend together. Let's *do* get some ground rules straight. First, I don't take crap from anyone, including clients. And as for the kiss, you didn't exactly fight me off. Maybe your ice princess routine has left you in need of a warm-up."

Marla gave him her best arched-eyebrow stare. He was really getting on her nerves now. "That kiss was all an act," she snapped.

He grinned and folded his arms in a self-satisfied gesture. Marla crossed her own arms in self-protection.

"And no bullshit either," he said. "Besides,

there is no way you can convince me you aren't weak in the knees from that kiss."

"You are full of crap," she countered.

"No, no crap; crapless. Remember?"

"*Stop that!*" She raised her voice.

"When was the last time you got kissed anyway? Your pals in there acted like lightning had struck. They say you pretty girls spend most of your nights alone. Well, don't take it out on me, Ms. M., I'm just the messenger."

Marla seriously considered slapping Tom Riley, but decided it was beneath her. She felt the heat in her face. No words came out of her mouth when she groped for a properly scathing comeback.

Tom smiled in that way people smile when they think they've won, and walked right by her, apparently expecting Marla to follow him.

"You . . . you don't even know where you're going." She swung away as he passed and walked in the opposite direction. "This way, Mr. Riley. Your first day is only six hours from being over. I'm going to see what I can do to make them the worst six hours you've ever spent."

"You've obviously never met my ex-wife."

"Anything she dished out on you was undoubtedly deserved. You are one of the rudest men I've ever met."

"Maybe you should go slumming more often. Increase the research quota, you know?"

"Maybe I should call your company and tell them what kind of man they have working for them, cancel my policy, and take my chances with another not-so-bright insurance man. I'm sure there are more of them out there. What do you say to that, Riley?" Marla delivered that last bit over her shoulder, then flipped her done-up hairdo head back around and marched forward. Unable to resist, she looked back around to see his face.

He looked completely exasperated, but, feet shuffling, followed her anyway, his hands stuck in his pants pockets. Which made him look, she decided, like a sulking teenager. Anton was never going to win this one, and just for resisting the totally resistable Mr. Riley, she was going to get some great photos at the end of this month. Yes sirree.

Chapter Three

HERE COMES
THE BRIDE

Tom was used to the cold backside of a woman beside him, but the limo ride from the agency to the hotel was one of the chilliest fifteen minutes he'd had in a long time. Damn that woman for honing in on the one thing that would shut him up. He'd do anything to keep this contract alive, even put up with Marla Meyers for another six hours and twenty-nine days.

He pulled up the collar of his trench coat and braved the February wind, which felt warm compared to her. How did a perfectly good-looking girl like that get so nasty?

There must be some nicer women out there. Maybe *he* should increase his research quota.

Maybe he should think on dating again. His stomach soured at the thought. What, would he take a woman out for a nice frankfurter at a Nathan's stand? That was about the extent of his dating budget.

Marla walked a car length ahead of him, wrapped in fake fur. He quickened his step to catch up with her, which pissed him off even more. This spoiled-brat woman was going to be running his life for a month.

God, why did he always end up with women from hell that twisted him around like a pipe cleaner? Sisters, aunts, a wife, and now this. He must have been a bad boy in a past life.

After *this* was over, he was going to throw himself into his career and crawl out of the financial slump the last year had brought. He'd been so down over the divorce, and over his dad's death, nothing seemed to work.

Of course, it didn't help that all the clients he took over from his dad *died* on him, leaving Granite paying up on life policies every other month.

This dry spell was going to have to end. His son deserved more. Of course, he'd still rather spend time with Max than spend ten hours a day in his office making cold calls.

How did he end up in the most boring job in the universe? There had to be a balance out there somewhere, and he'd have to find it. Weirdly enough, Marla Meyers was giving him the most excitement he'd had on this job for the last ten years.

The backstage bustle was amazing. Marla had vanished, so Tom found himself a safe corner with a high stool to perch on and watched the scene, which included a large quantity of naked and half-naked women that no one seemed to take any note of except him.

Most of them were too thin for his taste; he liked a rounder woman himself. As a matter of fact, except for a few decent-looking girls—and some of them *were* girls—it was starting to look like willowy ghosts were haunting the place. Why did people think being this thin was a good thing?

And as for the makeup—when they talked about the smell of the greasepaint, well, this was it for sure. Max Factor to the tenth power. It all had kind of a strange scented-candle smell, like the incense at mass. But these sure weren't nuns, and he was no choirboy. He better stop staring or they'd throw him out.

When Marla reappeared, she had on a sheer bodysuit. He looked her up, and he looked her down. Every inch had cloth on it, but the sheer spandex did little to hamper his imagination. Now, how could a girl that delicious be such a snot?

She must have sensed his eyes on her, because she glanced nervously in his direction and crossed her arms over her breasts. Tom figured there were two layers there, anyway. Some kind of bra was holding those up.

The other girls paid no attention to him at all. Someone had pinned a GUEST tag on him in the midst of the confusion, and it seemed to be the magic invisibility badge as far as the other models were concerned.

But apparently he was not invisible to Marla. A crew person came by, slipped a dress over her head, and a minute later she looked like a jittery butterfly in some kind of painted silky getup. She was a stunning butterfly, though. Tom took out his book and his reading glasses, and tried to look like he wasn't looking.

Another butterfly came stalking across the room. She was dark, tall, and angry. Her auburn-colored hair sprang around her like wild Slinkys, and she was headed straight for Marla. Tom peered over the top of his glasses.

The dark butterfly stopped inches in front of Marla's chair and planted her hands on a slim pair of hips. "Meyers, I need those size-eight suede Helmut Lang's of yours. You know, the ones I borrowed for New Year's Eve?"

"Didn't anyone ever teach you the magic word?

What's your problem, Paris, hormones acting up again?" Marla's voice was calm.

"God, yes." The Paris girl seemed to relax a notch. "I've tried every Chinese herb ever made, and I just can't get that edge out of me, Marla. I just want to kill somebody for some relief. So where are the shoes . . . puleeeease?"

"I broke a heel. Then I must have . . . oh, I left them in Tom Riley's . . . apartment. Yes." Marla backtracked as she remembered the story.

"Tom who?"

"Tom—boyfriend Tom." Marla pointed at him.

"Who calls their boyfriend two names?"

"That was for your benefit. He's right over there. Oh, Tom . . . Tom!" Marla gave a little wave.

Tom acted surprised, as if he hadn't heard the entire conversation. He sauntered over to the Amazon butterfly girls. Standing next to the two of them was somewhat unnerving. He felt vulnerable. And short. He pulled his five-foot-eleven-and-one-quarter inches up as high as possible.

"Tom, this is Paris James. Paris, Tom Riley."

"My pleasure." Tom nodded to her.

"You're not very tall, are you?" Paris stared. "This is your boyfriend? Maybe you do need glasses, Marla."

Tom went from shocked to pissed in ten seconds.

"Looks like you have a mouth to match your height, there. Big and unruly."

Paris bent her head down to him and got right in his face. "Nice to meet you, asshole."

Tom would never smack a woman. Never, he reminded himself.

Marla cut between them. "Paris, shut up and go eat some soybeans. You are really getting out of hand, girl." Marla moved to Tom's side and looped her arm through his. "Besides, Tom, here, is as cute as they come. You're just jealous." Marla snuggled against Tom's body. Tom let her. It calmed him down. Paris backed down a little, but still stared right at him.

"Did Marla leave a pair of black suede shoes in your apartment?"

"Sure she did." Tom sneered. "By the way, where do you get your shoes repaired? That heel was really a mess. I know a place about three blocks from Fulton Street—the Shoe Doctor. He's an artist." Tom pointed in the air toward his end of town.

Now Paris and Marla were both staring at him. Paris opened her big, lipstick-slick mouth again. Tom watched an interesting shade of red climb up her cheeks. She seemed agitated for some reason.

"Tombo, if we break a shoe, we get new ones—like every week." She poked his shoulder with her finger. "Even when we don't break them, we buy shoes. Shoes are our life."

Tom clenched his teeth. "Whatever. I hear your keeper calling you, Miss James." Tom smiled a gritty smile. Marla actually giggled. Paris glared, then stomped off. She threw a comment over her shoulder like a flying rotten tomato.

"I should have been the bride today, Meyers. Blondes are boring."

"She's actually much nicer when it's not day twenty-seven," Marla said.

Tom looked confused. Day twenty-seven, so what? "Nicer than what, a cornered badger?" Tom headed back to his wooden stool and hid behind his book again. Then he got the PMS joke and smirked, flipping a page.

The insignificant detail caught my attention, a forget-me-not stuck in the lapel of the man in the coffin.

This was truly M. B. Kerlin's masterpiece book of the Mike Mason series. He shoved his glasses up, and read on.

Forget-me-not. Now, who didn't want the up-standing Mr. Lindt-Varney to forget them? It certainly wasn't his wife. I took a sideways glance over the widow's way and saw a tearless, well-made-up face. Mrs. Lindt-Varney seemed to be holding up well.

Tom looked up from the page again as a sound check distracted him. A lush, forties big-band instrumental version of "April Showers" grew in intensity out of a speaker that must have been three feet from his ear. He got up and started checking the place out. A typical mock-up stage runway cut across the center of the Plaza Hotel ballroom. Workers were checking electric wires taped over the white cloth-covered runway structure.

It all looked pretty treacherous to Tom, from an insurance claim viewpoint. Marla must be used to navigating through all this, otherwise she'd be worse off than she was. He stepped around obstacles and stood in the back of the room. Tables were set up on one side of the runway, with place markers at most of them. Maybe he'd see someone famous.

A lanky beauty walked down the runway and back, trying out a turn where she opened a colorful umbrella, then twirled her way back to the stage area. She wobbled on her three-inch heels.

The most insignificant detail suddenly caught in his thoughts. The shoe. Why was Paris James borrowing shoes anyway? Surely she had an

Imelda Marcos–sized collection herself? After all, shoes were her life.

And why had she gone all red in the face about it? He spun that thought around in his head for a while, pulling a hotel chair from the last table row over to his spot at the edge of the room.

Maybe Miss Meyers wasn't such a klutz after all. Maybe someone wanted her out of the way. She was a woman on the rise. There must be a lot of jealousy in a profession like this. Like that Paris bitch who wanted to be the bride, whatever that meant. She could commit a crime, no doubt about it.

Oh brother. He'd definitely been reading too many detective novels. Life just wasn't like that.

"Lunch!" a voice called from backstage. Tom jumped out of his thoughts into the image of a nice pastrami on rye with sauerkraut. He strode across the room to answer a bigger calling than his wandering imagination. Free food.

Cold red potato salad was the closest thing to a good deli sandwich he could find. Even that had Italian salad dressing instead of mayo. Not even as good as his Aunt Rose's.

At his family's gatherings, the quality and uniqueness of potato salad was the source of a never-ending war that occasionally ended in one aunt not speaking to another for at least a month.

Sweet pickles vs. dill pickles; that came around every time. The celery debate was only once a year. In Tom's Irish and Italian family, food ruled.

Tom made do with his pile of potato salad, and a Dr. Brown's cream soda. He declined the fresh-squeezed wheatgrass Meyers offered him. What was he, a cow?

It was hard enough to eat with all those girls back in their hardly-anythings, not eating anything at all. Way before he could finish his large portion, the lights flashed on and off, scattering the girls like the bats he and his cousin once stirred up under a dark overpass. He couldn't see Marla at all. Close to the runway was probably his best vantage point.

Making his way to the side camera area, he found a safe spot to stand. Tom just hoped Marla was in a safe spot too. Marla, my face, my dear, don't ruin my life and break your nose. He stuffed the rest of his salad down and hid the plate under a nearby table set with a huge bouquet of flowers.

Taking out his novel, he leaned against a pillar and read several chapters before things started happening again. Lights dimmed. The noise from backstage ceased.

By now the crowd was settling in. He scanned for famous faces, and thought he saw a few. The well-dressed ladies in their big jewelry talked among themselves, sometimes even to the stray male companion. Tom had been to the opera before with his Italian mother, but he'd never seen a runway show live.

The music came up with an old Les Brown tune. The models started appearing dressed in suits that looked just like the forties to Tom. Everything old is new again, he guessed. Marla wasn't in that set, but pretty soon the set music changed, and she came out with her butterfly outfit.

Paris James was right behind her. More like a bat out of hell, Tom thought nastily. They both spun several times, making Tom extremely nervous. That platform was only about five feet wide.

He edged closer between the cameras. Marla Meyers was a stunner for sure. She moved with a dancer's grace. The dress was wrapped tight around her waist and bust, and showed them off well. She made it fine back down the runway, and Tom relaxed a little.

Two more sets finished before he saw Marla again, this time in a classic black velvet evening gown. Boy, there was the dress to wear to the Oscars this year. Tom caught himself having a fashion moment, and rubbed his temple. Hey, even if she was on the chilly side, the woman was stunning. So, hey, he was just looking. Who was he trying to convince here? He shut himself up.

It was hot between the cameras and lights, and he finally stashed his topcoat, muffler, and hat under the same flower table. Three more sets, and even the guests looked exhausted. The oohs and ahhs were thinning out. Then the stage lights went to a pale pink, the house lights practically black, and an old recording of Les Brown's orchestra playing "Sentimental Journey" swelled up. Tom knew his old jazz.

Behind him some men in tails rolled in a wedding cake big enough for Marla to jump out of, and for a minute Tom thought she might. An interesting frosting fantasy popped to mind. They parked it at the end of the runway, no doubt to cut for the guests. This must be the end. Tom let his shoulders roll back, stiff from standing still so long.

The bride was Marla. She walked in rhythm with the music. Her hair now had a veil attached to it that ran about six feet behind her and billowed in the breeze of a large fan they turned on her. The dress itself, while he'd never seen a pink bride, was an architectural masterpiece, if Tom did say so himself. A train came from the back of the dress, extending practically a football field behind her.

The crowd regained their oohs and ahhs. Paris James took up the rear in a blue dress, and a few more girls followed, one in lavender, one in pale green. Oh, this was the bit Paris was snipping about. Always the bridesmaid, Paris, he thought with a smirk.

His own wedding to Doris had been at a justice of the peace. She'd been wearing a maternity dress. He remembered the unrelenting fear that gripped him at the time, and the sadness he'd had knowing he'd gone and quit college, and his dream of the police academy, and would start work in his dad's insurance office on Monday morning. But he knew that baby deserved his father.

After the baby was born Tom remembered holding Max's tiny fingers in his own and just not caring about whether he was madly in love with Doris or whether his job was less than perfect. Insurance men didn't get shot in the line of duty.

Max was his son, and Doris needed him. That was enough to keep him with Doris for eight years. So they'd fallen into a routine and made the best of it. Hell, he'd still be there if she hadn't called it a day. It takes a crowbar to move a good Irish-Italian man such as himself out of a fairly livable marriage.

Change made Tom nervous. At this point, women made Tom nervous. They all wanted to change him. But he needed a change. He was in a rut. A big, boring insurance business rut.

Marla held a large bouquet of gardenias. He

could smell them all the way down the runway. Nice. One was in her hair too. She was near the end, and the scent grew stronger the closer she got to him. Now, that was the face of a woman you'd want to see coming down the aisle to you, if you really had to.

Her skin was like creamy porcelain, with a hint of a blush so natural Tom couldn't tell if it was her or the makeup. Her golden hair was framed with light. Her clear blue eyes shone, and she caught his gaze, then smiled a quick, luscious smile . . . right at him. She was an angel. Tom felt heat rush through his body. Holy shit. He had the hots for Supergirl.

Then it came. For some reason, Marla stopped dead in her tracks. Next came a terrible ripping sound, and Marla's body seem to jerk backward like a ball on elastic string.

From his position, Tom could see two things. One was a thin power cord yanked up out of position like a trip wire. The other was Paris's high heel planted firmly on the train of Marla's dress. Paris looked down, yipped, then took a tiny jump backward.

Too late, too late, Tom's mind screamed. Marla seemed to be rebounding from the backward pull, but in her efforts to continue forward, forward was where she was continuing.

He ran as close as he could to the end of the

stage, but could only reach for air as she took a nosedive, straight down into the top of the cake. The crowd hushed, then went wild, some laughing, some trying to reach Marla. Paris and the other girls seemed stunned into bridesmaid statues.

Tom jumped up on the end of the runway and grappled with yards of fabric until he had her around the waist. Lifting her up, he lowered her to the stage floor. She sat up right away. He knelt down beside her. She swiped at her mouth, gasping for air.

Pulling off his short-sleeved shirt, Tom started clearing frosting away from her face. His precious face! She was sputtering like a kettle about to boil over, still wiping at the frosting herself. Apparently her main concern was air passages.

There wasn't a scratch on it, he decided.

"Thank God, thank God. Your face is fine," he yelled. Marla stared at him through eyes surrounded by rings of white frosting. Even her eyelashes were tipped in white. Her hair was coated, and sported one or two pink frosting roses. "What if they'd had a bride and groom up there? What if that?" Tom ranted.

"Tom, shut up before someone hears you," Marla hissed stickily.

Paris stood nearby, but all she could say was, "I'm so sorry, Marla, those damn trains. Damn trains! This is why I'll never get married." She had flecks of white all over her blue gown.

The stage manager came out and encouraged everyone to calm down. Tom gave him some sort of signal that Marla was all right. The face was all right. Man, he was going to have to watch this girl like a hawk from now on.

Marla Meyers, clearly not one to take things lying down, got up, bowed to the audience with elbow-length gloves dripping frosting, and shooed the bridesmaids back down the runway. She rose to her full height, paused, and made a spectacular exit, waving like a beauty queen on a float, to thundering applause, flipping frosting in every direction.

Tom found himself standing on a high-fashion runway in his undershirt. He jumped down and attempted to make his way backstage before she reached the curtain. He'd only gotten a short glance and really needed to see her lovely, intact frosted face there to greet him. At least there weren't any obvious bumps. Tom thanked the saints above several times for preserving his commission check. He felt . . . lucky.

The media camera people seemed to be going somewhat insane. Getting by them was like trying to reach the forty-yard line with a sea of New York Giants in the way. Tom fought valiantly through the crowd and found his moment to dive backstage.

Wrestling through the heavy velvet curtains, he found himself in another sea, this time of semi-hysterical females. He moved through, searching for Marla. A flash of pink caught his eye. When he got to the spot, it wasn't Marla he found, but a perfectly round pile of a pale pink frosting-covered silk wedding dress, with a hole in the center where Marla used to be. He stared at it, expecting her to reappear.

Then a slow, sickening feeling ran through him, worse than a gulp of castor oil.

She was gone. His Marla face was somewhere he couldn't watch after it. Damn, damn, damn. Hand on his suddenly aching forehead, Tom ran through the last few minutes in his head. Had Paris done this on purpose? She was as nasty as they came, that was for sure, Medusa in a pretty package. Why had she stepped on Marla's train? Was it just an accident? He hadn't been able to gauge her reaction during all the panic onstage. But a jealous woman was a force to be reckoned with.

Man, what if she went to finish the job? But then what about that power cord? He hadn't seen the other side of the runway, with the lights in his eyes. Did someone pull it on purpose?

"Whassamatter, boyfriend, lost your gal pal?" Paris James stood just behind him. He turned quickly, catching her sarcastic smirk. Well, that was one theory shot. Paris didn't have Marla hostage-handcuffed to her at the moment. His mind went in a very weird direction.

Tom snapped out of his fantasy. "Where is she?" he demanded, almost eye to eye with her.

"How should I know? Who are you anyway, Ryetack?"

"That's Riley. You heard her, I'm her new boyfriend." Tom straightened up, realizing he had an ancient Yankees T-shirt that doubled as his undershirt on, and blobs of frosting stuck all over him. He wiped his hands on his T-shirt. Tom got the feeling she didn't believe him. "What happened out on that runway anyway?" Tom kept his eyes steady on her.

Paris shrugged. "Search me, she stopped walking, and I didn't. She deserved it, though. I should have been the bride today. It was just bad karma on her for taking my spot." Paris stuck her chin in the air and walked away.

That only answered one question. Paris hadn't kidnapped her or stuck her in a freezer backstage or something. One thing was for sure: Whatever happened, Tom knew he had to find Marla right now. Someone might actually be out to get her.

What would Mike Mason do at a time like this?

He stared at the pile of dress and guck. That was it. Follow the frosted footprints.

Somewhere was a practically naked woman with pretty good-tasting stuff all over her, and he had to find her before she . . . showered.

Chapter Four

SHE'S GOT
STEAM HEAT

Marla tipped up her face and let the hot water run over her. The shampoo washed what was left of the frosting out of her hair. Then she took her sea sponge and slowly went over every inch of herself. The heat of the water and the softness of the sponge made her tired muscles relax a little. The ache in her legs started to fade.

She turned and let the shower massage away the knots in her neck and shoulders. The delicate scent of her body wash was a marvelous vanilla, white ginger, and jasmine blend she had specially made for her. It always reminded her of St. Thomas, and the white-sand beach she had escaped to after her breakup with Derek. The island had given her back a sense of herself, and that's just what she needed a reminder of right now.

Pushing her hands against the tiled wall, she arched her back into the hot water stream. She closed her eyes and . . . mmmm. A foggy image of a dark-haired man swam into her steam-heated mind. His strong, imaginary body pressed up against her from behind. She daydreamed his strong arms reaching around her, caressing her.

Melting into her fantasy, Marla let her dream lover whisper in her ear and kiss the sides of her neck. She let herself feel aroused, and ran her hands softly over her own breasts. Two years with no lover was a long, lonely time.

"Ohhh, Tom," she heard herself moan. *Oh, Tom?* Oh no, oh *no*. She turned the water to ice-cold and danced up and down on the tiles for fifteen seconds, shaking her head and blubbering, "Brrrrrrrrrrrrrrrrr."

Shutting off the water, Marla stepped out and grabbed her thick pale green oversized towel. This was the shower that was supposed to cure her headache. Well, it had taken the edge off, but tomorrow her headache would be back. What the hell was she going to do with this crazy man Tom Riley?

She grabbed another towel, wrapped her long hair, twisting it up on her head, then slipped out of the big towel and into her white Turkish terry robe.

What she needed was a distraction. Her bare feet felt good on the plush wool area rug that took up most of her living room floor. She crossed the room and turned on the CD player. A slow jazz piano piece filled the air. Keith Jarrett.

In the kitchen she opened the Sub-Zero refrigerator wine drawer, took out the bottle she'd already uncorked, and poured herself a cold glass of Latour Montrachet 1996.

Rolling the lovely stuff around in her glass, she let the air get to it a bit. Then she took a long sip and let the wine dance in her mouth. She needed a drink. She just needed to relax tonight. I mean really, she didn't fall off the end of a runway during one of the biggest charity fashion shows of the season too often.

More to the point, she didn't usually find herself fantasizing about odd insurance men.

Settling into her favorite overstuffed beige velvet club chair, she turned out the lights and sipped her wine slowly. She gazed out at the Manhattan skyline that sparkled like a thousand diamonds in the darkness. She loved New York.

In some ways it was like the huge starry sky over her dad's farm in Indiana. When she was little, her dad would sit with her on the porch steps in the dark and point to a star that was a little brighter in the heavens than the others.

"That's your mom's star, honey, she's watching

over you from up there now. And I'm watching over you down here."

Those words had helped her so much. But then he'd gone and married Ivy. How could a man as kind and wonderful as her father not see what Ivy Richardson was really like? How could he have *married* her, and most of all how could he not see how cruel she was to his daughter?

Marla sighed. Probably because he was working from dawn till dusk and because Marla never told him what her days were like with old Poison Ivy.

At least it had all finally been resolved. Dad was free of Ivy now, and so was she. So why was it on her mind so much? She'd had plenty of therapy to get her head sorted out, but here she was, still going in little head circles over it all.

Time for a break. What was that Anton had said? Oh yes, the pink balloons. She closed her eyes, put Ivy Richardson in a big pink balloon, and let her go flying over Manhattan.

Then she stuffed Derek Stiles in another one and mentally pushed him out the window. That one didn't float as well, she noticed. She pretended she was primordial wind woman and gave the Derek balloon a big whistling gust of air. It floated up in the sky until it disappeared.

Wow, that actually worked. She felt better. She'd have to tell Anton.

Marla leaned back in the chair and let the wine tingle through her body. It was rushing through her bloodstream and up to her head pretty fast. She realized she hadn't eaten dinner.

The intercom buzzed.

"Miss Meyers, it's Carl the doorman."

"Yes, Carl, what is it?"

"There's a man down here to see you. Riley. Should I buzz him up?"

Damn. Well, there was no escape, because Granite Insurance had to love her *and* love her face so she could keep working and sending money to Dad. Running a farm was an expensive, unpredictable project. No matter how much her father reassured her, Marla would never stop contributing to its maintenance.

"Sure, send Mr. Riley up, please," she surrendered.

The twelfth floor was the top, and that's where Marla lived. This was one of those old Stanford White hotels that had been converted into upscale condos. Tom had even had coffee in a small café a few blocks from here on one of his afternoon city prowls through the Village.

Marla's street was tucked between West Eighth and Washington Square Park. It had a north-facing view and Marla's building was one of the few that caught some city lights.

Expensive, he mused. What a difference between her place and his rent-controlled rattrap on Rivington above a used furniture store.

The elevator opened to a red-carpeted hall with art deco touches. He was a man on a mission. Armed with her address, which Anton had unbelievably slipped to him in the backstage chaos, Tom was determined to have a chat with Marla and one more face check. He'd be receiving his commission check and was damn determined not to be asked to give it back only twelve hours into the deal.

As if Granite would be able to squeeze it out of him. He'd done a touchdown happy dance when those funds showed up.

Dangling that extra bonus at the end of thirty days was pretty smart of them. Bastards.

Apartment 12C. He rang her buzzer hard, then stood waiting with that sense she was staring at him through the peephole. He took off his hat and ran his hand through his hair, where it sort of stuck in a few places on leftover frosting. He must look like hell. Who cares. Enough with the look-over. He buzzed again, longer.

"Okay, okay. Hold on, Riley," her muffled voice came through the thick door. He heard three sets of locks turn over. At least she was smart about some things.

The door swung open and gave him the full body shot of Marla. Tom couldn't help but drink her in. She must be buck-naked under that white robe. She awkwardly retightened the belt around her waist and pulled the lapels up.

"Riley, you're drooling on the carpet. Come in and shut the door. It's bad enough you're here; let's not give the neighbors more to see. What do you want anyway?"

"What do I want?" Tom took a quick stride past the door, then closed it behind him. "You really are a piece of work, lady. I'm responsible for your . . . well-being. Did that slip your mind already?"

"Mr. Riley, you are standing in my home. I'm not going to tolerate any verbal assault from you. Obviously my face is fine, I'm unharmed, so you can leave reassured you have done your duty. I suppose you got my address from Paris?"

In her stern outrage, Marla had put her hands on her hips, and Tom was now focused on the cleavage he was treated to. Kind of made it hard to concentrate on bawling her out. He refocused.

"I beg your pardon, Your Highness, some of us have more than spa money riding on the outcome of the next thirty days." He stopped and made an attempt to soften his voice. It was getting mighty warm in here. He unwrapped his muffler from around his neck. "*Anton* gave me your address. But you already gave it to me on the insurance form, remember?

"Look, let's just sit down for a minute and talk.

I've got some serious concerns about your accident tonight," Tom continued. He kept removing things—his hat, then his coat—until she let out a great sigh and took everything out of his hands, hanging them on a very stately antique hall tree.

"All right, but make it quick. I've had a bad day, in case you didn't notice, and frankly, Riley, I don't know you all that well to be standing here in my robe, and it's late."

She walked ahead of him into the living room and gestured toward the sofa. She looked nervous, grabbed a glass of wine from the nearby end table, and stood by the window with her arms crossed.

"I could use a drink myself." He sat down on the fine pale green wool brocade of her sofa and felt like he was at his Aunt Lizzie's house. Everything was pale green and beige. He shifted uncomfortably. This was not going well. But he had to warn her about what he'd seen.

"What can I get you? Wine? Bourbon? I'll bet you're a beer man." Marla marched toward the kitchen behind him.

"Just pour me whatever you've got open." He heard her tinker with a glass, pop open something that sounded uncorked, and pad back across the thick carpet of the living area to where he sat.

She bent over slightly to hand him the glass of wine, and he watched a fat drop of water slide from a curled strand of her wet hair that had escaped the towel, down her neck, over her collarbone, and between her completely luscious breasts.

He took the glass and downed half of it in one gulp. It was smooth as . . . he leaned back against the sofa and let the wine go to his head.

"Geez, Riley, that's expensive stuff. Savor it." She curled herself up into her beige velvet chair and wrapped her robe around her. She sipped her refilled drink and seemed to wait for him to speak, her large exotic blue eyes fixed on his mouth, her head tilted slightly.

Tom leaned forward. "Miss Meyers, I don't think this was an accident today, with the cake and the fall and all. I was standing on the camera side, and I believe someone pulled up one of the power wires and made you fall."

He sat back, somewhat self-satisfied, and took another sip of wine. Damn, she was right; this was the good stuff: hint of oak and a smoky pear undernote. He heard the click of her glass as she set it back on the marble tabletop.

"Riley, I've been doing this modeling thing for eight years now. I've done hundreds of runway shows from Milan to Paris. I've seen plenty of girls go down. I've taken a few falls myself. It's an occupational hazard."

"Let's not mention that to the Granite home office, shall we?" His insides jumped. What had he

gotten himself into? "All I'm saying is I saw something. Let's call it a gut instinct. I think we should
at least consider—"

Before he could finish, she jumped out of her
chair, flashing a little leg on the way up, and paced
over to the window again.

"No one is out to get me, Riley. What possible
motive would they have? Remember what this is
all about. Me, the klutz, needs to reassure the
agency with an insurance policy. It's not that unusual, really."

Riley looked up when he heard her slur "un-
ushhual," and noticed her steady herself on the
windowsill. Maybe she'd been at that wine all
evening. Probably all she'd had to eat was cake.
He got up and came over to her. She looked at him
with a kind of hazy, puzzled expression.

"Meyers, go throw some clothes on. I'm gonna
get you something to eat. I won't take no for an
answer, so save your breath, for once." He took
her arm and guided her past the furniture. Bloody
hell, didn't most accidents happen in the home?
Amazingly, she didn't argue with him.

"Japa-nese," she hiccuped.

"Chinese," he countered.

"No deep-fried anything." Her voice trailed off
as she wove toward her bedroom.

"Fine, fine, Szechwan, then." Tom went to look
in her fridge for a quick appetizer. There were live

veggies in the crisper, an entire door full of vitamins, and tofu. Yuck. He hoped Shun Lee's had a table open. Boy, drinking that Coke the other day must have been like committing a crime for Tofu Tessie, here.

Marla's head was doing a little dancing-light thing, and she fought off a major attack of the giggles. She grabbed her favorite black jeans from a drawer and rummaged for her boyfriend-sized black cashmere V-neck sweater. She couldn't remember which boyfriend it was, but she always seemed to end up with a sweater from any guy she dated more than three months. Gee, her sweater drawer was getting low.

Putting on socks proved to be way too much for her. She flung on a big black wool coat and stuffed the socks in the pockets.

This proved to be very amusing, along with finding two shoes that matched. She started thinking about middle school and wearing two different-colored socks one day. Clothes had not been her thing before modeling. Then there was the static electricity moment, when her already minidress turned into a belt, revealing more to her date than he'd bargained for. Both of them mortified to see her underwear. Oops, forgot the underwear. She saw herself in the mirror and started laughing really hard in that silent kind of over-the-top way. She sat on the floor in a dizzy heap, laughing harder.

"Meyers, I hope you're decent 'cause I'm coming in there." Riley's voice was getting louder. God, was she decent? She tried to stop her hysterics by putting her hand over her mouth. It didn't work.

The great Marla Meyers sat in the middle of her room-sized walk-in closet, legs sticking out straight in front of her like a Barbie doll. Blotto Barbie. Tom let a snorting laugh escape him, then tried to keep a straight face.

"You're not much of a drinker, are you?" he said.

"Nope." She shrugged. She had two mismatched shoes near her bare feet, and Tom saw socks sticking out of her coat pocket. He bent over and pulled them out, then gently rolled them onto her feet.

Extending his hand, he gave her a lift up. She seemed to stand all right. Maybe he wouldn't have to send for take-out after all. He put his hands around her waist and let her hold her balance while she slipped into the loafers. So what if one was brown and one was black? She'd find out later.

"There, now I'm a regular New York girl, dressed in black from head to toe." She stood back and started to spin.

"Let's save the dancing for later, Miss Meyers. Here, put a hat on. It's cold out there." He grabbed a knit hat from the wall and helped her stuff her slightly damp hair into it. Both the towel and robe had been lost on the floor.

"Call me Marla, Riley." She went to give him a chummy slug in the arm, missed, and started to fall. He caught her in his arms. That was it. The feel of her cashmere sweater, and the heat of her body underneath it, her beautiful, shapely body, were more than he could brush aside.

He ran his hands under her coat, down her back, across her gorgeous ass. Oh God, she had no panties on, unless they were thong. His mind broke on that thought, and he pressed her gently into him, which she responded to by putting her arms compliantly around his neck.

"I'm gonna hate myself in the morning, Marla," he whispered in her ear, then slid his mouth down her neck, and slowly back to her waiting lips. He took her in like the fine wine she still tasted of. He teased her tongue with his own, and her mouth opened for more. She moaned and pressed her hot, cashmere-clad body up against his until he wanted to lay her down on the floor of the closet, right there, and taste every inch of her.

Once more, he held her close and covered her hot, beckoning mouth with his own, hard and deep, until she moaned and pressed up harder against his burgeoning erection. She slid her hand across him and a wildfire ignited between them. She bit the flesh between his neck and shoulder, then kissed him again.

His hand slid under her sweater and found the satin-covered fullness of her breast. She arched against him and his name slid through her lips. "Tom . . . Tom."

Tom's brain had departed his head for other parts of his body and she was following the trail. She pulled up his shirt and ran her hands over his chest, and down.

For some ridiculous, ancient, parochial-school reason, his head cleared when she slid her hands down to his top pants button and undid it. He stepped back and gently took her hands.

"Marla, believe it or not, I'm a gentleman, and you are suffering the effects of some really good wine coupled with no food. Now, there is a bowl of hot and sour soup with your name on it just four blocks away. I'm going to take you there and forget this ever happened. I doubt you will remember it anyway."

Marla looked a little stunned. There was a look in her eyes—*lust*, that was it. But she rebuttoned his button and gave him a funny smile.

"Yes, sir, Riley." She saluted him. He stuffed his shirt back in his pants and came around beside her. With arms linked, they marched to the door, grabbing his gear on the way out. He needed some really cold, fresh air right now.

"Got your keys, Meyers? Is this your purse? Out we go." He guided her to the elevator. In the lobby, Marla gave a little wave to Carl the doorman, who tipped his hat back on his head, raised his eyebrows, and winked at Tom. Tom smiled and kept to his task of keeping Marla going forward.

The cold air blasted them both, and Tom felt a sobering shudder run through Marla. Shit. She was going to be mad as a pissy alleycat when the wine wore off. He was surprised when she moved in close to him for warmth.

They moved quickly, and Shun Lee had a nice dark booth in the back open. Thanks, whichever saint watches over dumb insurance men who kiss their clients, Tom offered skyward.

Harry Lee was maître d' and Tom signaled him hello. He saw Harry size up the situation, call over the waiter, and order up Tom's usual. Special Shun Lee hot and sour soup, broccoli beef in a spicy black bean sauce, kung pao shrimp. Steamed rice. In ten minutes, the soup was at the table; in twenty, the rest arrived.

Marla's giddy state had moved to include a ravenous appetite. He watched her maneuver expertly with her chopsticks. She raved about the soup. It was one of the best batches Tom had had here in years. Harry probably brought out the good stuff for beauty, here, Tom mused. He sat back and enjoyed watching Marla indulge herself. She really could go from hot to cold in sixty seconds flat. Well, it had been almost an hour, and she was still on the happy side.

He might as well relax now, because as soon as she remembered that kiss . . . well, those nine kisses . . . the Ice Age would return. Brrrr. He had another helping of kung pao shrimp to warm himself.

Three shrimp bites in, he saw Marla pause. Her chopsticks poised in midair as her face slowly rose to look at him square on. Her eyes got very wide, as if she'd bitten a chunk of red pepper out of the soup. She sat up straighter than a nun and turned white. Tom decided to keep his mouth very, very shut. Her pallor lasted a full minute, and her face twisted into about three different emotions. Unable to decipher *which* emotions, Tom considered taking cover in the men's room.

Then she spoke in clear, precise tones.

"Dinner is on me."

Chapter Five

THE TROUBLE
WITH ANGELS

"You kissed him."

"I did no such thing."

"Yes, you did, I know it as sure as the sun do rise. It's written in your aura." Anton spun her around in the chair and stared straight into her eyes. Damn him.

"Damn you! I was drunk; it didn't count. Where'd you get that all-seeing thing anyway?" Marla squirmed under his unbroken gaze.

"From my Grandma Lucia. She had Hungarian gypsy blood mingled with Italian. And yes, it did too count. Honey, I'm gonna look fabulous in pink chiffon." Anton gestured, breaking his stare-down.

"A kiss isn't the same as sex, and when I realized what I'd done, I was completely disgusted. So stuff that in your crystal ball. Besides, I'd never make my bridesmaids wear pink chiffon." She faked a huffy roll of her eyes.

"You kissed him, you kissed him," Anton sang at the top of his lungs, and boogaloo'd her chair back round.

Marla could never really be mad at Anton for more than ten seconds. She deeply suspected he planned last night's entire encounter, starting with giving Riley her address. Damn that wine. Damn Riley too. Of course, he *had* stopped himself, which was much to his credit. Most men she knew who found themselves in her walk-in closet wouldn't have been so gallant.

"Look at you. You're a dream, you're an angel. This is that angel-in-her-undies shoot today, right?"

Oh crap, crap, crap. This was not a good follow-up to the lip-lock evening. Riley watching her cavort in her Angel Undies. If they weren't paying her a small fortune, she'd never do this gig. What was a nice girl from Indiana who could write mystery novels doing in an underwear ad? She'd have to call her literary agent and see if her next six books could get a better advance.

Never mind, she was a professional. This was business. She'd just ignore him. She pursed her lips together and had a vivid flash of sensation. The incredible hot and sour soup at Shun Lee's. That was it. Her lips were still tingling from the red pepper. Where was he anyway?

Tom Riley woke up with a big, huge hard-on. He removed the pillow from his face and enjoyed it for a minute. Must have been a good dream. The numbers on the Big Ben wind-up clock were glowing in the semidarkness, but he couldn't make his eyes focus enough to tell where the hands were.

Why hadn't the alarm gone off? Whatever residual REM memories he'd had deflated quickly. Big Ben had been with him since high school, and never failed him, even after being thrown across the room a few times. It had to be user error. He'd forgotten to pull the alarm stem out.

"Here I come, you ugly bugs," he shouted, flashing the light switch to warn the cockroaches away. He heard the telltale skittering of a dozen tiny roach legs. "Someday, Tom, someday soon," he promised himself out loud.

It was a good thing he'd taken a cold shower last night because there was no time for that now.

Angling sideways to fit between the cramped bathroom fixtures, Tom grabbed his toothbrush and squeezed the last of the Crest out of the tube.

He brushed vigorously with his right hand while combing his hair back with his left. Where the hell was his comb anyway?

Clothes . . . clothes. He hadn't yet made his monthly trip to the Laundromat last week. Yesterday's stuff was practically standing on its own with the frosting's help. Rummaging through his top drawer, he managed a fairly decent pair of boxers, blue with a white stripe. He'd have to go into the archives for pants and a shirt.

Ignoring the mothballs, he grabbed mustard-brown corduroys and a plaid polyester shirt from his dad's leftovers he stored in a cardboard box in the closet. Tom was actually grateful his place had no full mirrors for him to accidentally look in. He threw his overcoat, hat, and scarf on, and bolted out the apartment door.

The air outside was like a slap in the face. The bitter cold curled into his nostrils as he drew in a breath. Running for the subway helped get the blood moving, and once inside, he wedged in between a few people and grabbed a strap. Body heat. Not bad.

Tom closed his eyes and instantly remembered Marla's kiss from last night. Man. Underneath that slightly aloof but stunning exterior beat the heart of a passionate woman. Unfortunately, men like him did not attract girls like that. Marla was a champagne-and-caviar kind of babe. He was beer nuts and Budweiser.

Not that he was pond scum. Under this pile-of-shit clothing beat the heart of a truly passionate man. He read all the time; okay, he read detective mysteries. He liked opera and jazz; well, he liked jazz for sure. Women like Marla just naturally gravitated toward the upper crust. He couldn't even afford a Pop-Tart at the moment.

This thought was good. It would help him focus on his main objective. Making sure her face stayed out of harm's way for thirty days, and getting his extra bonus check. The initial commission was good, but it just paid the back bills and redeemed the office equipment.

He put the remainder aside to make sure he could keep paying Doris that monthly support. That bonus check would really get him on his feet.

Max's birthday was coming up in March; maybe he could take him somewhere special. Best of all, Tom loved toy shopping. At ten, Max would probably only have one good year left of Hot Wheel car tracks and Mystic Knight flying dragon planes. After that it would be video games and stereo equipment. Not nearly as fun, and ten times the price.

For a minute Tom hit that place in himself that hurt because he and Doris hadn't had any more children. He had all but begged her. She'd flatly refused.

"I'm the one who has to have it, and giving birth to Max was enough pain for this body to last a lifetime. Besides, I have career plans," she'd said. And how could he argue with that?

That would mean they'd have to have sex. Not Doris's favorite thing. They'd stopped doing *that* four years ago.

Anyway, if he'd won the argument he'd have two children suffering through a divorce.

"Hundred-eighth," the driver announced loudly. Tom bolted for the opening subway door, half asleep, still walking. When he emerged from the tunnel, the February air was filled with tiny dry snowflakes. He turned up his collar and headed toward the studio address Marla gave him.

"Hi, Tom . . . honey!" This boyfriend thing was really wearing thin, and it was only day two. Marla's ears got hot around the edges, embarrassed at the poor lie she was asking everyone to swallow. She adjusted her giant angel wings, and lost a few feathers on her way back up to the shoot area.

When she positioned herself and turned back Tom's way, she remembered that the only thing she had on besides wings was a pair of shimmery pink bikini underwear, and a matching push-up bra. Not to mention the extremely uncomfortable surgical tape under her boobies making them *front and center*.

She remembered because Tom's eyes went as big as a cartoon character's.

"Marla, angle your shoulders toward me . . . that's right. Amy, could you fluff her wings a little on that side?" Patricia Shires was one of her favorite photographers, and if Marla had to do an underwear shoot, better it be with Patty than with some of the other, male photographers.

"That's it, you're an angel, darling." Everyone in the studio tittered with laughter. Ten more minutes, and Patty needed to reload the camera for the "double angel" shots. Marla got up and stretched herself as many ways as possible. Where was Paris anyway? She'd been late to their last shoot too. Shielding her eyes against the lights, Marla saw a shadowy figure with giant wings just behind Tom. So Paris was here.

Marla took a mineral water from Patty's assistant Amy and chugged most of it down. Got to keep the fluids up under the lights.

"Ouch, ouch, ouch." Paris stomped over to Marla. "This tape is like some medieval torture device."

"We're lucky now. The old fifties girls used duct tape I hear. At least this stuff leaves most of your skin on when you pull it off," Marla said.

"Yes, Little Mary Sunshine, the pioneer women had it harder. I know. Just acknowledge my pain; then my rant is shorter. Haven't you learned that yet?" Paris tried to sit on the stool next to Marla, but her wings kept getting in the way.

"Shit. Help me out, here, will ya?" Paris fussed. Marla came around and adjusted the wing contraption so Paris could sit. Her nose started itching from the tiny flying feathers.

"Achoooooo," Marla sneezed.

"Eccchhh. Get me a tissue, quick, and one for her." Paris wiped at her left arm.

"Ah-ah-ah-ah-choooooo." Marla took the offered tissue. She must have a feather up her nose.

"Achoo, achoo, achoo." She took the whole box from Amy.

"Makeup, over here," Amy called. Marla let out six more sneezes in a row. Patricia came over to her, looking concerned.

"Marla, you aren't allergic to goose feathers, are you?"

"No, no, I used to help pluck them back home," Marla managed between sneezes. Patty laughed.

"I didn't know you were a farm girl. Well, hon, we are going to have to take a break, because your eyes are swollen, and some red blotches are creeping up your neck. I'll do Paris for a while. Let's see how you look in an hour. Get some cold compresses for her, will you, Amy?"

By now Tom was edging up to the set. A steely chill swept through him. There were more ways than one to ruin a model's face. Here was Paris again, at the scene. Marla was a blotchy, mascara-stained mess by now. She couldn't seem to stop sneezing either. She'd take two steps and start a sneezing fit again. He reached out and took her hand.

"Marla, it's Tom. Walk this way." She didn't even fight him. Then again, she had a false eye-lash hanging over one eye. He led her to a large overstuffed sofa against the studio wall, but her wings were in the way. He fiddled with the straps.

"I—I don't know what's wrong. I've never been allergic to anything," she sniffed. Her face was re-ally going for the big puff now. Amy came over with a cold cloth and unhooked the wing contrap-tion from Marla's back.

"Better get her to the washroom and go for a rinse-out. Irrigate her eyes, particularly. I've seen this before from makeup. It's right down the hall," Amy said.

"Marla, we're going to head for the ladies' room and get you washed off. Take my hand, I'll lead you." She followed, holding the cold cloth against her face.

"Anybody in here? Man alert," he called in the door. The room echoed empty, and he led Marla in.

"Okay, Meyers, you're not going to like this, but I had to do this to my son once when he rubbed his mother's skin toner in his eyes. Bend your head in the sink this way." He pulled a small chair over to her, sat her next to the sink, then turned on the water and got a paper cup from the dispenser on the wall.

With as much finesse as possible under the circumstances, he irrigated her eyes till he thought she'd drown. It took every ounce of self-control he had to keep his eyes and hands off her nearly naked body. Her breasts were six inches away from his face and looking more puffed than her eyes. Steady as she goes, man, he advised himself.

"Auuuuuugghhhhhh," she moaned, obviously miserable.

He looked at his watch. "Just a few more minutes."

Then he was done, and Amy showed up just in time with a towel for Marla's head and a thick terry robe. He tucked the robe around her shoulders and legs with great relief. She emerged from the sink looking like an alleycat in a rainstorm. Her eyes were almost swollen shut. Amy stared, then politely left.

"Marla, someone did this to you." He let his thoughts loose.

"Oohhhhhhh brother. How do you figure that,

Riley? I had an allergy attack." Marla rolled her hair into the towel.

"I'd like to have Paris's wings tested for some substance. Itching powder or something."

"Riley, you're nuts. How could I ask for that? They'd think we were both crazy. There's more than one way to lose a job, and one is for them to think you're nuts." Marla started crying. That was a surprise. Tom felt helpless, then knelt down to her chair level and patted her on the shoulder.

"Come on, Meyers, buck up, now."

"*Buck up?* I'm a mess. I've lost this shoot. That's thousands of dollars I could actually *use*, Riley, plus I could default on my agency contract and not be able to get more work." She stopped crying and blew her nose on four more tissues from the box she still clutched.

"Noooo, no. You're right about one thing, Meyers, we aren't going to mention this conspiracy theory to anyone. You just got a feather up your nose. Neither your agency nor my home office needs to hear about this. But you have to promise me to think about what I am saying. Now let's get you some clothes."

"They're in the third dressing room down this same hall. No one will see me." They left the ladies' room, and she slipped in the dressing room door.

"I'll be right back. I'll tell your photographer something."

Patricia stepped over to Tom when he returned, and they had a quiet conversation. Over Patricia's nodding head he could see Paris straining to hear. What was the real story here? Mike Mason wouldn't let this slip by.

"Thanks, Ms. Shires, I'm sure she'll be better if you want to reschedule with the agency." Tom walked past her and over to Paris.

"Ripley. Believe it or not." Paris smiled her Cheshire cat smile.

"That's Riley, Miss James. Marla's going to rest her eyes and reschedule the rest of the shoot for another day."

"Poor little thang, looks like her winning streak has taken a little dip." Paris put on a fake pity face.

"Of course, you as one of her best friends must feel terrible about that. Right?" Tom looked Paris right in the eyes. Green as sin.

"Why, of course. I'm just kidding, Riley." Paris broke the gaze uncomfortably and squirmed in her shimmery blue underthings. Funny, she just didn't have the same effect on him as Marla. *That* scared the shit out of him.

"You might want to think about what you say, Paris. Coming in as someone who doesn't know you well, it sounds more like you wouldn't mind at all if Marla was out of the picture," Tom said.

For once, big-mouth Paris stood there in her underwear completely speechless. Tom felt the victorious moment run down his body. It was a swell feeling. " 'Bye, then, we'll see you soon." He swept around the back of her wings and swiftly plucked a feather out, sticking it in his pocket before she could even take note.

" 'Bye, boyfriend." Paris tried to turn his way, but she was pinned by the awkward wings.

Tom took out the feather, sniffed it a little, then sneezed. Hmm. He replaced it in his shirt pocket, then ran to the men's room and washed off his hands. He sneezed four more times. Taking a tissue, he plucked the feather out of his pocket and wrapped it up. In his other pocket was a packet of crackers in a plastic container. Setting the feather down, he emptied the package and replaced its contents with the feather, wrapping the whole mess in a paper towel.

He loved this detective stuff. Back in his pocket, the lumpy clue made him smile. He knew a nerdy friend from college who became a pharmacist. Tom knew just what to do with the magic feather. He also would bet money it had something on it.

How was he going to get Marla to listen to him? Two days into this deal, and already the worst had happened and her face was out of commission. Thank God it was temporary. Thank God they agreed to keep it quiet, and thank God she was getting dressed. The faster he took her home, the better. A man could only take so much of an angel.

Chapter Six

OH SWEET MYSTERY OF LOVE

The night was dark and stormy. Rain slammed against my car windows. I slouched down in the backseat of my black Jaguar XJ6 as I saw the shadowy figure emerge from the barbershop. O'Shay. Who was this guy following? What an amateur. The man had the classic trench coat and fedora that gave away a greenhorn every time.

Not to mention if I knew him as a reporter for the Seattle Daily, so did the murderer. Time to clue this loser in before he gets sent to the bottom of the bay with cement overshoes.

The night was dark and stormy? Marla highlighted the entire paragraph, hit copy, and pasted it into her *spew* file.

Her work was getting stale from lack of practice. This whole month was really cramping her style. Setting her laptop aside, she slid down farther and stretched her legs out under the covers. The soothing feel of her 320-thread-count cotton sheets eased her mind some. This was just what she needed. Downtime. Time to roll out a couple of chapters of Mike Mason, in her bed.

Her publisher wanted to see *Murder on the News* in four months. Usually that wasn't a problem. Even though modeling had an unpredictable schedule, Marla had managed to create order in her life around the chaos. She set herself weekly goals, and kept them.

But now she had chaos on top of chaos. She snuggled deeper under the down duvet. Maybe she'd take a nap first. The sun shone through her miniblinds, making horizontal stripes of light on the bed.

Hey, she slept under goose down every night. Obviously something else had gotten to her. It would be nice to know what she was allergic to, so she didn't get into it again. It was probably Riley's cologne. Or was that just the scent of bargain shaving cream? Most likely. Oh brother, now she was thinking about Riley again.

It should bother her that this man, with whom

she supposedly had a professional arrangement, had managed to kiss her twice in three days. But strangely enough, since the first one was cover for their boyfriend story, and the second time was . . . well, clearly her fault, she felt perfectly justified in not worrying about it. She'd just continue with the rest of the thirty days as if nothing had happened. Best possible idea. Absolutely.

Heaving a huge sigh, she threw back the bedcovers. Farm girls from Indiana never could sleep in. There might as well be a big ol' red rooster in her apartment crowing at the crack of dawn. She looked at the clock. Seven-thirty. She'd better get up, shower, dress, make a fruit smoothie, and work on the office computer. See, she thought, a nice regular routine. Her life. She straightened the pants of her blue silk man-pajamas, and put on her fuzzy white slippers.

In the bathroom, Marla looked in the mirror tentatively. She'd taken a huge dose of Vitamin C last night, ignoring the over-the-counter antihistamines Riley had picked up at a drugstore on the way home. Her vitamins and some power-cleansing, detoxifying herbs seem to have done the trick. Her face looked a little puffy, but not bad. In another day, she'd be back to normal. Maybe they were dodo bird feathers. Go figure.

Her hair looked like complete hell. She grabbed a scrunchy and pulled it all back in a ponytail. She took her electric toothbrush, stuck on some baking soda whitening toothpaste, and cleaned her teeth for a good ten minutes. Smiling into the mirror, she admired her handiwork. It was nice of her dad to give her braces as a kid, undoubtedly a huge strain on the budget.

On her days off she tried to avoid makeup to give her face a break. Just a little moisturizer. She opened a jar and dabbed the expensive cream under her eyes and over her cheeks in little dots.

The intercom buzzed. Well, for sure it wasn't Riley because he never got up before eight in his life, she thought with a giggle. She punched the bathroom speaker button.

"Yes?"

"Miss Meyers, its Carl." Carl had a habit of stating the obvious.

"Yes, Carl," Marla answered patiently.

"That man is here again. Mr. Riley. Do you want me to let him up?"

Riley? No, please. Not on her day of order.

"Put him up to the speaker, Carl."

"Okay, Miss Meyers." She heard some rustling and assumed Tom was at the speaker.

"Riley, you can have the day off. I'm not doing anything today."

A croaky male voice crackled through the old speaker system. "Meyers, can we talk about this for a minute? How about a cup of coffee?"

"No, thank you."

"I mean me. Can I come up for a cup of coffee? I haven't slept all night."

That explained the early hour. Not wanting to continue explaining things through the speaker for all to hear, Marla agreed.

"All right. Let him up."

"Are you sure, Miss Meyers? He looks very unsavory today."

Marla suppressed her laughter. "It's okay, Carl, he's a friend of mine," she replied. Unsavory. What horrid outfit did Mr. Riley have on today? she wondered. Lost in imaginings, she walked into the kitchen to put some coffee on.

Pulling her French press from the shelf, she measured out three tablespoons of Italian roast coffee. That ought to get Mr. Riley going. She filled her copper kettle, put it on the stove, and fired up the gas burner. Then her doorbell rang.

She opened the door and stared at Riley in the same unbelievably terrible clothes he'd had on yesterday, but even worse, because he'd obviously slept in them—or laid around, anyhow—his eyes were bloodshot from lack of sleep, and he had a day's growth of beard. *Unsavory* was definitely the word.

She couldn't help herself. Covering her mouth with her hand, she tried to keep the laughter in, but it overtook her. Then again, he was staring at her like she was Dick Tracy's Moon Maid. She drew her hand back and saw blobs of lotion stuck to it.

"Ha. We're even," he said, and trudged toward the smell of coffee grounds in her kitchen.

We will never be even, Riley, she thought. She rubbed the lotion into her face on the way to the kitchen. Of course, it wasn't her place to tell Riley what a total fashion aardvark he was—except she was telling everyone he was her boyfriend.

"Riley, we need to talk about your presentation." Marla entered the kitchen area and reached in the cupboard for a coffee mug and her cup. As she turned back to him, she caught a strong whiff of mothballs. It made her nose wrinkle up.

"That's not what I came here to talk about, whatever it is you mean. Just listen to me for a few minutes."

Ignoring him, she poured boiling water into the coffee press, stuck in the gizmo, and tapped her fingernails on the marble countertop while the coffee steeped a minute. "If I'm going to masquerade you as my boyfriend, you are going to have to clean up your act. Are you willing to put yourself in my hands?"

"No, I'm not. I'm sorry if you find me offensive. I've been doing some research and going over the events of the last few days in my head. Besides, since I took this job on, I haven't had time to do anything . . . like sleep, or shave, or get my laundry done. I don't have all day, I have to pick up my son after school, and he gets out at three o'clock. Isn't there a faster way to make that?" Tom snapped.

"You have a son?"

"Yes, he's ten. Max."

This was an interesting tidbit about Mr. Riley. He was a father. Marla plunged the press down hard, and the hot steaming coffee was ready for Tom's mug. She poured it in and handed it to him. "Look, how about you just drink this down, go lock yourself in my bathroom, and take a nice hot shower? Basically, I'm not going to listen to you until I can stand being in the same room with you. It's the mothball cologne, you know? I know this is unusual, and I'm trying to be as polite as possible, here, but that's it."

She assumed an uncompromising stance, but Riley just stared at her. She handed him a spoon and the sugar bowl, which he waved away, then gulped some coffee and finally spoke.

"Let's see, I've known you a few days, and you're telling me I smell too bad to talk to and should take all my clothes off and get in your shower?" He took another long drink of coffee. "I don't think so, lady."

Marla had a plan hatching in her head, and there was no way in hell Tom Riley was going to get around it. She decided to turn on the charm. Men, simple creatures that they were, were basically helpless to resist the wiles of a truly determined woman.

"Tom." She smiled while she poured coffee in her special cup, then added a cube of sugar and a dollop of cream. If she was going to indulge in coffee, she liked to make it a treat. "You're tired. And you said yourself you've got to pick up your son later. I suppose you could go back to your place, but I'm offering you a nice, warm, clean place to shower. I'll even listen to whatever you have on your mind if you'll clean up some. How does that sound?" She leaned against the counter, sipped her coffee seductively, and batted her eyes a little.

A barely audible grumble came from Tom's stomach, but that was the only sound he made. A stroke of inspiration hit her. "How about I make you some breakfast while you're in there?"

"Well . . . only if you will listen to me when I'm done," he agreed reluctantly.

"It's eight in the morning, Riley. We have time. I promise I'll listen. Now take your coffee in there," she ordered, pointing toward the bathroom.

Riley poured some more in the cup, then headed down the hall. "All right, but no scrambled tofu. I've seen the inside of your refrigerator," he called over his shoulder.

"I promise. There are clean towels in the cupboard in there. Use the pink ones."

"Women," she heard him mutter.

As soon as the bathroom door closed behind him, Marla reached for the portable phone. She pressed autodial 2, balanced the phone on her ear, and headed for the fridge. Grabbing cartons of eggs, cheese, butter, and assorted vegetables, she waited for her call to connect.

"Hi, you've reached 555-6545. Leave a message, please."

"Anton, pick up, pick *up*," Marla hissed into the phone.

"Marla, I'm here. What is it, hon, having a shopping attack? I can be there in ten minutes. I've already got my britches on and had a bowl of Cocoa Puffs," Anton's perky voice came through the phone.

"I have to talk fast, sweetie. Tom Riley's in my shower."

"Yikes, girlfriend, you lost the bet in two days? Tsk, tsk, I am so surprised at you. No, I'm not, I told you under those hideous clothes Mr. Riley was Mr. Right. I win, I win," he singsonged his taunt.

"So sorry to disappoint you, but he came over here to talk business. I tricked him into the shower. I can't go on passing him off as my boyfriend looking like he does. I've got an idea, but I need your help."

"I'm still imagining you tricking him into the shower. I think I know what you have in mind, but I warn you, when I'm done, you're not going to like it."

"What are you talking about? Anything will be an improvement."

"Just mark my words, dear. Now, I've got some wardrobe here. He's taller than I am, but Warren left some of his things here before he ran off with that Argentine prince. Boo-hoo. Of course, these are just divine, since I bought them for Warren myself. I am the queen of shopping, after all." Anton giggled.

"Just hurry. I've got to go steal his clothes and make him an omelette."

"We'll have a long talk about this later, sweetie. I'm on my way."

Anton hung up, but his teasing rang in her ears. That goose. As if. He'd just have to wear that pink chiffon at someone else's wedding. Marla grabbed a screwdriver out of the kitchen drawer and snuck down the hall. She could hear the shower running. Oooh, she was on a dangerous mission now!

As quietly as possible, she turned the doorknob lock with the screwdriver tip and slid in the door. Steam billowed around her, and she could see his hazy form behind the glass door. His clothes were piled on the floor, uncomfortably close to the shower. She made a dash for it, grabbed the pile, and made it back to the door.

Pausing, she turned back to see Tom's behind come into focus. My goodness, he *was* well put together. Somehow she'd imagined him as . . . less. Then again, he did have great biceps, and he did catch her in his arms, and his eyes were that great chocolate brown. The steam clouded up the room again. She instinctively turned and flipped on the fan switch. It started up with a whir.

"Huh? Hey, Meyers, what the—" Tom started, but she slammed the door to avoid seeing any full frontal nudity. That would be rude.

"Meyers, what are you up to? Hey, hey! Give me back those clothes." Riley's voice went down a notch and sounded menacing. "Marla, what do you think you are doing?"

"Relax, Riley, put on a towel. I'm leaving a robe outside the door. Breakfast will be ready in a few minutes. Oh, there's a new disposable razor in the sink drawer and a few other things. Help yourself," she called through the door.

"Have you completely lost your mind? Are you planning on keeping me prisoner?" Tom sounded like he was trying hard to keep his voice calm.

"Can't hear you . . . I'm in the kitchen. I'll just throw those clothes of yours in for a wash." Marla went and stuffed the insufferable brown cords and polyester shirt in her front-loading washer.

Humming as she worked, she wondered what had befallen Tom Riley, that he should be so out of touch with his appearance. After all, this was New York, and fashion surrounded them. Cheap fashion, even. He had said something about his recent divorce. Maybe he wasn't used to taking care of himself.

She was probably being horrid. Well, breakfast would help. She'd make him a great omelette, and he'd forget the whole thing.

He really didn't know her that well. She could have just pretended to be a sane person. He could be in the clutches of a psycho-model. Tom dried himself off and wrapped the towel around his waist. Carefully opening the bathroom door, he spotted the robe folded neatly within his reach on the floor. A quick grab, and he had it. Thank God it wasn't flowered silk or something. A little short, but it would pass until he figured out a way to get his clothes back.

He opened the sink drawers and found the disposable razor pack. Next to it was aloe shave gel. Chick shave. Oh brother. Things could be worse, he reasoned, as he spread the soft gel on his beard and watched it change to foam. He could be in the clutches of Paris. Hmm, even that wouldn't be so bad. And he smelled some mighty good smells coming from the kitchen. Could Miss Granola be cooking bacon?

Okay, he reasoned with himself. A gorgeous model has you trapped in her apartment and has stolen your clothes, but she's making you breakfast. No matter how he turned it around, Tom couldn't find anything bad about it.

"She wants me. That's it. She's decided to make me her love slave. Never mind I came in here looking like a bum. She's just sex-starved," he said to himself, then wiped the steam away from the mirror and examined his face as he shaved. Not a bad-looking guy, really. It could happen. Hence the shower request. Obviously that wine-induced kiss stuck with her.

Tom decided he was willing to be her boy-toy, even if it only lasted an afternoon. Kind of unprofessional, but as far as he remembered there wasn't an oath taken by insurance men not to acquiesce to the sexual demands of their clients.

He rehearsed his entrance. Maybe a nice stroll-up behind her with a neck-nibble? Or should he just turn her around and go for a kitchen-counter encounter? Tom was getting turned on just thinking about that one. It sure was hot in here. Time for some fresh air.

He set the razor down, toweled off with a wet face towel, straightened the belt on her robe, and strode out toward the kitchen. "Down, boy," he whispered to Mr. Big, as he affectionately referred to his manly parts.

"This is just too delicious, you wicked girl. I haven't had this much fun since Warren danced naked in the fountain at Santa Marguerita, that little Italian village we stayed in, you remember?" Anton sat on the counter stool, close to Marla.

"We might have to get him drunk or something. How about I spike the coffee?" Marla added.

"Oh . . . no . . ."

Marla and Anton turned simultaneously to the sound behind them. There was Tom, with his hands waving out in front of him, backing away, his face stricken with a kind of reddish green pallor.

"No . . . nooooooo, you don't. I resign. Give me my coat. I'm outta here."

"Whatever is the matter with him?" Marla turned to ask Anton. "Tom, if you don't like eggs, I can make you some waffles or something."

"Aaaaaaaaaaaa! Help!" Tom continued backing away. Anton turned to Marla.

"Hon, I'd say, from the look on his face, Mr. Riley is suffering under the delusion you want him for a ménage à trois starring *moi*. And, of course, you." Anton gestured grandly toward the players.

"A what?"

"Oh Jumpin' Jehosefat, Marla, you are so naive sometimes. Your farm roots are showing, hon. He thinks you want him for some kind of kinky sexual adventure. A threesome."

Marla choked on her sip of coffee and spit it into the air laughing. Anton jumped off the chair and walked toward Tom.

"It's your hair she wants, Sampson. Delilah wants me to cut your hair. Just a nice trim around the sides. . . ." Anton made a square with his fingers like a filmmaker and sized up Tom's head shape.

"I have a barber, thanks anyway." Marla could tell Tom was trying to recover his dignity.

"Go easy, Anton. One thing we learn on the farm is to approach a newly caged animal slowly," Marla said.

"Mr. Riley, your barber . . . well, I hate to tell you, but he died in 1979. That's his ghost cutting your hair," Anton retorted in a completely serious tone.

"Very funny. Look here, Anton, I'm sure you are great, but I'm not financially equipped to take an appointment with someone of your caliber."

"From the looks of things, you're equipped quite well." Anton was getting silly.

"Anton, stop that. You're scaring him," Marla warned.

"Mr. Riley, this is a favor I'm doing for Marla. Besides, I hate to see a really gorgeous man such as yourself running around without realizing his full potential, speaking in an appearance way."

"What is he saying?" Tom turned to Marla.

"It's free, Riley," Marla replied. Tom seemed to perk up at that thought, but she saw a shadow cross his eyes. Then he spoke carefully, and sternly, to Anton.

"All right. I'm game. But Anton, you can't do any of that flirting stuff with me anymore or I'm leaving. I know you're Marla's friend, but I'd rather keep things purely business, if you don't mind. Agreed?"

"Of course. I acknowledge that you are destined for another." Anton turned his head and gestured. "Now let's get to work, I have appointments in three hours. Some of us have regular jobs, you know."

"Fine, then, in the interest of playing Marla's supposed boyfriend while I watch after her, I agree to a haircut. A free haircut." Tom looked hard at Marla. "Now could you please give me my clothes back?"

"Well, no." Marla walked over to the garment bag Anton had brought with him. "But here are some new ones. On the house. Consider them a bonus benefit for doing this job," Marla said. "I really am grateful that you're helping me get this policy accepted, Riley."

Tom sighed and took the bag.

"Don't put them on just yet, Mr. Riley. There's no use getting that thick, lovely hair all over that cashmere sweater."

Marla watched Tom give Anton a look.

"Oh, sorry. I'm trying." Anton shook his head and tsked at himself.

Marla interrupted. "Now have a bite of your breakfast, and we'll get to it in a while."

"Thanks, but if you don't mind, I'll just put on some underwear. Is mine available or does that come with the deal?"

"I took the liberty of putting a few pairs in with the clothes, Thomas. Take your pick. Also socks and a nice pair of Italian loafers in a size ten. My former boyfriend left a perfectly fine wardrobe behind when he . . . ran away from the best thing he's ever had," Anton added with a deep sigh.

The deep sigh was echoed by Tom, who set the garment bag on the back of a love seat. He pulled out a pair of bright purple silk boxers and sighed again. "I'll be right back. Did I smell actual bacon?"

"Well, you smelled prosciutto ham I warmed up and put in the omelette." Marla flew around the kitchen gathering breakfast.

"Close enough. Thank you for the breakfast. Sorry if I've appeared . . . ungrateful," Tom said as he stepped out of the room. He reappeared in a few minutes, then settled at the table. Marla brought him the omelette, more coffee, and some toast.

"Anton?"

"Just coffee, hon; a little sugar and cream—you know." Anton sat across the table from Tom.

Tom sank his fork into the savory omelette and took a bite. Hell, she could actually cook.

"So, Marla tells me you're recently divorced?" Anton set his face in his hands and looked at Tom inquisitively.

"Yes, I am, two years now." Tom stopped for a second. Anton wasn't going to weasel a bunch of information out of him. What the heck was that about anyway? Maybe he was just making conversation. At any rate, it just served to remind Tom he had something to say, and nothing was going to stop him. Not even Anton.

For some reason—gut instinct, probably—he didn't consider Anton a suspect. Tom took a swig of the strong coffee. He continued talking between bites of breakfast and slurps of coffee. "Listen, Anton, you're one of Marla's best friends, right? She seems to trust you."

Anton nodded.

Marla came over with her cup of herbal tea. It smelled like mint.

"Anton is the only person I really trust, Riley, he's been through eight years of modeling with me. I even lived with Anton for a while in my early days." She reached over and patted Anton's hand. "We have no secrets."

"Meyers, you promised if I took a shower you'd listen to me, and since you feel that way about Anton, I'm going to make him listen, too. Maybe he can help."

"All right, go on, then." Marla sat back with her tea.

"Here's the thing. Let's look at the events of the last few days. Since you walked into my office Monday, you've fallen down my stairs, tripped into a cake, and been exposed to a chemical irritant on the set. That's mathematically nearly impossible."

"Unless I really am accident-prone, Riley. I've had other things happen, particularly in the last few weeks." Marla set her tea on the table and rubbed her forehead with her hand. "Maybe I need glasses or have a brain tumor or something." She looked suddenly vulnerable to Tom in her pale blue pajamas. He noticed her fingers were long and slender, like a musician's or an artist's.

Tom stopped and thought hard about what she

said. "It is possible that you are just accident-prone. I know you said you've had other mishaps. All I can tell you is that I have a gut feeling this is different." Tom got very serious. He wanted her to know he was serious about his theory.

"I want you to know I think that your shoe was tampered with, that someone deliberately pulled up a cord on that runway and made you trip into the cake, and . . . listen up, because I spent most of last night with my friend who works in a lab. I took him a sample of that feather. He says there was something on it, we're not sure what yet, but it was a highly irritating substance. You'd have to be very close to it, even touch it, to have it affect you."

He'd also spent the night getting his stuff out of hock, setting up his office, and writing checks. Then playing the trombone to sooth his nerves. The theories built up during all of that mindless time.

"What makes you think it was meant for me? The feathers were on Paris's back."

"It's just a feeling I have." Tom plunked his coffee cup down on the table. "I know it doesn't sound right, but I've seen it with my own eyes. I might be wrong, but if I'm not, then someone wants you out of the way."

Tom noticed Anton had grown more restless as

he listened. Now Anton stood up and paced beside the kitchen counter bar.

"What would be the point of getting me out of the way, Riley? Who would have a motive? Every crime has a motive," Marla pointed out.

"I'm not sure yet. You and I are the only ones who know we are on a thirty-day trial, and that I'm watching you." Tom turned and looked at Anton carefully. "Besides you, Anton. Anyone else aware of the policy would assume if you're injured and can't work, the agency would collect three million dollars. I think we should look at who would benefit from that. Is there anyone else?"

"Rita knows. But she promised to keep quiet so I wouldn't be embarrassed. Hopefully the boyfriend story is selling," Marla said.

"Rita Ray. That's right. She'd be the person who would benefit the most, the agency collecting all that money," Tom said sharply. "Is it standard for the agency to request this kind of policy on certain models? I know some of them have their legs insured by Lloyd's of London. It has to be someone who understands the procedures of the agency, and has something to gain by you having a policy and having to use it."

"But I don't see how collecting on the policy is as good as me bringing in the agency's percentage over time. Besides, Rita is one of my dearest friends. Just don't go off half loaded, Riley."

"I see what you mean, but three million dollars in a lump sum is better than two years of fifteen percent."

"You know, about the wings . . ." Anton finally spoke from his new perch on the bar chair. "The Angel Undies promo people had those delivered by a prop company on Water Street. We sent someone from our own agency to pick them up, which was highly unusual."

"Can you find out who?" Tom got up animatedly. He cleared his things, grabbed up his empty breakfast plate, and took it into the kitchen to stand across the counter from Anton.

"Anton, you aren't actually believing this, are you? There are perfectly reasonable explanations for every one of Riley's suspicions. My heel just broke. The cord was just loose. The prop was accidentally exposed to some cleaning chemical. The best explanation of all"—Marla gestured widely—"is that I'm a klutz!"

Anton turned back to Tom. "Give me some time. I'll dig some information up for you." Tom saw the serious look on Anton's face and nodded. He looked down at himself and realized he still had Marla's robe on and nothing else but purple silk boxers. He tightened the wrap belt. "Can we get to where I get some clothes on now, folks?"

"Haircut first. You, princess, you still have your jammies on too." Anton pointed at Marla.

"It's my day off." Marla made a face at Anton, but walked toward her bedroom closet obediently. That was Tom's favorite spot in the house so far.

Jumping down from the stool, Anton directed Tom around the kitchen until he was stationed on a chair in the middle of the tile floor, shoulders wrapped in a sheet.

"No wild stuff, there, Anton. No shaved initials or wedges or whatever all that stuff is called. Just a little off the sides."

"Oh, Mr. Riley, just shut your eyes. I'm going to turn you into Adonis."

"No Greek stuff either."

"Quiet. I'm creating." Anton's scissors flew around Tom's hair like quicksilver. Tom surrendered and closed his eyes. He was tired. Finally someone believed his crazy theory, even if it was only Anton. He was going to have to get some sleep after this and try to sort it all out. That and a few dozen other things.

Chapter Seven

BEFORE
AND AFTER

Marla gasped. "Anton, this was a twisted and devious plot."

"Takes one to know one, hon." Anton stood back, looking terribly pleased with himself.

"It's not that bad, is it?" Tom was dragged to the full-length mirror. He turned his head a few angles to check out the haircut. It was far from his usual cut, but truthfully, Anton had a gift. When was the last time Ernie had cut his hair anyhow? Fall?

The black cashmere sweater and tailored slacks, well, they were undoubtedly the best-quality stuff he'd had on since he scraped together enough to buy his first suit in college. He had to admit, the clothes and the cut felt great.

Come to think of it, that suit was pretty cheap. Its specialness must have been the sense of accomplishment he'd felt paying for it himself from his tiny salary as a trombone player in a weekend jazz band. The pre-Doris suit.

"Riley, you look like a new man. The clothes definitely fit too." Marla was acting kind of squirrelly. She sure looked great, though, slim black slacks and a soft red sweater. She had on bright red lipstick that reminded him of the fifties. Altogether, Marla Meyers could stop a speeding freight train in its tracks.

"You two look simply delish. How can you deprive Manhattan of a look-see?"

"You're just not playing fair, Anton," Marla said. Tom couldn't figure out the special secret language of those two.

"Marla said you are going to pick up your son after school today. Why don't you all go on an outing? It would be a thrill for Riley, Jr., to meet a real model, and you could keep an eye on Marla at the same time. After all you've said, you don't really want to let her out of your sight, do you?"

"Anton, that is completely rude of you. I'm sure Mr. Riley doesn't want his time with his son interrupted." Tom watched Marla glare at Anton. "Besides, I had some other things to do today, *darling*."

"Oh, you work too hard anyway. What do you say, Tom?" Anton replied.

Tom had been thinking this through, and the idea of bringing a fabulous woman like Marla over for Doris to see him with had its merits. Either that or he was feeling suicidal. Max actually would be thrilled, and he had planned an outing to the museum. Max liked to check up on the dinosaur bones at least every six months.

On the other hand, Doris might think he was holding out on her if she saw him all decked out with a babe on his arm. As if he would compromise his son's comfort level for a new wardrobe—or a woman, for that matter. He could tell her the absolute truth, and see how that went. What the hell.

Then there was that point about him keeping an eye on Marla as much as possible. Considering how much was at stake, his job, his check, his neck.

"Marla, I'd appreciate it very much if you would agree to come with me today. If you don't mind a museum outing with my son, Max. I'd feel much better about our arrangement if I could have one day go by without an incident."

"See?" Anton interjected. "That was a big speech for him. Look outside. It's freezing, but the sun is out. You could use some fresh air."

"Fine. Riley, I like kids, I love the museum. I'm sure we'd have a nice, relaxing time."

"Well, then, that's settled. Thomas, here's a coat I brought for you. Marla, bundle up, hon. Y'all can pick up a little lunch to go at Zabar's. Be

sure and get a couple of those cream cheese Dan-
ishes with the apricot. They're to die. Little Riley
will love them. Bring me a couple too, will you,
dear?"

"Max is more of a Nathan's dog kinda guy.
Thanks for the haircut, Anton, and the loaner
clothes." Tom put on the loosely tailored black
leather jacket. "You're all right."

"No loan, Thomas, they're a gift, for watching
over my Marla. I'll bring the rest of poor Warren's
things over here later tonight."

"Thanks," Tom said. Poor Warren had great
taste.

Marla came out in a black fake fur coat with a
matching hat. Here we go, thought Tom, *into the
lion's den*. Relaxing. Sure.

At two o'clock Marla stood with Tom outside
Glen Oaks Elementary waiting for Max to come
running out the double doors. Tom seemed nervous with her standing beside him. A few of the
other parents glanced their way, and a few
women openly stared. Marla wondered if they
had an interest in Tom. This could be pretty bad
for his social life, hanging around with her.

Marla felt a little guilty. Well, heck, she'd be out
of the picture in less than a month, and maybe the
makeover and the short-term girlfriend bit would
improve his pickings. She couldn't tell from Tom's

expression whether this was just incredibly embarrassing or incredibly ego-fulfilling.

"Dad! Wow, you look great! Who's your friend?" Max appeared out of a sea of children's faces, ran right into Tom's leg, and held on tight. Tom lifted Max up like a rocket, then held him eye to eye.

"Hey, little man, this is Marla Meyers. She's a client of mine, and she's going to hang around with us today. Is that okay with you?"

"Are you kidding? That's great, Dad. Hey, Miss Meyers, are you my dad's new girlfriend?"

"Nope, sorry. We're just friends. Can I come with you to the museum?"

"That's great, but I'm starving. Dad, can we get a hot dog downtown? Let's go catch the bus, guys."

"We get to take a cab today, son, in honor of Miss Meyers."

They got back in the waiting taxi and hung on for dear life while the driver tried for the land-speed record across the Long Island Expressway. He mumbled something about beating the mid-town traffic. The cab dropped them off a few blocks from the American Museum of Natural History, right by a Nathan's hot dog stand. Max jumped out as Tom paid the driver.

Marla followed Max as fast as possible. Somehow her Midwest childhood still left her with a sense of wariness about the city, and she felt protective. Instinctively, she grabbed Max's hand. He looked up at her and grinned. He didn't let go, and his kid-sized hand kind of snuggled into hers.

"Want a hot dog, Miss Meyers?"

"You can call me Marla."

"I've seen you on magazine covers. My mom gets piles of them from the place she works. She does women's nails. Once this lady asked her to put little pieces of hundred-dollar bills on her nails. Mom said it was gross, that she could have bought a new refrigerator with it instead. Have you ever put money on your nails?"

"No, I haven't. It does sound gross. I did have stars on mine once, though."

"Max, what are you two yakking about?" Tom stepped up to them, looking worried.

"She had stars on her fingernails once. I'll have the usual, Dad. That's a pickle dog," Max explained to Marla. She looked into his extremely cute face. He must take after the mother. His eyes were hazel, and his hair was reddish brown. But his face shape was very . . . Riley.

The dog ordering commenced, and Max was reminded by Riley not to wolf down his sweet-pickle-relish-smothered hot dog. They went a few doors over and got papaya drinks to wash it all down. There were some swivel stools in the Papaya King, and "Stewy" said he didn't mind them eating there. Max had gotten the counterman's name in about ten seconds.

Tom handed Marla her dog, and she breathed in the aroma.

"I didn't know you had it in you, Meyers."

"Haven't you ever seen anyone eat a chili dog, Riley? Chili is good for you, all those beans and . . . and . . ." Marla fumbled for an excuse, but truthfully, she'd always had a weakness for chili.

Her dad had made a ritual out of preparing his pot of chili in the winter months. Cold weather always brought that out in her. She watched the steam rise off the hot dog smothered in spicy chili with a squeeze of some sort of cheese product squiggled on top. Better not think on it too much. She took a big bite and enjoyed herself immensely. Her eyes opened to see Tom grinning at her over his own chili dog.

The other thing she was finding enjoyable was the new Tom Riley. Now that Anton had provided him with some decent clothing, those intense brown eyes and the wavy hair that gave him the classic look of the dark Irish were even more appealing. She felt a little shallow about it all, seeing him in a better light just because his hair was neat and his clothes upscale.

It seemed like Tom Riley was awakening to his new self too. More than once she'd seen women turn and give Tom the once-over as they passed. He looked . . . taller.

Of course, this was all a plot on Anton's part to prove to her that Riley was her cosmic destiny. She wasn't about to forget this man undoubtedly had nothing in common with her at all. Nor that he was New York born and bred. In Marla's book, that was a recipe for disaster. Hmm, *Murder Bakes a Cake*, about a murderous chef. She was going to have to change her title run. She was sick of thinking up titles that rhymed with *blues*. What, *Murder Over the Pot Au Fues*? Marla finished her chili dog and slurped down the rest of her great papaya drink.

"Ready for those dinosaurs, buddy?" Riley stood and started cleaning up the mess surrounding Max . . . and Marla.

"Welcome to the American Museum of Natural History. In our Hall of Vertebrate Evolutions, we meet the world's tallest freestanding dinosaur exhibit, Barosaurus. Here we have re-created the Barosaursus, an enormous plant-eating dinosaur that lived a hundred and forty million years ago, rearing up to protect its young from a fierce, attacking Allosaurus."

The tour guide snapped her gum and led them through the exhibits. Marla was truly awestruck. How could she have gone ten years without visiting this museum? She'd gone to the Guggenheim, and MOMA, and dozens of other galleries, but never here. What the heck *had* she been doing for the last ten years? Suddenly Marla felt her biological clock kick her in the rear. Ouch.

Marla heard herself saying "Wow" about as many times as Max. There were displays of dinosaur bones everywhere. She felt like a kid again; a kid from Indiana.

"Wow, Marla, come and look at this. This is the Tyrannosaurus Rex. He's the baddest dude. He ate everybody else. That one over there is an Apatosaurus." Max pointed at the skillfully reconstructed bones. He obviously knew everything in the known universe about every kind of dinosaur. Marla enjoyed his commentary more than the museum tour.

"Where did you learn so much about dinosaurs, Max?" Marla asked.

"My dad and I are really into it. He reads me books, and we've been coming here for, like . . . my whole life. We saw a movie about a dig in Argentina where they found a dinosaur nesting ground with thousands of eggs. They were fossilized with the baby dinos still in there. They think they were these ones called Titanosaurs. Big huge plant-eaters. Cool, huh?"

"That is cool, Max. Your dad's pretty cool too." Marla looked up at Tom, who shrugged casually.

"Boys like dinosaurs," said Tom.

"Max is really a great kid, Tom, you've done a good job with him." Marla and Tom walked side by side as Max bounced ahead of them. They broke off from the tour group and let the boy lead them along.

"Thanks, I enjoy being the dad dude."

"You know, Tom, I feel like that Liechtenstein cartoon where the woman says, 'Damn, I forgot to have kids.' Right? I was just wondering where the last ten years of my life have gone. I did get to see Europe and went to college here in New York, but somehow it all just feels like a blur."

Marla hesitated. She was being pretty revealing with Riley. That wasn't like her. Maybe Riley would make a good friend, since there wasn't going to be any romance between them. After all, could two people get more different? She decided to continue.

"I would've liked to have gotten married and had some kids. My whole focus has been to help my dad keep the farm going. I always felt guilty about not being the son that could stay and work the farm and all."

"Daughters can stay and work the farm; you're just better at this. I don't think your dad would want you to sacrifice yourself and your career to stay on the farm, even if you weren't a woman. Do you?" Tom looked over at her with his wonderful brown eyes, and his great new haircut, with true interest in what she was saying. Marla felt a flush run over her cheeks.

"Modeling isn't really my heart's desire, Riley; it's just a job I got into to pay for college. The money was really good, so I stayed with it. I tried a few other things the first two years I was here. The starving student thing wore thin."

"Well, what is your heart's desire, then?" Tom asked.

"I can't tell you yet. Hey, Max, what's that one, a Gigantosaurus?" Marla changed the subject before she opened her mouth about her writing. She and her literary agent had decided long ago not to let people know a woman wrote the Mike Mason mystery series. Men were her biggest readers, and they just couldn't take the shock of finding out M. B. Kerlin was really a *Marla Beth*.

After the museum Marla surprised herself by stuffing down a truly decadent handmade ice-cream sandwich coated in chocolate, washed down with a Coke. Tom seemed amazed at her capacity to stray from healthy food.

To give Max some excitement, Marla called the agency limo driver and asked if he'd have time to run them back out to Queens. In about a half hour he pulled up on their block, got out, and opened the door for her.

"Wow, Dad! I've never ridden in a limo ever! This so cool. I wish Russell could see this," Max said.

"Russell—best friend," Tom translated. "You didn't have to do this, you know."

"Oh, relax, Riley, it's fun," Marla said. "Here you go, Max, sit wherever you like."

Max popped into the limo past the surprised driver and tried three seats before settling on the backward-facing one.

Marla buckled in beside Tom. She watched the excitement on Max's face and felt really happy. Once the driver was back in, she pushed the intercom button. "Terrell, how about we rock out on our way to Queens? Something a ten-year-old would appreciate?"

"Yes, ma'am." She could see Terrell's grin in the rearview mirror.

Tom wrote the address down on a pad in the back and let Max hand it through the driver's partition when Marla lowered it. In just a few seconds the bass beat of the Backstreet Boys was pumping through the compartment. Max obviously knew all the words, and was singing along kind of off-key but cool.

Tom joined in, pretty much faking the lyrics. Marla felt a strange lumpy voice rise out of her as the chorus came around. They did the sitting "frug" for that one, then switched to a "swim" as the tape moved over to an old Beach Boys tune.

Marla thought she would pee her pants laughing at their combined bad singing voices.

The limo pulled up in front of Doris's house just as they finished woofing to someone letting some dogs out.

Doris's eyes—with their press-on lashes and iridescent pale green liner—opened very, very wide. He noticed her usually bright red hair was in a straight platinum blonde ear-length bob. Aside from all those shocks, Tom couldn't believe it when he saw Doris actually extend her hand to Marla.

He also couldn't believe he'd just gotten out of a limo with the slightly flushed Miss Meyers who had just finished woofing like a dog.

"Marla Meyers. *The* Marla Meyers. I am so pleased to meet you. Doris Riley. I'm a big fan."

"It's very nice to meet you, Doris. I'm one of Tom's clients," Marla politely replied while Doris continued to shake her hand. "You sure have a great boy, there."

Tom let his shoulders relax a quarter of an inch. Amazing. He was prepared for Doris to blow a gasket.

"Marla came with us to the museum, Mom!" Max came in beside Tom. "We had a great time. I showed her all the dinosaurs. Look what she bought me. It's a model of the Stegosaurus. I'm gonna to put it together tonight."

"That's swell, Max. I'm sure Miss Meyers had a great time," Doris said. She ruffled Max's hair.

"Cut it out, Mom. Dad, let's go in my room and set it up."

Tom hesitated. Could he leave Marla in the clutches of Doris?

"Yeah, go on, there, Tom. Miss Meyers and I will have a cup of tea and chat while you two play." Doris shooed Tom down the hallway after Max, then turned back to Marla. "Miss Meyers, let me take your coat. Would you like to stay for dinner?"

"Oh, I'm sorry, I've got something scheduled for later tonight, but thank you for the invitation. It smells wonderful," Marla replied.

What the heck could she have scheduled for this evening? Tom hadn't seen evidence of any active dating. He listened with curiosity as he slowly moved toward the hall and Max's room.

"Thanks, it's my lasagna. Can I get you some banana bread or a piece of rhubarb pie with that tea? My mother dropped over some baked goods today. Not that I never bake, but you know how it is. We career girls don't have much time for these things."

"I sure do know what you mean, Mrs. Riley. I can hardly find time to order out."

Tom heard Marla's answer. This from the

omelette queen? He walked slowly toward Max's room and left the bedroom door open as he went to help Max set up his model.

It had been a little embarrassing to have Marla buy his son a gift at the museum store, a place he usually steered Max away from to avoid a purchase. But he couldn't deny she was genuinely excited to pick Max out a present, and he sure couldn't say no to Max's eager face. He was so used to saving every dime, he'd forgotten there was any in the bank.

The sound of female laughter drifted through the house. Tom strained to hear more, but everything else was muffled. There was something extremely strange about a woman he'd recently necked in a walk-in closet with having civilized tea with his recently ex-wife—and laughing, yet. It gave him the willies.

"Don't worry, Dad, they'll be fine. Mom would've already killed her if she was going to," Max said dryly.

Tom stared at his son in surprise. "Max, my man, you are getting so wise for your ten years."

"Marla's cool, Dad. You should marry her."

Tom stuck a rib bone into the Stegosaurus spine. "I can't afford her, son."

"She's got plenty of money. She doesn't need yours. You need a new wife, Dad; someone to cook you dinner and wash your clothes and stuff.

Marla already fixed you up great, see?" Max tugged on Tom's cashmere sweater. "I know you and Mom aren't going to get back together. Besides, Mom has a new boyfriend. Howard."

Tom was still catching up to the "new wife" concept when he got sucker-punched by the "new boyfriend" part.

"Howard?" Tom repeated.

"Yeah. He's okay. They go to Thursday night bingo. Grandma Anna babysits me. Hey, here's the head." Max lost interest in his parents' social lives and focused on the model.

Tom felt very strange indeed. What was all that Doris had said about finding herself and not wanting to be married anymore? Hell, what was he even concerned about? If she found someone new, she might stop driving him crazy. Tom thought on it for a few minutes while he assembled a leg bone.

The truth was, his real concern was his son and how someone new in Doris's life would affect him. How would that person treat Max?

He and Doris were going to have to have a long talk about this. God, how he wanted to take full custody of Max. But he'd needed a better living space, so he hadn't brought up the subject. Plus, he didn't want Doris to suffer. She loved Max, and Max loved her. Maybe with a little more time things would work out.

High-pitched shrieks erupted from the kitchen

area. Enough to make Tom jump and run down the hall to see what was happening, with Max right behind him. There sat, or squirmed, Marla and Doris, doubled over, laughing so hard they couldn't get a breath in sideways. Another round of shrieking laughter spilled out of them as Tom and Max looked on.

"Would you like to let us in on your little joke, girls?" Tom asked dryly.

"N-n-n-o," Doris managed to choke out. She grabbed a cloth napkin and handed it to Marla, then took one for herself. They wiped at the tears rolling down their cheeks and took turns smothering renewed fits into the towels. Tom got the distinct impression the joke had been about him.

The sound of a phone ringing interrupted any further conversation. Marla dug around in her black bag and pulled her cell phone out. She excused herself and went into Doris's small but extremely clean living room. For once Tom had some appreciation for Doris's neatnik tendencies. Max followed Marla.

"So what was that all about?" Tom eyed Doris.

"None of your beeswax." Doris smirked and started clearing the tea things. "Oh, but it was very nice of you to bring her along. She did tell me you thought I might like to meet her."

Tom sat down on the kitchen chair, caught off guard. "Sure."

"She also explained the new you—clothes and hair and all—and how you had to watch her for the month. By the way, you look terrific. I always told you if you tried for a better class of clientele you'd get somewhere."

Tom sighed, put his bent elbows on the table, and planted his face in his hands. Here we go again. Well, he definitely owed Marla one for having the perception to supply some excuses to Doris about things. Which reminded him . . .

"Max told me about Howard."

"Oh, well, I was hoping to be the one to tell you." Doris busied herself washing cups out. "It's nothing serious. We're just dating."

Max's voice came from the direction of the refrigerator, "Sorry, Mom, it just popped out."

"It's okay, Max." Tom stood up and walked closer to her, lowering his voice. "I'd like to talk to you about Max's place in all of that sometime. Not now."

"Tom, I'm sorry to interrupt, but I think we need to discuss something." Marla came in from the living room. "And seeing as it might affect Max, I'll just tell you here. I've been called to do a three-day shoot in the Bahamas. It was scheduled for later in the month, but the weather seems to be perfect right now. I fly out tomorrow, which means I guess that you fly out tomorrow too. Max, I hope you don't mind. I've got to borrow your dad for a few days. I know you guys probably hang out on the weekends."

"It'll be okay. Spring break is coming up and we can make up for it. Right, Dad? You should go, Dad." Max jumped up and down.

"Don't worry about it, Marla, it'll be fine. I can get tomorrow off easy," Doris added in a smooth, cooperative voice.

Damn, Tom thought. So that's what it sounds like when Doris is agreeable. This was all getting too spooky. Then there was the flying to the Bahamas thing. Suddenly Tom's missed night of sleep caught up with him. He rubbed his forehead and sat back down abruptly. His head was swimming with details.

"How many days?" he asked.

"We'll be back Monday evening."

"Max, I'll come and see you as soon as I get back," Tom said. "I'll call a cab and get you back home." He headed toward the kitchen phone.

"Riley. The limo is outside waiting for me. I told Terrell I'd be a while. I've got some things to take care of tonight. I'll give you a lift to your place."

"See?" Doris hissed at him, her elbow in his ribs.

Tom winced. "Hey, Max, let's go have a man-to-man talk in your room." He headed for Max and scooped him up over his shoulder, carrying him down the hall with Max squealing and shouting in delight.

"Max, I'm gonna miss you for three days. I don't know how much I'll be able to call, but I'll try. I love you, guy, and I'll think about you every day."

"I love you too, Dad." Max gave him a bear hug that made Tom's throat choke with emotion. He would have stayed with Doris forever just to have time with Max. Ten-year-olds were so funny. They flipped back and forth between being little boys and big boys at least once every two hours. Lucky for him, the little boy part still liked hugs.

"Don't worry, Dad. Go take good care of Marla. I'll see you when you get back."

"Okay, champ." Tom and Max both heard the limo honk in front of the building. Tom gave Max one more hug and headed for the door. He stopped, turned, and gave Max a thumbs-up. "Pals?"

Max returned the gesture. "Pals."

Tom slid into the limo seat beside the great Miss Marla Meyers. She was absorbed in her cell phone for a while. Terrell piped in some slow, easy Miles Davis. Miles and his smooth-as-a-woman horn.

Marla ended her call and seemed to relax some.

"Would you like to fix us a drink, Tom? Neither of us is driving, and the bar is fully stocked." She pointed to a square on Tom's right. He slid open the rolltop and saw twenty little airline-sized bottles in their holders. A larger circle held little cans of mixers. A stack of glasses took up one corner and the ice bucket hole contained a bucket of ice. Ready for anything.

"Wow."

"I'll have a scotch and Drambui on the rocks, please," she said.

"Rusty nail coming up, ma'am." Tom opened a couple little bottles, palmed a glass, popped a few cubes in with tongs, and expertly poured the appropriate amounts in.

"Nice work, Riley. Not a drop slipped."

"I did a short stint as a bartender for my cousin's catering business. Just before Doris and I got married." Right away he wished he'd left out that part about Doris. He finished up his own drink and took a gulp.

"You really married young, didn't you? Doris said something about that tonight. Tsk, tsk, you're gulping again. My theory is that on the rare occasion I have a drink, it's the best I can find, and it's a thing to relax and savor."

Her comment made him take another gulp of his scotch. "What did you and Doris talk about in the kitchen?" he asked, a queasy feeling coming over him.

"Women get right to the heart of things very quickly, Tom. We talked about her job, your job, your divorce, and how she'd decided to let you go because she wanted both of you to find true love. It was a very hard decision for her. That's what's made her so cranky with you lately. She feels you haven't made any progress toward that goal, while she has. The unevenness of it gets on her nerves."

"Holy shit. Did she discuss our sex life too?"

"Pretty much."

Tom thumped his head back against the seat. "We were only there sixty minutes."

"Women talk." Marla smiled a knowing, closed-mouth smile at him, sipped her drink, and changed the subject. "Don't you love this music? Terrell keeps a big jazz selection for me. He loves it too. Get with the groove, Tom."

"I give up." Tom got with the groove. He leaned his aching head back against the warm leather seat and closed his eyes. "This is one of Miles's best platters, you know. *Birth of the Cool.*"

"It's my favorite. But I love vocals, so I'm partial to Cleo Laine."

"Oh man, that's for sure. Cleo is the Miles Davis of vocals. Betty Carter's fun, of course Billie Holiday, but she's depressing. . . ." His voice faded off as he lost his train of thought. The jazz was flowing, the liquor was expensive, the woman was beautiful, even if she knew far too much about him and was way too driven and bossy. No doubt about it, this was good.

* * *

Marla watched Tom sleep. She curled up side-ways and listened to his steady breathing. A dark tendril of hair sprung up as he shifted slightly. With the tip of her finger she wove it back into place. He brushed at his forehead when she did, but went back into a deep sleep.

The black cashmere sweater and the dark jacket brought out Tom's strong features. The light and shadow played off his face. He was so very good-looking, and he had no idea.

Doris had told her much more than she'd let on: how much he had sacrificed for them, how de-voted to Max he was, spending as much time as possible with him. Tom was a good father.

Doris also told her how he was stuck in a hold-ing pattern with his job . . . and his love life. Marla smiled to herself. If you ever want to know the truth about a guy, go talk to the ex.

Not always true, though; if Derek had it to tell, she probably was the horrid witch who wouldn't give up her money and insisted he sign a prenup. Who could blame him for hitching a ride on the next gravy train?

What would have happened to her if he'd stuck around and married her? She had a sudden chill and turned to hike up the heat a little. No doubt he would have had a mistress on the side before they got back from their honeymoon.

So she should count herself lucky. She was free and happy. She'd never thought about being lonely much. Until Anton brought it up the other day.

But she didn't want to change anything in her life. It was peaceful. Safe. She was tired of being pursued by larger-than-life pushy East Coast heads of companies who wanted to "acquire" her. Maybe she'd be an eccentric mystery-writing spinster with twenty-seven orange Persian cats instead of children.

Maybe she'd meet some ordinary guy and have an ordinary life. Plant some snapdragons. Have a baby.

The ice in her drink had melted and she stirred the last of it with her finger, then sipped it down. She might as well forget about writing tonight and just pack her bags.

Miles was playing "Moon Dreams." Out the limo window she could see the not-quite-full moon traveling with them. She laid her head on the soft leather and watched Tom until they reached Rivington Street.

Chapter Eight

STRANGERS
IN PARADISE

She hated takeoffs. She hated landings too. And turbulence. But a nice smooth sky ride in the fluffy clouds with the sun coming in the windows was fine.

Riley had done his usual morning slump over a large cup of coffee from a Starbucks stand in JFK Airport. Now he was asleep under his gray fedora hat. He let out a short snore and settled back against his first-class seat. She was sure spending a lot of time observing Tom's sleep patterns.

She snuck out her black leather notebook and a good pen and started making book scribbles.

Mike Mason had missed her. She'd be damned if she'd let the three hours before they connected in Florida go by without writing.

It was that rose that bothered me. It wore a hole in my brain like I wore a hole in the carpet pacing for an hour.

I remembered a film from 1951 starring De-lores DelMarco. Shadows of the Night—*or something like that. Delores played a demented woman who was tormenting her former husband by masquerading as her own ghost. Making him think she had died in a fire that he had set. That was it. The husband had murdered her, so he thought. But she had escaped. She'd been burned badly. And in the movie she kept dropping those red roses with black ribbons all around.*

Finally the guy had . . . jumped off the balcony of the mansion ruins as she walked toward him, scared out of his wits. Yep, that was it.

Now, what the heck did that old movie have to do with Randall Crantz's death? I sat back in my office chair and scratched the back of my head with my pencil eraser. Looks like I'd be spending my day watching old movies. That, and some re-search on ol' dead Randall. Maybe I'd try the Seattle Daily*'s archives. Crantz had lived here for quite a while.*

Which brought me to the reporter. O'Shay. Ah, yes, O'Shay of the Daily. *Now, what did that boy know that had them on the same trail? And who was his tailor? A good-looking guy like that running around in a sloppy suit.*

Oh brother. Did she really just write that last section about O'Shay's tailor? Marla glanced over at Tom. His dark brown eyes were wide open. Startled, she quickly slapped the notebook closed in her lap. He pushed his hat back off his face and grinned, then moved his seat to the upright position, along with himself.

" 'Dear Diary'?" His voice was husky. Sexy, even.

"Travel notes. Keeping track of my mileage." It was sort of true; she did have some mileage notes on the back pages.

"I should've figured. Well, Meyers, at least you've got a brain in that pretty head of yours."

"Full of compliments this morning, aren't you, Riley?"

"You know, you didn't have to put me up here in first class. Specially on a six-thirty A.M. flight. I could have slept just as well in coach and saved you the bucks."

"Now, how would that look?"

"It'd look like two months to pay you back instead of six."

"Don't be ridiculous. It's on the agency." Marla stuffed her notebook and pen back in her tote bag and ignored Tom's perturbed look.

"Can I get you some coffee?" the stewardess interrupted. "Can I take your coat and hat, sir?" Tom handed them over and took the fresh coffee offered.

"Can I get you a pedicure with that coffee, sir?" Paris's voice replaced the flight attendant's. She moved around and sat on Tom's aisle seat arm.

"Good morning, Paris," Marla said.

"Good morning to you, good morning to you, good morning dear dunce-head, good morning to yoooooooooooo," Paris sang.

Tom moaned and took out the in-flight magazine to hide in.

"My, we're in rare form today. What's up?" Marla asked.

"Just greeting your boyfriend. Good morning, Rattly!"

"It's Riley, Paris, and you know that. Now go back and sit with B.B. and behave yourself," Marla admonished her.

"He's no fun. He fell right over. He's asleep." Paris actually giggled.

Marla glanced over at Rita's idea of a chaperone, her son, B.B., and laughed. "We'll be in Florida in thirty minutes anyhow. Why don't you go tickle B.B. and see if he'll wake up?"

"Oooh. I like that idea." Paris blew a kiss at Tom, then headed back to her seat behind them.

Obviously Paris's PMS had lifted. But good moods were rare for her. It probably wouldn't last more than another short, uncomfortable flight.

"Are you two actually friends?" Tom asked.

"It's a complicated relationship. She knows I don't take her seriously, so she can act out all she wants. Paris is a very insecure woman deep down."

"I don't suppose you'd consider her having enough motive to drop-kick you in a cake?" Tom asked sharply.

"No way. Subject closed." Marla put on her headphones and turned on some spunky jazz station. Tom went back to his magazine.

For the rest of the flight, layover, and bumpy trip from Florida to Nassau, Marla considered Tom's theory. It seemed to her that she'd have a sense of it if someone were really out to get her. No matter how she turned it around in her head, she couldn't find anyone with a motive.

Rita loved her like a daughter and would never want anything to happen to her. She'd never sell her out for money.

As for Paris, it just didn't follow.

From her own experience as a mystery writer Marla knew the basic elements of crime. None of those elements existed in her life as far as she could see. Still, Tom seemed so convinced.

It was sweet having him worried about her. It almost seemed like he really cared, instead of just caring about his policy.

Tom knew he was in trouble the minute they stepped off the plane. A tropical breeze picked up the edges of Marla's wrap dress and gave him a damn fine view of those gorgeous legs of hers. The moist, hot air put a flush on Marla's slender neck and she'd taken to licking her lips every so often while they waited in line, probably thirsty. Somehow all of this was driving him crazy.

It amazed him to think that Nassau was just a short flight from New York City. He let the heat fade the chill of early morning Manhattan that still hung on him like a bad tie. He'd truly landed in another world. A warm, sensual, palm-swaying world.

They moved through the customs lines slowly. Paris, Riley, Marla, and Rita's son, B.B. Ray. Marla had told him it wasn't unusual for B.B. to tag along on shoots, supposedly as a kind of chaperone for the girls, but that his interest in the trips had a direct correlation to whether there was a casino nearby. Since they were staying at the Atlantis Resort and Casino, B.B. was hot to trot.

"Move it along, Riley. I have no idea why Marla is so compelled to drag you everywhere—you can't be that good of a lay." The sharp voice of Paris cut through the bustle of the airport.

"It must be my other talents," Riley snapped back.

"I'm trying to visualize that, but I'm getting nothing," Paris retorted.

Tom clenched his teeth and kept his mouth shut. So much for Paris's good mood.

"Hurry up, all of you, I'm sweating like a pig in this humidity, and I'm starved," Paris groused loudly.

Marla turned and, much to Tom's delight, zinged Paris back. "Paris, stick a sock in it. Not every girl gets a free vacation to the islands. Most of our friends are stuck in the city with slush splashing up their legs."

"Free? We'll be working our butts off." Paris stalked off toward the waiting limo driver with a sign reading RAY AGENCY as soon as they sprang free of the customs line.

What a foursome. Wouldn't you know he'd end up on a tropical island with a gorgeous model, only to be joined by her pal the Queen of the Underworld and Igor the idiot son of her boss?

What was he thinking anyway? He and Marla may have had two accidentally intimate encounters, but under it all, she was headed for some multimillionaire real estate mogul, and he was headed for . . . what? A snarling pet bulldog and a bachelor apartment?

Was he ever going to get married again? The thought of Doris versus a new wife in his life brought up images of his childhood cat Fluffy, with her mouth full of feathers, his sisters screaming in their high-pitched girly voices, and the empty parakeet cage, its little door ajar. He chuckled to himself.

As they slid into his second limo in two days, another thought came to him that made a deadly chill run down his spine, right down to his big toes. Was he ever going to get laid again?

He looked over at Marla, her body well defined in a silky turquoise-blue wrap dress. She settled in and leaned back against the seat, her eyes closed, her lips slightly parted.

Maybe he was approaching this all wrong. Tom thought of the hungry need she'd showed when they'd kissed in her closet. Now, here was a woman who could use some safe, uncommitted sex for a few weeks. They were probably in the same boat on that one. Two deprived souls. Sure, he wasn't her ideal guy, but now that Anton had spruced him up . . . well, he was at least do-able.

This was an excellent plan. Tom ran his hand through his hair in a macho kind of lion's mane gesture and sat up. He'd just provide her with a service. That was it. He'd let her know there were no strings attached, and that he was willing to . . . be there for her.

Suddenly Paris's bare foot was between his legs. He jumped like a spooked cat.

"Rub my foot for me, will you, Riley? These heels are killing me," Paris said. "Geez, a little jumpy, aren't we?"

Tom looked up into Paris's face and saw a sly, sexual smile spread over her lips. Holy shit, she was coming on to him. She must have radar. Then he noticed Marla slowly open her eyes, take in the scene, and arch her right eyebrow way high up on her forehead. Her mouth took on a pinched expression. Then she turned a very distinct shade of red. There it was. She was jealous.

He picked up Paris's foot and started to rub it. This was a good plan. Very good.

Marla stood by as the hotel staff gathered up her luggage, and B.B., no doubt attracted by the sound of slot machines, uttered the third sentence she'd heard him say since they left New York. He flicked his dark glasses down, then tipped the bellboy a few dollars and said, "Later."

That left her with Paris and Tom. The nerve of that crazy redheaded woman, coming on to her supposed boyfriend right in front of her. She felt the heat rise up in her again. For some reason, this time Paris's antics really bothered her.

She'd draped herself all over Tom in the limo. Talk about motives, right now Marla wanted to strangle that hussy. And Tom. Of course, he was just a mere man and couldn't help himself. But a double murder wouldn't be out of the question.

Marla stalked pointedly ahead of them toward the front desk. Not that she should care. In truth, Riley was a free agent, but still, she didn't like her charade being challenged.

"May I help you?" the desk clerk asked.

"Meyers. The Ray Agency party," Marla answered, distracted. Out of the corner of her eye she saw Paris go into her helpless act, loading Tom up with her big lime-green leather tote and her matching shoes. Paris was barefoot. Marla's nails dug into the strap of her purse. That bitch!

The clerk returned with four keys. "I've put you and your companion in one of our view suites. The other two in your party are across the hall in two deluxe rooms."

"What?" Marla came out of her rage and paid attention.

"Your agency faxed the arrangements to us. Is that acceptable? We can change if you like." The clerk smiled.

"No-o-o," Marla answered slowly, letting it

sink in that Rita's secretary had booked Tom with her in one room. This was very good for her current purposes. "That's just fine, thank you." She took the two suite keys in one hand and kept the others separated.

Marla turned around and put a little action in her walk. The heels of her favorite Manolo Blahnik sandals tapped a staccato against the marble floors. She caught up with Riley and Paris and did a step-slide next to Tom. "Paris, here's your key. I'm sure you want to rest those swollen feet of yours. Oh, and here's B.B.'s key. He's probably on the blackjack tables by now. Tom and I are in 3221."

With a quick movement, Marla removed Paris's things from Tom's arms and hooked them back on Paris, who was staring at her feet to see if they really were swollen. Marla waved at the bellboy, pointed at whose bags were whose, and practically dragged Tom toward the elevator. Damn, she loved the feeling of being in charge. The elevator doors closed.

Marla punched the third-floor button. "You don't mind staying in the same room, do you, Riley? It's a suite, so there will be plenty of space for us to keep out of each other's way. I think there are two bathrooms. We want to keep up our cover with Paris and B.B. along."

"I'm here to serve, ma'am." Tom saluted her. "Let me know if there's anything I can do for you, Marla—besides keeping you from harm, that is. I mean, after all, here we are, two lonely, single people in a room together. . . ."

"Exactly. That's what we want them to think. Paris doesn't need to know anything about my policy and these problems I've been having. She'd just love to torture me with it." Marla turned and looked Riley in the eyes as the elevator opened. "I would actually appreciate it if you'd keep up the act a little better, Riley. I don't think my actual boyfriend would let Paris get to him. She's a terrible flirt."

"You want me to keep the act up better?"

"Yes, if you don't mind. I mean, I know you didn't sign up to play my latest conquest, but, well, you see the position I'm in, here. We have most of the month left yet."

"I certainly do. I'll do my best."

Riley had a weird male tone in his voice, but at least he understood. She'd have to try and be nicer to him. He really hadn't known what he was getting into with all this playacting when he signed up to watch over her.

The bellhop emerged from the other elevator and came down the hall just as they reached the door of the suite. Marla dropped her black tote bag on the floor, put the key in, and opened the door. Just as she began to step inside, Tom scooped her up from behind, into his arms, and carried her in. As she turned her head to speak to him, he covered her mouth with a kiss. The hotel guy grinned, rolled the luggage cart in behind them, and past them into the bedroom area.

Tom strode over and gently deposited Marla on one of the queen-sized beds. He dug in his pocket and handed the guy a tip, then walked out with him. She heard door to the suite close, and they were alone.

"How was that? Better?" Tom came in toward her.

"Yes, but the hotel staff is not our main objective," Marla said as she sat stunned on the bed. Riley had surprised her on that one.

"Right. Just getting into practice." Riley put both his and Marla's garment bags in the closet and left her other things on the bench at the foot of the bed. He took his duffel bag over to the dresser and started pulling his things out and putting them into drawers.

"What are you doing?

"Unpacking. Suppose B.B. or Paris come over here for a drink? We want to make it look good, don't we? I'll take this top drawer; you can have the rest. Beautiful room, isn't it? Did you see that view of the lagoon?"

"Not really. You swept me up too fast."

"Shall we order up some lunch? You must be hungry. I saw your first meeting isn't until three."

"Sure. Have them make me a shrimp Caesar salad and some iced tea." Marla was losing her "in charge" feeling. Maybe she needed to eat. She stretched herself full out on the bed and enjoyed the feel of the satin bedcover for a minute.

Tom stood there for a second, then went into the next room. "Get whatever you want, Riley, it's on the agency. I'll just take a quick shower and be right out," she called after him.

Marla in the shower. Tom tried to focus on reading the menu. So, she wanted him to keep the act up better? This was undoubtedly her way of justifying her needs. Why else would she be jealous of Paris? And boy, was she jealous. For a minute there he thought Miss Meyers was going to have an old-fashioned hair-pulling catfight with Paris after that stunt in the limo.

No doubt about it, what Tom needed was an audience. He'd do an Oscar-winning performance as her boyfriend, get her warmed up, then when they were alone later . . .

He let a great shower vision of Marla wash over him while he had the front desk ring up Paris's room.

*   *   *

After her shower, Marla slipped on a pair of white shorts and a knit polo shirt with some sandals. Her stomach growled. She walked out to check on how Riley had done with the food.

Lunch was on a small table set on the terrace. The breeze from the water came in the open terrace door and ruffled Tom's wavy dark hair. She noticed he had some of Warren's resort wardrobe on: a knit polo and shorts almost the same as hers but navy blue. With the expensive clothes, and the new haircut, it would be hard to tell Riley from any well-moneyed guest at Atlantis.

At least her friends wouldn't be pulling her aside asking her if she'd lost her mind dating him. Unless his New York edge and rude manners came through unexpectedly. Then again, she'd known a few billionaires with the same rude manners. Rich snobs were not her type at all.

What *was* her type? Had she even given any thought to that? She knew what she didn't want, but what *did* she want? Most of all, was she willing to give it to herself? To step out of her orderly life and let her type in? Maybe get hurt. Maybe what she wanted didn't exist, whatever it was.

She stopped at the phone to call the front desk for messages. He seemed to be behaving awfully well on the trip so far. He hadn't tried to convince her someone was after her for the last six hours.

His completely messed-up mystery plot. There was just no one with a good enough motive to bother with her.

Oh, she'd heard of stalkers with some of the other girls, but stalkers loved to leave a calling card. Being anonymous was not their thing. She'd written one book with a stalker in it and done some research on the mind-set.

Which reminded her how she wouldn't be getting any writing done for the entire weekend. She'd scribbled a few pages on the plane ride, but it was going to take more concentrated time than that to meet her deadline. What was an author to do?

No messages. She remembered how hungry she was and walked toward the terrace.

Tom came over to her and, much to her surprise, slipped his arms around her waist and kissed her forehead. He brought her body close to his before she could shove him away.

"Darling," he said.

"What the hell?" She tried to step back a little, but he gently held her close.

"Shhhh," he whispered in her ear. "Paris is on the terrace."

"Oh," she whispered back, "thanks for the warning, Dr. Seuss."

"My pleasure." Taking her hand, he led her outside. "Here she is, all cleaned up."

"Isn't she just a peach," Paris said, taking a sip of what looked like a strawberry daiquiri. She was slumped in a plastic chair, a huge black straw hat shielded her face, and dark glasses covered her eyes. But nothing shielded Marla—or Tom, for that matter—from the black fishnet and lycra swimsuit Paris almost wore. Her long, tan legs were draped across to another chair. She wore black high-heeled sandals. Her whole demeanor was one very blatant come-on. Sheesh.

That was it. She and Paris had been friendly for years. She may sling one-liners around harmlessly, but it wasn't nice of her to go fishing for Marla's supposed boyfriend. That had always been the unwritten rule between them.

Tom slid a chair out for Marla. She sat down hard, grabbed her iced tea, and glared at Paris. He moved up close behind her and started massaging Marla's shoulders. It felt so good, she leaned back and sighed. She might as well play her part too.

"Oh, knock it off. You two are making me sick. Marla, you always get the guys. I'm sexually deprived. If you don't stop, I'll have to go after the tennis pro here."

"That's not how I remember it, Paris. I'm usually stuck with the best friend or distant cousin of your date. Let's take Ernesto's second cousin Tito. With the large teeth. Tito liked to tango."

"Hmmm. Good point. Score one for you, Marla. But spare me the massage. I'm eating." Paris sucked more red slush through a fat straw. Marla couldn't imagine hitting the liquor this early in the day.

"Tom, could you let me have a minute alone with Miss Congeniality, here?"

"Sure, pumpkin. I'll take my beer in the bedroom." Tom picked up his frosted glass and stepped back inside.

"While we're on the subject, Paris, can you manage to keep your mitts off Tom? It's not neighborly of you to try and steal him right in front of me."

"I'm just horny." Paris stretched out in the sun. "Hot weather makes me think of sex. And he looks so much better now. He's yummy. Besides, you two seem so . . . so *not*."

"We are not *not*, we just have self-restraint in public," Marla snapped. "Besides, I might have to drown you in the pool if you don't stop." She stabbed her salad and stuffed some in her mouth.

"Well, I'll say this for you, 'pumpkin,' I've never seen you get jealous of me with any of the men we've shopped and dropped. Riley must be special. Go figure you'd fall for some boring insurance dude. In that case, I'll transfer my lust onto some unsuspecting fool I take a fancy to. I can only flirt anyhow until I finish my stupid period."

"How about B.B.?" Marla asked straight-faced. They both practically tipped over their plastic chairs laughing, and Paris got a brain freeze from inhaling her daiquiri slush too fast. This was more like it. Marla was pleased she had solved their differences and that she had made herself clear. Boundary setting was important.

"Poor B.B., surrounded with women all day long. He's like a eunuch in the harem." Paris tried to sound sympathetic.

"Poor B.B. No wonder he gambles. Rita needs to cut those apron strings, though. I've tried to talk to her, but she's just not there yet."

Tom stuck his head out on the terrace. "Are you girls done?" He stood near the sliding door.

"Yes, I just need to finish my salad." Marla took a little less aggressive poke at her shrimp Caesar. "Paris, the wardrobe is set up in room 2335. We're doing a swim shoot, then the glittery stuff tonight. Lori Spencer is the photographer, you know. She wants that sunset and something at the roulette table after dark." Marla went into her business mode, taking bites between phrases. The food was helping her think. She was back in control.

Paris rose from the table and straightened her swimsuit so the fabric would actually cover her right breast.

"All right, *Marletta,* my dear, I'll meet you over there. I've got a few stray hairs to wax. These swimsuit shots are *trés* ouchy."

Marla watched Paris pause near Tom. She shot Paris a "kill you now, or later?" look. Paris sighed and kept going. "I'll try and behave. 'Bye, all." She waved, then wiggle-walked out the room door.

Atlantis was paradise as far as Tom was concerned. It was without a doubt the most luxurious hotel he had ever stayed in.

Eighty degrees, a slight breeze, the sound of the waves; days like this made you wonder what had been keeping you in your tiny rut back home.

There were plenty of times that he could have taken a trip, and even had the money. Well, at least a fair amount. Seemed like the last ten years were a blur of bills, school events, and Doris's discontent. Maybe his own too.

He'd made a big effort to be a good father to Max. The last two years hadn't been easy. Max seemed to be pretty well adjusted. It was his own adjustment that was taking so long.

He wasn't sure how he felt hearing the news from Marla that Doris had let him go so they could both find happiness. What about his son's happiness?

But deep down he knew that bickering parents didn't provide Max with what he needed either.

The most important thing was to get along with each other now. Somehow, for the first time in two years, he felt resolved with the Doris situation after what Marla had told him.

He parked himself poolside by the huge Aztec temple water slide. This was where the first shoot was supposed to take place. What a blast Max would have here. A spark of guilt burned at his stomach. How he wished he could give Max more: more opportunities, more of his time.

A waiter appeared to take his drink order. Tom asked for a soda. He wanted to stay on his toes and make sure nothing else happened to Marla.

The warmth of the Bahamian sun penetrated deep into his muscles. He stood, stripped off his polo shirt and shorts, then leaned back on the poolside chaise. Man, this felt great.

The waiter reappeared with his soda and Tom signed for it. Taking a long sip, he thought about his options.

Maybe when this was all over he'd talk to Granite about becoming an insurance investigator. Then he'd be on a bigger payroll and that might improve things all around. He could see bringing Max here, or to Disney World. Max should come first.

New women just weren't on the agenda. Not yet. He'd spent eight years married to a woman he didn't really love. The next time he took that step, it would be different.

Tom took another cool drink and tried to relax more. He needed to relax.

The photo crew had started setting up, and he hadn't even noticed. A few guests were in the pool, but his attention had drifted to some twentyish girls who came shooting out of the waterside. When they emerged from under the water, they waved at Tom and then swam off.

Geez, he must look better than he thought. He sucked in his stomach. Warren's Speedo suit was a little more revealing than his usual loose boxer-style swim shorts. But when he dragged the old ones out to pack last night, there was a rip in the crotch.

He was actually grateful Anton had thought of everything for the trip, sending along a suitcase full of Warren's summer clothes with Marla. Yes, he was well dressed for his roll as Marla's boy-toy.

And all of a sudden Tom wished he'd ordered a gin and tonic.

Marla tugged at her swimsuit bottom. It felt a size too small. How they loved to squeeze her into things. Her feet stung on the hot pavement. She quickened her pace and danced around a bit. Finally one of the crew handed her a pair of yellow thongs.

Marla followed Paris across the promenade toward the faux Mayan temple. There were two other girls along at the shoot too. Paris and Marla were both dressed in white swimsuits, with a gold Aztec-like motif. She had to admit, the red-headed Paris was quite stunning in white.

She spotted Tom on his chaise by the pool. Aside from the fact that he was pale as the white cotton cover he lay on, he looked incredible. Boy, she'd been right about those muscles. He had 'em, all right, and they were all in the right places. Her gaze roved over his body: the broad shoulders, highly developed upper arms, well-defined abs—which he seemed to be sucking in for no reason. He was looking good in that skimpy suit.

When she got down to his great legs, she paused. Sexy? Yes, except for the socks with his sandals. Marla rolled her eyes and stifled a huge laugh. You could take the boy out of the city, but not the nerdy fashion sense out of the boy.

The sun felt divinely good. Her pallor had been covered up by some clever bronzing makeup. The slight breeze ruffled her hair up around her face. She should come here more often.

Marla felt suddenly tired. Approaching a long set of shoots, changes, posing, being forced to emote whatever notion the photographer had in her head, it was all getting to be too much after eight solid years. The last time she'd taken a vacation had been after she and Derek broke up, and that was years ago.

"Marla, dear, so nice to see you." Lori Spencer came up and shook her hand.

"Nice to see you again, Lori, it's been too long. What have you been up to?" Marla replied.

"Doing a documentary on Cuba. You'll have to come to the screening. But I needed some money, so it's back to fashion for a while."

"No kidding. I've been thinking about getting out. . . ." Marla's sentence trailed away as something caught her eye behind Lori's shoulder. There was Paris over with Riley, and *over* was the position she was in. Riley was sure getting a chest X-ray view of Paris's cleavage! An unsettling angry ball started forming in her stomach.

Lori's voice brought her attention back. "Marla, let's get you a nice fruity Mai Tai or something. You look a little scrunched around the edges."

"No, thanks. Make it something virgin." There was no way Marla was going to let herself get tipsy and lose control of the situation again. Besides, she'd need her strength to push Paris off the balcony later. She'd have to shut it out of her mind for an hour to get through this shoot.

"And let's just go down and *up* out of the water one more time, girls! One, two, three . . ." Lori sounded like a swim coach. Marla took a breath, dropped under the water again, then rose like Venus on the half shell for the tenth time.

"Yes, yes, yes! Perfect, perfect. Okay, girls, that's it for the water torture. Get cleaned up and I'll see you in the casino by the baccarat tables in one hour."

Slogging out of the pool, Marla glanced up at the brilliant streaks of pink, yellow, and red painting the sky behind her. No wonder Lori had been so thrilled with the shoot. She definitely got her sunset.

A good-looking crew member stepped over and wrapped a thick white towel around her shoulders. He smiled and spoke to her with a great Australian accent. She looked into his handsome face and marveled at his sea-blue eyes. He seemed to be flirting with her. He also sounded like he was underwater.

"S'cuse me," Marla croaked, then bent sideways, stuck her finger in her ear, and shook her head. A rush of warm water cleared out of her right ear. The handsome Aussie laughed and gave her naked back a rub with his warm hand.

"Rory!" Lori's voice called from behind a pile of equipment. That tone made Marla figure Rory was hers.

"Coming, love." He winked at Marla, then turned toward Lori.

Men. They were dogs! Just no-pedigree mutts run by their mating instincts. At least she could hear now. Marla shrugged the towel back over her shoulders and marched toward the hotel.

She jumped as Tom Riley took up with her step and put his arm around her. After her initial reaction, his touch began to calm her frayed nerves. He'd put on his shirt and shorts again and the heat from the sun seemed to have soaked into them. She warmed herself against him.

"Long session, hon, you must be tired," he said, loud enough for the crew and Paris to hear.

Paris cocked her head and stared as they walked by. She was looking a little frizzy. Marla smiled. The humidity will get you every time.

"How about a nice cup of tea?" Riley continued. "Let's go dry you off before the next set." He chatted amicably with her, holding her affectionately as they walked. It almost made Marla sad. How nice it would be to have someone do this in real life. She actually felt herself get choked up. Damn, she must have gotten too much sun. Or jet lag.

"Thanks, Riley," she said in a low voice as soon as they were out of earshot of the others. "You're definitely improving."

Tom looked into her watered-up blue eyes and saw something there. Before they reached the outer doors, and while they were still in view of the crew, he stopped and gathered her up in his arms.

"I do have my talents," he said quietly, his lips

close to hers. She tipped her head slightly, and her mouth parted in invitation. Her eyes closed for a moment.

Taking his time, he kissed her softly, then ever so slightly ran his tongue between her lips and teased her with it. Her eyes flew open, and he stared straight into them. If he was going to play-act, he'd go for the Oscar. She surprised him and leaned in, her arms sliding around his waist. It was she who kissed him this time. A long, sweet, sad kind of kiss.

Feeling her tremble, he broke off the embrace, touched her cheek a moment, and held her against him. "Are you cold?"

"No. Yes." Her voice was muffled against his shirt.

"Come on, I'll get you that tea."

Chapter Nine

SOME ENCHANTED EVENING

The chandeliers blazed like fiery crystals above them. Marla, Paris, and the other models glittered as the light danced on their sequined swimsuits.

They each wore matching long gloves and feather plumes in their hair, and were, as they say, absolutely dripping with diamonds and gemstones. Marla squinted against the tiny reflections coming off all of their finery.

Positioned around a roulette wheel, the four of them looked like fifties glamour girls out for a night of gambling, except they had on swimsuits instead of evening gowns. They'd put Paris in midnight-blue to compliment her red hair; the other girls were dressed one in silver, one in gold, and Marla herself in a deep blood-red. Marla was often asked to wear red, with her forties looks, blonde hair, and lips that took to crimson well.

She tugged at her long red gloves and admired the three-tiered diamond pave bracelet. In her personal life she wasn't too inclined to deck out in jewelry, even for big events. She had her standard fat gold bracelet and a beautiful round gold locket that had belonged to her mother. It was about the size of a silver dollar and held a picture of her mother as a young bride. Marla had picked out a wonderfully faceted gold box chain to hold the locket.

Everyone who knew her well knew this was her standard dress-up uniform. Her necklace, a black dress in the appropriate length, and black suede velvet shoes pretty much covered her nightlife. When was the last time she'd even gone to a real party?

What was it Tom had said about her shoes? His most far-fetched theory so far, she remembered. The tampered heel theory. She thought about how that would play out. She'd trip and fall flat on her face, right? Was the elevator shut down by someone so she'd have to take the stairs on her wobbly tampered-with high heels? Wait a minute—why would someone be after her that day anyway, before she even had the insurance policy in force?

She was going to have to ask Tom how that fit in. Her Mike Mason mind just wasn't working tonight.

"Speak of the devil," she whispered out loud to herself. Unfortunately, Paris was right next to her.

"What devil? Is B.B. around?" Paris asked.

"That's not the devil I was speaking of. I meant Tom," Marla said.

"Now, why would you be calling ol' sweet Tom a devil? Trouble in paradise?" Paris arched her right eyebrow at Marla, and put her blue-gloved hands on her hips.

"It's just an expression," Marla said blankly.

"Wow, he's sure looking good enough to eat. You let me know when you're done with him; I'd like a snack," Paris purred.

Marla's blood did an instant hot boil. She grabbed Paris's gloved wrist and turned her around so they were face-to-face. "I should be talking about you, you she-devil. I ought to rip those dangly rhinestones right out of your earlobes. I thought I told you not to mess with Tom. I saw that lean-over act you pulled by the pool."

"Ouch! Okay, already. I told you I get horny when it's hot. I can't help it," Paris whined.

"Well, *help* it," Marla hissed. "Redirect, girlfriend."

"I promise! Now let go."

Marla gave Paris's wrist a healing rub with her other hand, then dropped it like a limp noodle.

"Sheesh! I swear I've never seen you so wacko, Marla. You must be in love."

Marla didn't know what she was. She'd never felt so riled up about someone horning in on her supposed territory before. Even with Derek it was more like a business deal gone bad in comparison.

"I'm sorry, Paris, I don't know what's come over me."

"I do. You need sex. Don't tell me you and Rizzo boy haven't done the nasty yet? Actually, don't tell me. I can't bear the burden. If it's true, then now's the time, Marla. It doesn't get any hotter than the tropics."

Marla felt her cheeks go hot and kept her mouth shut. She spotted Tom in the crowd and found herself very glad to see him.

Tom approached their table dressed in a sharply tailored white evening jacket, black bow tie, pleated tux shirt, and black formal pants. He looked fabulous, like he just stepped out of a movie. His smile was so genuine, she'd almost thought he was glad to see her too, instead of just glad she hadn't broken her nose and screwed up his contract or something.

Paris sidled up to him. "Wow, Thomas, you clean up good. What's the occasion?" Marla came over to the other side of Tom, and Paris took a step back. *Okay!* she mouthed to Marla.

"Ms. Spencer asked me to be a background figure. I guess I play the guy who brought you." Tom struck a pose that sent both Marla and Paris into a good laugh.

"Well, then, Daddy Big Bucks, we'll lean all over you and make it look good." Paris looped her arm through his, and Marla grabbed the other one.

"Just relax and act natural," Marla advised him. "Lori is a good director." The three of them approached the roulette table, and Lori got her camera in action.

"That's great! Keep walking this way, you three. Tom, look at me, tilt your chin up a little . . . good! Hey, he's a natural, girls. Pipper and Kimberly, you two come and join, one on each side. Silver by the blue, gold by the red. Super! Tom, look at the roulette dealer and start acting like you're going to make a bet there. See that stack of chips? Just stick it on a number at the center of the board."

The dealer proceeded to play out a fake game, and Lori kept her directions coming.

"Red, number twelve," the dealer sang in his usual manner.

"Hey, we have a winner!" Paris pointed, and sure enough, Tom's pile of chips sat on red and twelve.

Lori looked up from her camera for a minute.

"Damn! Too bad they're house chips," she said with a laugh.

Everyone seemed to be enjoying the shoot, but Marla's feet were starting to ache from the red satin sandals they were squeezed into. The hot weather was making her swell.

Lori must have noticed the telltale crease in her brow, because next thing you know she had her up on the roulette table stretched out on her stomach, knees bent, legs in the air like a classic girl-on-the-piano bit.

"Oh, *trés* fifties, Marla, you are just my blast-from-the-past girl. Roll up on your left hip, will you, dear?"

Tom stood back and watched Marla do her thing. Paris was saying something to him, but he didn't hear because he couldn't take his eyes off the blonde in red.

"Kind of sounds like sex when they do that, doesn't it?" B.B.'s voice came from behind Tom's left ear, along with the distinct odor of bourbon. "'Roll on your hip, now move, honey.'" B.B. snorted a sleazy kind of laugh.

Tom swung around and faced him. He wanted a good look at B.B. Maybe under that bland expression lurked a man with a motive. What he saw was the haze of alcohol settled over B.B.'s eyes. His Hawaiian shirt and Bermuda shorts didn't conceal the fact that B.B. was soft. He had a pretty well-cultivated beer belly, and his neck was getting some double-chin action. That, combined with shifty eyes and thinning dark hair slicked back with gel, gave B.B. the look of someone who had nothing good going on in his life.

B.B. gave Tom a wry smile, raised his glass back up to his mouth, and took a healthy slug of booze. Tom didn't even grace B.B.'s comment with a reply. Then he thought better of it and went for some information. He knew the liquor would either shut B.B. up and make him sullen, or get him loose-tongued. He was betting on loose at the moment.

"Man, you sure do have the luck going on these shoots with the girls. Quite a job you've got, there, B.B."

"You said it, Riley, just one long eye-candy trip. And I get my pick of 'em too."

Tom whistled low. "I'm gonna call you Lucky from now on. What's your cover?"

"I'm a media escort. Keeping an eye on the goods." B.B. puffed up. "Being the son of the agency owner has its perks. Someday I'll take it over from the old lady and make some changes. You know, branch out into some film work."

Tom had the urge to accidentally stuff B.B. into

the men's room toilet face first and see if he liked "branching out." He casually looked for the nearest restroom sign.

B.B. took another drag off his bourbon. The ice tinkled in the near-empty glass and, like a psychic, the bar girl was there to replace it. She must just hang in B.B.'s circle, ready with another whiskey and water. B.B. handed her his empty, signed a ticket, then grabbed the new drink and waved her away.

"Rita's looking pretty healthy at this point, B.B. Are you up for the wait?" Tom watched him intently.

"Sure. As long as I get gigs like this, what's to complain?"

"Well, as long as she's paying, I see your point. You've got yourself the dream job, man."

"I'll say this for you, Riley, you've cracked the toughest nut on the tree. Marla, there, doesn't warm up easy."

"You speaking from experience?" Tom tugged on his tie and undid his collar button. The answer to this one could make him a little nervous. "Not that I mind. It's understandable."

"I thought on it. I'd rather stay loose. She's all or nuthin'. Not my type." B.B.'s eyes shifted to Marla, and Tom saw something far away nudge B.B.'s thoughts. It looked like pain to Tom. The kind that comes with rejection.

"I guess that makes me lucky too, then," Tom said.

"Yeah, I guess so. We're just two lucky guys. How about a drink, Riley? I'm buyin'. It's on the agency's expense account."

"Sure, I'll have a beer. Whatever's on tap," Tom replied. Might as well keep the game going.

B.B. waved the bar girl over and passed on the order. This time, when he signed, Tom saw him add a hefty tip. B.B. sure was loose; loose with the company's money, that is. B.B. pointed to a table stand, and the girl left the bottle of beer and a frosted glass for Tom. Tom walked over and, just as he'd hoped, B.B. followed.

"Want to get in on a little action tonight, Riley? There's a poker game upstairs with some guys I know."

"No, thanks, that's a little rich for my blood."

"What is it you do anyway? Besides Marla." B.B. choked on a laugh and slapped Tom's shoulder.

"Insurance."

"Oh yeah. Well, how about the blackjack table? I've been havin' me a pretty good streak tonight."

"Maybe later. I promised Marla a foot rub after the shoot." Tom was baiting him with that last comment, and watched a flicker of jealousy rise in B.B's expression.

"Suit yourself. I'll be at the tables until ten.

Poker's in room 1492." B.B. took one last long drink, set the glass down hard on the table, tipped his hand in the air, then walked off into the crowd.

Tom poured the rest of the beer into the glass and glanced Marla's way. The glitter girls were still going at it, lined up like bathing beauties from the Follies. He let the beer run down his throat and clear the smell of B.B.'s heavy cologne and drinking out of his system. What a piece of work that guy was.

Tom wondered if Rita was fully aware of the amount of money B.B. sent through the agency expense account. She had to know; surely the accountant had shown her the cash flow. And who was picking up his gambling expenses? Lucky streaks had a tendency to . . . end.

"I'm fine." Marla smiled weakly. She had sequins sticking her in the armpit, bad red shoes, and an aching head. She was also a professional.

"Okay, then, big smile now, everyone; let's try one with teeth, girls." Lori waved her hand in the air. Marla and the others followed her as she led their gazes first one direction, then another. Would this shoot never end?

"Marla, you're being too stiff. Get your elbow out of my ribs," Paris hissed.

"Sorry, sorry." Marla would rather get it all done than take a break and extend the torture.

What the hell was the matter with her anyway? She rolled her shoulders a little to get the kinks out. She looked up and saw Riley standing nearby. His bow tie was untied, and he'd popped open a button on the top of his collar. It made her smile.

"That's great, Marla. Paris, girls, give me that sweet kind of closed-mouth smile. Think about something you like. Chocolate cake or sex or something." Lori clicked a dozen more times, then straightened up. "Okay, that's a wrap. Thank you all. I've got individuals charted out in the war room for tomorrow. Check your schedules tonight, please. Good work, ladies. Go to bed, will you?" Lori joked. Marla knew she meant it for her, though. Their eyes met, and Lori winked.

"I feel like Robert Palmer, with all you gorgeous girls around me." Tom came up and put his arm around Marla.

"In that suit, it's *you* who's irresistible, Mr. Riley, sir," Paris teased. "Tom, will you take care of this girl tonight? She's really off her beat. If I didn't know you better, Miss Meyers, I'd say you had the dreaded PMS. Of course, nothing so ordinary as hormones ever ruffled your feathers till now."

"It must be the climate change or something." Marla didn't even have enough energy to play girlfriend to Tom's boyfriend act. She reached down and took off the horrid shoes. "Tom, how about I go change? Maybe we could have a little supper."

"You two party poopers go on. I'm going to slip into something less comfortable and go dancing. Pipper, Kimmie, come dancing with me?" The other two glittering beauties agreed, and they went off in a trio to change out of their spangly swimsuits, then make some local men crazy.

"Are you in a dancing mood, Marla?" Tom asked.

Marla walked along with Tom to the elevators. "Not really, my feet are killing me." She sighed. "Lots of times at these location shoots all the girls go out dancing together in the evening. It must be a sight for the regulars, to see four or five great-looking women dancing with each other."

Marla drifted into a story while Tom listened. "Then sometimes we'd all play this game and find the dorkiest-looking guys in the place and ask them to dance. It gave the guys such a thrill. I think they got a big kick out of it."

"Is that what I am, Marla? The dorkiest-guy syndrome? Is that the game you're playing with me?" Tom said all that very calmly, while he pushed the elevator button. Marla was speechless. The elevator door opened, but she just stood there, until Tom grabbed her arm gently and pulled her in.

Was she that shallow? He sure didn't look like the dorkiest guy right now. He still had a hold of her and he was looking in her eyes, waiting for an answer. His moody eyes seemed to reach into her heart. She could feel his powerful arms gather her in, and she could feel something inside her break like a brittle twig. She wanted to say, *No, Tom, that's not how I feel about you.* But how *did* she feel about him?

He didn't kiss her. He let go of her and she slipped over to the side of the elevator. Her head ached with confusion. Maybe ten years in the city had turned her hard. Maybe it was the eight years of bending to everyone's perfect pose, being sewn into dresses, and caked with makeup. Whatever it was, Marla knew she was tired of it. Bone-tired.

Then it was their floor. Silently, he walked her to their room and opened the door.

Inside, she tried to talk. "Riley, you aren't the dorkiest guy. You are a good friend."

"Isn't that the same thing?"

"You're more than that. . . . I mean . . . I don't know what I mean," she stammered. They stood close to each other but didn't touch. She could feel his body heat radiate out to her, warming her cold skin.

He reached out and put one finger on her lips. The fire concentrated wherever he touched. His eyes never left hers. She parted her mouth as he circled his fingertip over her like a kiss. He brushed the very edge of her tongue, and she let him.

A deep ache rose up in her. Desire. So bad. She'd never felt anything like it in her life. It burned deep and made her skin rush with sensation all over her body, blooming like tropical wildflowers across her lips, across her breasts, and down to the heat between her legs.

He took his finger off her lips.

"Okay, Marla." His voice was as deep as a jazz bass, and it resonated in her body, each note a vibration. He reached directly behind her to a low table and picked up the black leather hotel guide. "Let's have the hotel fix us a little supper. I saw some tables out by the beach. We could just relax for the rest of the evening."

Marla stood very still. It was hard to move when you were on fire.

"Why don't you take your shower and change into something comfortable? I'll wait for you and take my turn. I'll make us a reservation at one of the dining rooms. Does outside suit you?" Tom kept talking in that voice.

Marla came up for air. She felt the words come out of her tingling mouth, but they were so disconnected from her. "Whatever sounds good. Light. Seafood, maybe?" By the time she finished talking, she had come thumping down to earth.

The ache was still there, but was fading like a dream.

"Got it. A little pasta aioli with some grilled prawns. I saw that on the Fountain Garden's menu." He broke their close proximity and walked over to the desk. "Go on. I'll call."

"I'll be quick." Marla slipped away through the bedroom door, shut it behind her, locked it, and leaned against the wall, rolling until her forehead stuck on the grass-cloth wallpaper.

Then in one quick movement she stripped off the sequined swimsuit and pressed her naked body against the coolness.

What the hell was going on between her and Riley anyway? She tried to organize it, list it all in her head: the pretense, the bet with Anton, and then the emotional carnival ride she'd been on all day. But the list fell apart when it got to the part where she wanted Tom Riley to rip her clothes off and plunge into her.

She peeled herself off the wall and headed for a hot shower. Or a cold shower. Whatever was going on, the only way to sort it out was to walk straight into it. No more pretenses. And to hell with Anton's bet. She didn't need new photos that bad. Marla was sure of one thing: She needed something. Something to fill the empty ache. Maybe even . . . Tom.

Chapter Ten

FROM HERE TO ETERNITY, AND BEYOND

Moonlight became her, Tom thought. Everything became her, really, because Marla was just naturally beautiful. She was graceful . . . well, sometimes. She was intelligent, and underneath it all, she was as hot as an alleycat in heat.

It had been a long time coming, but about an hour ago Tom remembered one thing he was very good at. Everyone had natural talents. He'd just forgotten what his was, until the look in Marla's eyes, as he touched her lips, reminded him. Here they were, miles from home. This was the perfect place. He wanted to share it with her. Set her free from the cage she seemed locked in, if even for only one night.

The umbrella over their small table rippled in the warm breeze. There were lights strung all around it, and they cast a golden light over Marla's blonde waves. "Stardust" was being piped in from the lounge out to the patio. They must have a trio inside—bass fiddle, piano, and clarinet—playing old jazz standards. Mighty smooth. He loved the old songs.

Several other couples were at similar tables in a semicircle around a small fountain and patio. The tinkle of crystal glasses and light laughter made a kind of music of its own.

They had eaten almost in silence. Marla was sipping her champagne, her blue eyes on him every minute. He'd ordered the Roederer Cristal, best bubbles on the menu. He'd pay back Rita later. The steady streams of effervescence made the long tulip-shaped flute glass look like a light show in her hand. She set the glass down and smiled at him.

The band started playing "Moonglow." A perfect swing-low clarinet love song made for dancing. Tom extended his hand, and she took it. He led her out from under the umbrella, onto the patio, and into his arms.

"I'm not a very good dancer, Tom."

"That's impossible. You just haven't danced with the right man."

"Remember me? The trip-and-fall queen?"

She was stiff as he tried to move, that was for sure.

"All right, we'll have a dance lesson. First, you gotta get with the rhythm." He put the palm of his hand up for hers to rest on. She followed his move and put her palm against his. The electricity between them traveled through their touching fingertips.

Then Tom let the beat of the bass find his body. It was a slow, easy song. He slid his left arm around her waist. Not too close, just enough. Her feet started moving with the music as he guided her.

"Very good. Now, here's the second thing." He leaned up close to her ear and whispered, "You've got to surrender." He brushed his lips as lightly as champagne bubbles against her cheek on the way down to her full, coral pink lips. He only let her have the suggestion of a kiss. He teased her. She closed her eyes and let him, leaning her head back to give him her neck. He teased more kisses across that graceful neck and down a few inches to her bare shoulder.

His hand moved over the blue silk halter dress she wore, to the small of her back. He pressed her in closer as he led her into the dance. And then a very small miracle occurred. She surrendered. He took that moment and moved her like easy jazz music across the patio. She was there with him all the way.

When the last phrase of "Moonglow" came down, he spun her out slowly, then back into his arms, their bodies only a breath apart. Her eyes were wild and blue and begged for more. Her heartbeat was wild too.

They stayed as they were, and when the next song swelled up, he showed her the feel of the music until she fell into step with him again. Her hips moved in an easy sway this time, and he ran his hands over her waist and let them rest there. She wound her arms around his neck and kept up the rhythm. Tom's brain exploded into champagne sparks until he could hardly take a breath, from the hurt of wanting her. It hurt so bad, he let it. He took her closer and let her feel it too.

When they'd danced four more songs, he danced her back to their table, picked up their two glasses of champagne, slung her tiny bag over her shoulder, and danced her out to the smooth sandy beach. They danced until they couldn't hear the music anymore. Then they walked, holding hands, until the lights from the patio and the hotel were like stardust.

The secluded section of beach was deserted. They sat by some palms close to the shoreline. Even if someone walked by, they would hardly see the two of them.

The moon still looked remarkably full, reflected

in the calm waters. They both sat gazing out at the gentle waves.

She set her glass in the sand and stretched herself out, resting on her elbows. Her head lolled backward, her hair dangling behind her.

"You're a terrific dancer, Tom. How'd you get so good?"

"The nuns at St. Mark's were wild women. They taught me everything I know. Sister Margaret used to be a ballroom dancer before she joined the order."

Marla giggled. "Well, thank you, Sister Margaret, wherever you are."

Her voice was so very sexy, and the heat of the night made his body . . . vulnerable. He moved over to her and sat down behind her on the sand.

"Come here, I'll rub your shoulders," he said. Tom was trying very hard to keep his cool. After all, a dance was just a dance. A kiss was just a kiss. Marla pulled up her long hair and twisted it forward, then moved between his legs. His cool got harder.

Concentrating on her shoulders, he started stroking the muscles, shoulder to neck, then down again. Marla let out a moan and leaned herself backward. Every movement she made only served to ignite his primal urges. The little sounds she made. The softness of her skin. The fragrance of her hair, like jasmine. Her hips between his legs. Moving.

He ran his hands up her neck and onto her temples. By God, if he was going to get this hot, she was too. Gently he worked on her forehead, neck, and shoulders. He did a slow, smooth move and unzipped the back of her dress. Her skin was like fire wherever he touched.

She had nothing on under that dress. He slid his hands down to her waist and up, nearer her breasts with every stroke.

"Riley?" Her throaty, velvety voice was full of desire. He could hear it, and feel it.

"You missed your calling."

"How do you figure?" He moved closer behind her and spoke low.

"You should have been a masseuse," she breathed heavily, "or a gigolo." She was almost whispering.

"I've seriously considered that. Gigolo, that is."

"You could dress in white suits, live in Florida, and escort well-preserved women to the opera." Marla took a very long time to get all of those words out.

"I look bad in white suits." He ran his fingers down her naked spine. He could feel her body respond to his touch. Her skin was moist with heat and so very sexy it made him get more aroused, if that was possible. There was no way she didn't feel his hardness, close as she was.

To his surprise, she moved her body ever so slightly against him. He about lost his mind as she pressed into him. She meshed her fingers with his, pulling his hands forward, under her dress. His fingertips softly brushed over breasts, then pressed her hardened nipples. Marla's responsiveness was . . . shocking.

She broke away from him, flipped over quickly, and pushed him down on the sand. He stared up into her tropical sky-blue eyes. What a completely delicious woman. He opened his mouth to say something. Before the words could come out, she graced him with her luscious red lips, which were, he noticed right away, on fire. While she was kissing him, she unbuttoned his silk sport shirt with very skillful fingers.

Those lips of hers traveled from his mouth, to his ear, to his neck, and down across his chest. Joining them quickly was her tongue, then her hands. Her long blonde hair fell across his belly. Tom felt the hardness and heat between his legs shoot up twenty degrees as she licked first his right, then his left nipple—who knew that was a great place on a man too? he thought with his last few moments of sanity as he felt her tongue continue down his stomach. A southerly movement.

She reached behind her neck and untied the halter string of her dress, letting it drop to her waist. The round fullness of her breasts was glorious in the moonlight. She leaned down just enough to let them touch his bare chest. She was driving him completely insane.

He pulled her against him, and rolled her over as fast as a man could, in one quick, strong movement. Now they lay on the sand together. The waves lapped up behind them; sea foam rushing between them. Cupping her head in his hands, he let his desires go and kissed her with the passion that had been building for days, weeks, maybe years. She melted underneath him and wound her legs up with his.

"Make love to me, Tom," Marla begged.

"Are sure about this?" he said between kissing her and trying to think clearly, which was really impossible. He made a mental note to smack himself for asking that. What an idiot. Why ask a woman about to have an orgasm if she's *sure*?

But he wanted her to be really clear about what was going to happen.

"Yes, yes." She ground her body into his with complete abandon. Her breasts burned against his skin. He cupped them with his hands and put his mouth over first one sweet nipple, then the other. Marla almost screamed with pleasure.

He had never wanted a woman as much as he

wanted Marla Meyers at this moment. Tom had a vision of walking through the lobby with a huge erection. Transportation problems. But could he take her right there in the sand?

Hell, yes. He stood up and scooped her off the ground, moving back under the trees. Her arms wrapped around his neck and a primal sound came out of her. She nibbled his neck with her teeth slightly bared. Geezuz, what planet was in his house of lust? Or maybe it was hers. Miss Virgo was definitely rising tonight.

"Oh, Marla. Oh *shit*, Marla."

She stopped squirming on the ground and looked up at him with a pleading in her eyes, arms stretched out toward him. "Tom, I need you."

He flopped down next to her and put his arms around her so they faced each other on their sides. "Marla, we have no . . . raincoats. No protection. No condom."

Marla's eyes widened a little. "Oh God, Tom, I guess it's been a long time. I mean . . . well, you know."

He put his fingers to her lips. "Don't talk. Let's just go up to our room and continue this where we left off. There's a drug shop here; hell, they have them in the men's room. I'm just sorry to break the mood. Moonlight becomes you." He stroked a lock of her hair back over her forehead.

"Anton sang that to me once. We had a shoot with a fake moon." Marla giggled. Then she sat bolt upright. "Anton," she repeated. Then she frowned. "Thirty days. Oh my God. I'm crazy."

Tom watched all the hot fun drain out of her in one swoosh. What the hell made that happen? Then again, what made her hot in the first place? His "two lonely people" theory had been working so well up to this point.

"Let's go, Riley." She gathered her dress and tied it back behind her neck. He helped her zip the back, then went over for her bag. He was thinking, let's go as in *let's go*? Or let's go?

This did not look good. It was more than a condom problem now, although he couldn't believe that incredible oversight on his part. Somewhere in his head he probably hadn't expected her to move this fast. He'd underestimated her.

But beyond that, he must have said or done something. Probably his brilliant question: Are you sure? Maybe back in the room things would resume. Oh, let that be true, Tom thought. He tried to remember the patron saint of getting laid, but that seemed like some kind of Catholic contradiction. How about St. Jude, patron saint of desperate causes? Yep, that was the one.

Determined to salvage some of the better moments of their evening, Tom strode up to her, took her hand, and pulled her back under the palm trees.

Pressing her up against the trunk, he slipped his hands behind her shoulders and kissed her silky, sandy skin all the way up to her wet, sweet mouth. He was lost in the taste of her. She tasted tropical, and sexual, and . . .

It seemed such a rare thing for Marla to surrender to him that he knew he'd better savor her—like dessert. His blood pounded in his head with longing for her. He wanted all the way in. He looked into her eyes to see what his chances were.

She smiled at him and touched his lips with her finger. He opened his mouth and sucked on her finger until her eyes glazed over again and she pressed against him. She was still hot. He went in for the kiss that would convince her to take him into her bed. Perhaps all was not lost.

A rustling in the treetops above them distracted Tom from his mission.

Marla heard it too, froze, and leaned against the tree for support.

Looking up, he couldn't see anything in the darkness, even with the moon. Must have been a bird or maybe a monkey. He shifted his gaze back to Marla. Her beautiful face was there, waiting for him, lips moist with his kisses. That was the last thing he saw before the darkness swallowed him.

* * *

"Tom, Tom! Wake up. *Please* wake up." Marla shook Tom's shoulders, shouting in his face. She shouldn't move him, right? But that was for a spinal injury, not for someone who got knocked out by a coconut.

What the hell was she going to do with him? Drag him toward the hotel? Panicking, she ran to the shore, scooped up a little lagoon water in her hands, ran back, and splashed his forehead with what was left. He didn't even stir. Now he was unconscious and wet too. That was useless! She was *not* a useless female. She *would* help her friend.

Kneeling over Tom, she felt for a pulse and found one. She tried to open his eyelids but couldn't see well in the dark. He was breathing—alive. At least that was clear.

Then she heard the distinct sound of someone shimmying down the palm behind her. Adrenaline rushed through her body. What if Tom had been right all along? Quickly she positioned herself, grabbed Tom around the chest, and with the strength of a woman frightened for her life, dragged his unconscious body over the sand. It seemed like miles, but she made it to one of the large overhead lights that illuminated the hotel garden.

"Heeeeeeeelp!" she screamed at the top of her lungs. Immediately people began coming toward them. Marla collapsed behind Tom's body. What a time for her "protector" to get knocked out. She stroked Tom's temples. Poor guy, she had been about a minute away from losing the bet to Anton and letting Riley take her to bed. Her loneliness, Tom's great dancing, and his incredible kisses had gotten the better of her. She could feel the excitement and emotion that led her into Tom's arms tonight change into fear. She choked back a sob.

Oh great, here she was with a damp, unconscious man in her lap, feeling sorry for herself. What self-respecting Indiana farm girl would indulge in that weakness? Running her fingers through Tom's hair, she bent over him to see if he was coming around. Then she felt the warm fluid on her hands. Holding them up to the light, Marla could see bright red blood smeared everywhere. Oh God, Tom.

"Somebody help me!" A man in a hotel uniform gently pulled her away from Tom, nodding to another woman, speaking French. The woman had a towel with her and they elevated Tom's bleeding head, the woman checking Tom over to see if he was breathing.

A series of shouts between staff members eventually brought a medical person of some kind. He told Marla in French he was the hotel physician.

"A coconut fell out of a tree and hit him," she replied to his questions in her rusty French.

"Madam, that is extremely rare."

"Yes, yes, I know. Someone was in the tree!" Marla insisted. A guest who had run over wrapped a robe around Marla's bare shoulders.

The doctor checked Tom's pupils with a small light. "I need more light to be sure, but it appears he's just knocked out. We'll take him in to the infirmary. Are you his wife?"

"N-no, no. Just a friend," Marla stammered.

The doctor stared at her with a kind look, then talked into a tiny cell phone, in French again, asking for a stretcher crew. In a few minutes, Tom was being transported into the hotel. She followed as they took the service elevators to a clean, white-painted infirmary with smooth white sheets.

"He needs some stitches. I will wake him first. I don't think he has a concussion, but he will have a very bad headache. You will need to watch him for the rest of the night." The doctor was young and black and wore a starched white coat. He spoke in soothing tones and made her feel better. Seeing the towel soaked with blood, she felt a little woozy. She decided to go look out the window while they prepped Tom for stitching.

Outside, a strong breeze had picked up. The palms swayed wildly, and she could see whitecaps out on the water. She hadn't even noticed the wind before. She'd been lost in Tom's embrace.

She had wanted him to make love to her so badly. To feel him deep inside her.

And then what? Tom had another life. A complicated, unresolved life. She didn't see herself in that picture anywhere. She'd remembered because of Anton's bet that this was a short-term arrangement. That didn't fit her goals. If she was going to bring a man into her life, it was going to be for keeps. No more window-shopping. No more disasters. She'd have to be extremely careful. How could she have let herself slip so far tonight?

Paris was right. The heat was getting to her.

She pressed her palm up against the cool window and realized she hadn't washed the blood off her hand yet. Was that coconut meant for her? How could this unknown danger follow them all the way to the Bahamas? Maybe a local just went coconut hunting and slipped. Maybe it was a teenage prank.

Maybe she better put on her Mike Mason thinking cap and start paying attention to Tom's suspicions before she ended up dead.

Chapter Eleven

PROFESSOR PLUM IN THE DRAWING ROOM WITH THE CANDLESTICK

"He took a coconut for me," Marla replied.

"Oh God, they've just ruined your beautiful haircut. Look at that patch, it's not even disguisable as a wedge." Anton circled around Tom's head like a bee. He reached out with one finger to touch the bare spot.

"Ouch. Cut that out, Anton. It will grow in." Tom waved Anton the bee away, and put his navy-blue Yankees baseball hat back on. "The point is, Marla is not safe." Anton's misplaced concern about his hairstyle over his injury was less than becoming. These fashion people were something else. Tom's mouth formed a straight line of displeasure.

Anton sat down on Marla's pale green brocade chair and pouted. "Not to mention you, Riley. Just look what being around her has resulted in."

"Stop that, Anton, you sound shallow. And you both know that coconut could have just spontaneously fallen." Marla curled up next to Tom on the sofa and pulled her bright pink cashmere throw over herself like a child's blanket.

Tom put his arm around her. Anton's eyebrows shot up. Out of the corner of his eye, Tom saw Marla scowl and shake her head. These two were definitely up to something. He just didn't have time to go there.

Keeping Marla safe was his first priority. He had gone over every inch of her apartment when they got back and questioned Carl the doorman about security. Carl seemed to take his job seriously. At least that was a relief.

"I'm going to stay here with you, Marla. We are only one week into our thirty days, and things are not looking good. The doctor on the island said the coconut in question was hacked, not chewed or pecked off." Tom rubbed his forehead to ease the ache.

"Let's go over this slowly," he continued. "Someone is after you, Marla. Someone wants to see you out of the way. Who do you know that has anything to gain by your not working?"

Marla shifted away from Tom's arm, stood up,

and wrapped her shoulders in the throw like a cape. She paced the hardwood floors bordering the area rug. "That's the problem, Tom, I just can't picture what significance my working or not working has on anything."

"Phooey, Marla, I can think of several people who would like to see you out of the way. Let's take Paris. I love her to death, but she really wants the Lauren layout, and you know she's whined about it to everyone." Anton launched into a pretty good imitation of Paris's whining: *"It's just not fair, redheads can look just as vampy. I can look like a movie icon from the forties too!"*

"What would make her take the next step and actually hurt me, Anton? See what I mean?" Marla tightened the throw around her protectively. "As selfish as Paris is, she's not evil enough to plot my demise. Anyway, she'd never be able to keep it all to herself."

Tom started to stand up, but his head pounded like a drum. A mild concussion was not what he needed right now. He grabbed a plump sofa pillow and stretched out the length of the couch, chucking his sneakers off on the floor. The pain was making him think fuzzy. Damn!

"Let's go a little deeper, here," Tom said.

"Listen, Tom, I had this thought over the weekend. If these attempts to get me out of the way were related to the insurance policy, why did they start before I took the policy out? That doesn't make sense."

Anton leaned forward and directed himself toward the pacing Marla. "Because why else would you *get* the policy if you weren't having accidents? Someone had to make it look like you needed the policy. It's a pretty standard practice with the agency after a girl reaches a certain level. You weren't really quite there yet. Sorry, honey, no slam intended. We both know you have more talent than the average clotheshorse. The accidents pushed that decision along."

"Anton, you are brilliant." Tom would have kissed him, but bleeachhhh. Besides, he couldn't raise his head off the pillow very well. "Marla, do you think you could pour me some of that nasty press coffee of yours? Anton and I need to brainstorm more."

"Where's the magic word? You're acting just like an amateur detective. You two need your Dick Tracy outfits." Marla moved toward the kitchen even without the magic word.

"I was thinking more Watson and Holmes. I like the capes better."

"Anton, this is not a game. This is real-life danger. Who would benefit from Marla's policy paying off? The agency is the beneficiary." Marla dropped a spoon on the countertop, which clattered Tom's nerves to a fine edge.

Her voice was hard. "Rita is sole owner," Marla said. "But she would much rather get her percentage of my salary than a lump sum. Besides, Rita loves me. She's like a mother to me. There is no way she would do anything to hurt me."

"Someone would do anything, Marla," Tom said through gritted teeth. "You'd have to be blind not to see that at this point."

"Here's your damned coffee, Riley." Marla smacked the cup down on the end table right behind Tom's head. It rang against the glass insert. Tom flinched. "This is all crazy, and you know it. You know that the truth might be that I'm clumsy, and that's it," Marla said, too loudly.

"Now, Marla, honey, Tom's job is to keep you safe."

"Tom's job is to keep from having to pay off a policy and get his ass in trouble with his company. What happens after thirty days, Riley?"

"Technically speaking, you will no longer be considered high risk, and I can stop watching you. I even get a bonus for carrying through. Then, if you get into an accident, they'll pay up as usual. It just relieves me of the considerable strain of proving to them I wasn't an idiot for writing the policy up in the first place."

Anton leaned in closer. "What happens if it's within the thirty days? Can I have a cup too, sweetheart? Cream and sugar, of course."

"They'll pay up, but I'll be fired," Tom stated flatly.

A silence came from both Anton and Marla. Returning with Anton's coffee and one for herself, Marla sat down across from Tom in the other chair.

"I had no idea, Tom. I thought they'd just yell at you a little." Marla softened her tone.

"Nope. My ass is on the line."

"Look here," Anton interjected, "Rita may be like a mother to you, Marla, but she's got that son of hers to deal with. One thing is, Tom, it was B.B. who picked up and delivered those wings to the photo shoot."

Anton struck a pose and continued. "Plus, he's got big money problems. I happen to know she's paid off his gambling debts to keep him from getting in trouble with the Atlantic City people at least four times last year. I shouldn't be telling tales out of school, but this is an emergency. Maybe Rita really does need the money."

"I will never believe Rita would do anything to harm me. Nothing you say will convince me. Rita and I have a very special relationship." Marla sat back stiffly in her chair.

"Okay, okay." Tom rose painfully from his prone position. "I'll think about everything you've said. I'll even keep an open mind about the possibility I've read too many detective novels and am seeing plots where none exist. In the meantime, Marla, I'm going to camp out on your couch for a few days. If there is someone after you, they came all the way to the island to follow up on the job. B.B. was there. Didn't he have sort of a crush on you, Marla?"

"B.B.'s had a crush on every girl in the agency. Yes, he asked me out, but I turned him down nicely. I don't think there were any hard feelings left." Marla reached for her coffee and sipped slowly. "Why me, Riley? If this is true, why not any other girl at the agency?"

"I don't know." Tom looked into Marla's eyes and saw fear there. "I promise you that before this month is over I'm going to find out, Marla. I won't leave you with this hanging over your head."

Marla smiled weakly. "Thanks for that, Tom."

And what would happen at the end of the month? Would he just walk out of her life forever? Tom slouched down with his coffee cup. A miserable feeling came over him. He pictured his crummy apartment, his barely functioning office, his head with a bald patch on it. What the hell did he have to offer Marla Meyers?

She lived high. He lived low. She may have gotten carried away last night, but bottom line, she probably regretted it right down to her pink-painted toes.

*　*　*

It was Anton's turn to pace now. Oh, oh, Tommy boy was in the dumps. Anton's sixth chakra was tingling, and he couldn't sit still. How could he get these two twin flames to ignite each other?

Something had occurred, but from the looks of them, not the horizontal tango. Marla didn't look . . . satisfied. He moved over behind Marla and started rubbing her shoulders. My, she was tense. These two just needed a tree to fall on them, didn't they? Obviously a coconut just wasn't enough.

"I know this sounds melodramatic, but if Sherlock and I are going to solve this mystery, we've got to set a trap for the perpetrator. See, now, if we were playing the other game I'd have to call him Dick." Anton burst into a series of laughs. Tom and Marla didn't join in.

"Cut that out, Anton. It hurts when you laugh," Tom groused. "A trap would mean Marla as bait. I don't like the sound of that."

"I could help." Anton shrugged.

"They would have to think I was out of the way. Anton, come over here and stand beside me." Tom rose up. Anton trotted over and stood at eye level with Tom's chin. "Quite a difference. Do you have any platform shoes?"

"I like *this* game!"

"Can it, Anton. This is about height. We have to

make them follow you. See? If they think I'm out of the way, then they'll come after her here. But I'll really be with her all the time." Tom pushed his baseball cap back. "We've got some scheming to do. Marla, how about you order up some dinner, and we'll work this out together?"

"Make coffee, order dinner. Geez, Riley, did anyone everyone ever tell you what a chauvinist pig you are? I'm only doing this because I'm hungry, mind you. Anton, what's that Indian place you order out from all the time?" Marla asked.

"Elementary, dear Marla, it's the Taj Mahal Take Out."

"Miss Meyers, it's Carl here."

"Oh, Carl. We ordered out from Taj Mahal. The delivery will be here soon."

"Got it. You also have two guests here. A Ms. James and a Ms. Ray."

Marla took her hand off the intercom button and turned around to the others. "Oh my God. Tom, did you hear that? What are Rita and Paris doing here?" The last time both women had shown up to see her was around Christmas, and that was at a little agency party she'd thrown. This unannounced visit was unnerving.

What else was there to do? "Let them up, will you, Carl? Thanks." Marla felt guilty. Here they had been discussing Paris and Rita behind their backs, with Tom throwing accusations around everywhere. Plus Rita knew about Tom's real role as insurance guardian, but Paris didn't. If Paris found out Marla had been lying to her, she was liable to have a conniption.

"Ding-dong, Avon calling," Paris's voice carried through the door. "You'd look pretty in my pink passion nail polish, dearie."

Marla swung the door open. "Rita! Paris, how nice of you to come over without calling." Marla got her point across directly. She gave Rita a hug and glared at Paris over Rita's shoulder.

"I'm sorry, Marla, it was all Paris's doing. She got me all worked up about the Atlantis shoot and poor Mr. Riley taking a coconut in the head. Anton? Oh, Mr. Riley. There you are. I'm so sorry about your mishap."

"It's just a bump. Call me Tom, Mrs. Ray."

"Well, by all means call me Rita, Tom. Mrs. Ray was my last husband's mother, for pity's sake. Although he was my favorite husband." Rita moved into the room like a diva. Marla always admired the style that went with Rita. It was that classic model look from the fifties. Rita was quite the cover girl in her time.

"Paris, dear, come in, I'll get you a glass of wine." Marla put on her hostess face.

"Got any champagne? It looks like we have

most of a party here; Anton, Tom, Rita, and us girls. Bubbly is just the thing."

"Bubbles coming up." Marla moved to the kitchen.

Anton came over to Paris and fluffed her hair. "Paris, we need to brighten up that red of yours. That Italian dye just isn't holding as well."

"That's my real color, you traitor." Paris batted at his hand.

"Maybe when you were twelve." Anton turned on his heel and went to the kitchen with Marla.

"Flutes are in the glass-doored cupboard there, hon," Marla directed him.

"None for me, thanks," Tom called out. "Champagne won't mix well with the pain pills I plan on embracing later tonight."

Marla watched Tom find a safe chair. He looked like he was going to just observe the entire room like a Neil Simon play. It made her nervous. The cork popped up to the ceiling, and she couldn't manage to get to a glass fast enough to catch the spray of Dom Perignon that issued forth.

"Damn," Marla muttered.

Anton directed the bottle toward four fluted glasses, then handed them out one by one. "Cheers, everyone, here's to Tom's hard head." Anton raised his glass.

Marla's hand shook as she went for a sip. This

business of Paris suspecting Tom of being *not* the boyfriend, and Rita knowing Tom's real job . . . well, it was making her head spin. She liked Paris in a strange pain-in-the-ass sisterly way, and it would be a shame to get on her bad side. Paris had a very big bad side.

Tom watched Marla's hands shake. She must be cracking under all the strain of the pretense. On the other hand, Paris finished her glass of champagne in one long swan-necked swig. She would have made a great sailor. Rita perched herself calmly on a kitchen barstool and sipped like a lady. Which of these women would have the nerve to try and hurt their supposed friend? Sometimes, when Marla talked, he could almost see how ridiculous his theory sounded.

Then again, there was no denying his gut instincts. Never in his life had they steered him wrong. Someone, wherever, whomever, *someone* had it out for Marla. Tom made another sweep of the room and decided to pick a suspect.

"So, Rita, would the former and well-liked husband be the father of B.B.? He and I had some time to talk on the island. He says you have him travel with the girls?"

"No, B.B.'s father was my second husband, Bert. Not my favorite at all. That's why we used initials for my son. It was a better choice than Junior. Poor B.B. would have been Alberto Basil Manetti, Jr. We called him Bertie for a few years, but when he got big enough, well, the boy was always headstrong, even as a child. I'm sure he got that from his father, along with his Italian good looks. However, my third husband, Mr. Ray, adopted B.B. and we changed his name. It was easier for us all to have the same name. That didn't go down too well with the Manetti family, as you can imagine."

Rita looked into her glass for a full minute, with a definite scowl on her face. Tom had to think she was going over the sins of the father of B.B. It was obvious B.B. inherited the sins more than the good looks. Talk about a mug only a mother could love. And to think she'd told him all that in one breath with no prying. Sheesh. Marla was right. Women get to the heart of the matter.

Marla moved behind Rita, who was now sitting in one of Marla's white dining room chairs, and touched her shoulders protectively. For some reason this irritated Tom. Marla wasn't getting this at all. It's like she'd lean his way, then forget all about everything that had happened.

He wondered if that was her modus operandi in every aspect of her life: the amnesia effect. Like how she seemed to have forgotten that forty-eight hours ago she had pressed her naked breasts against him and begged him to make love to her on the beach. But that meant nothing to her now. A momentary slipup.

Steeling himself for the pain in his head, he rose and crossed the room to the expansive windows.

The sun was setting on Manhattan's majestic skyline. A strange rusted rose color, brought on no doubt by smog, streaked through the city. Darkness was right behind it.

Tom looked around him again at the characters in this little play. Anton and Paris stood by the kitchen counter. Anton was playing with Paris's hair; little braids were sprouting everywhere. Paris looked preoccupied with her champagne and the bottle she kept near her for refills. Marla hovered over Rita. Rita, the impeccably dressed icon for her successful agency.

These were the people in Marla's life, and one of them had it out for her. It had to be someone close to her. Worse than that, despite the fact that Marla had apparently filed their passion under "Unfortunate Tropical Errors," he actually cared. He cared more than about his bonus check, more than about his job. This cat-and-mouse game was going to end now.

"Listen up, everyone. Since you are all here, I have something to say."

"Tom, whatever you are thinking, I'd rather you discussed it with me first," Marla said. Her eyes were burning through him. He ignored her.

"Marla is in danger. It's my job to find out why. Accidents have been happening. Only they aren't accidents. One of you in this room knows something about it, and I'm going to find out who, and what."

The room was silent as a midnight mass. Now he had everyone's attention. Paris got a very suspicious look on her face, and Rita reached for Marla's hand on her shoulder. Anton stopped braiding Paris's hair.

Marla was genuinely agitated. "Riley, what is the point of this? It's just as likely they *are* accidents."

"What exactly are you talking about, Riley? Are you telling me you are some kind of bodyguard for Marla? Boy, you sure fooled me. Stupid Paris, tell her anything." Paris crossed her arms and glared at Marla.

"Paris, your professional jealousy is very apparent. I'm wondering how far you would go to get Marla out of the way," Tom continued.

Jumping up from her perch, Paris made quite a sight waving her arms, turning beet-red, with tiny braids flying around her like feathers. She was obviously so angry she couldn't even squawk. Tom stifled a laugh.

"You . . . you . . . *jerk*! Jealousy?" Seeing a six-foot Amazon woman coming at him was a little unnerving, but when she took her best shot, he caught her fist in his hand, moved her toward the sofa, and sat on her lap. She scrapped like a wild pig as he held her wrists gently but firmly.

"Let her go!" Marla took three long strides and grabbed Tom's arm, landing on his lap. He let go of Paris, who had calmed down enough to stop hitting him.

Tom eased Marla off his lap, got up, and turned to Rita. "Then there is the matter of your agency and the three million dollars you stand to collect if Marla gets hurt. That gives you a motive, Ms. Ray. Something about keeping the bad boys from breaking B.B.'s legs over gambling debts?"

Rita took out a handkerchief and put it up to her mouth as if to cover up a sob. Paris kicked him in the shins.

"O-o-u-c-h." Tom danced away from her, holding one leg.

"Rita, let's go," said Paris. "Marla, your bodyguard, or whatever he is, is crazy. I should have known—he was so not your type, being alive and all. And thanks for lying to me too. I thought we were friends." Paris swooped her coat up, grabbed Rita's arm, and pretty much dragged her to the door. In the blink of an eye, they were gone.

"Get out of here, Tom Riley. I never want to see you again." Marla's face was stone-white. She clutched the back of a chair for support. His shin ached, his head ached, and he'd had enough of this game all the way around. Screw Miss Meyers. Somebody should, because he'd never get a shot at it. Screw Granite. He'd go to work for Providence.

"If that's how you want it, fine. Watch out for falling pianos." Coat in hand, Tom stalked out Marla's door.

"Tsk, tsk. He got a little carried away, didn't he?" Anton put his arm around Marla's shoulder.

"Carried away? Tom Riley is a rash, ridiculous human being."

"The nerve, accusing your friends of plotting against you. I mean, is this his idea of protecting you? He's just gotten way out of hand. You'd think he actually cared."

"Right. Like he's not just in it to keep his job and . . . collect his bonus." Marla slunk down in a chair and laid her cheek on the whitewashed maple table. She saw Anton pull a flower out of the dried centerpiece arrangement of hydrangeas, roses, and pepper berries. He tickled her cheek with it a little, then slid it into her hand.

The intercom buzzed again. Maybe it was Tom coming back to apologize. She raised her head off the tabletop. Before she could get the intercom, Anton was at the door.

"Yes, Carl? It's Anton."

"Taj Mahal here in the lobby with some great-smelling cartons. Shall I let them up?"

"Oh, not now. Miss Meyers is indisposed. I'll pop down and get it.

"Indian food for three, at your service. Be right back, hon."

Then Anton was gone and she was alone. Damn that Riley. She folded her arms on the table and put her head back on them. A few tears escaped. They ran onto the wood and puddled there. Damn him for leaving her alone.

Chapter Twelve

SHADOWS OF
THE NIGHT

If he'd had his trench coat on, the rain wouldn't be soaking him through to the bone. This wool jacket would probably shrink to Max's size before he got home. Tom stepped out into the slick black street and hailed a cab.

"South Fulton. By the bridge." Tom slid into the dark cab.

"How are you tonight, sir?" The cabbie had a deep East Indian accent.

"Crap. I'm like crap."

"That can only be woman troubles."

"Bingo."

"Oh, gambling troubles?"

"No, no. Bingo. You hit it on the head. Woman troubles."

"Looks like it's you that has been hit on the head. Did she take a rolling pin to you? Whatever it was, you might as well apologize now, because every error in love is done by the man no matter what you are currently thinking."

"Does your fare include free advice? She threw me out."

"That is very unfortunate, yes, but what did you do to deserve it?"

"I tried to protect her. I tried to find out the truth. I took a coconut for her."

"Am I wrong in assuming you did this in a very brutish and unthinking manner?"

"No. You are not wrong in assuming that. I lost my head. Probably because it's cracked. Even so, we have a contract. She can't just throw me out."

"It appears as though she has done that very thing."

"Listen, what's your name . . . *Rama*?" Tom read the driver ID card. "She's not really my type. She's uptown, you know?"

"This uptown is not safe? You said you were protecting her. Yet here you are, walking in the rain with your woolen jacket all soaked up. And who will be protecting her now?"

"No, dammit, she's not safe. Shit. Turn around, turn around." Tom smacked his palm against his

knee in lieu of his head. He had never felt so confused in his life. Here he was, discussing his problems with the Cabbie Llama. The driver made a
sharp U-turn in the road. Tom grabbed the seat
and hung on.

"Geezus, Rama, we're not in a chase scene here,
slow it down."

"I sense that the time is auspicious. Have you
had any dinner?"

"No."

"I'll radio ahead to my cousin's husband. He
has a Chinese take-out place on the way. Chicken
chow mein okay?"

"Fine. So I guess we are hurrying to eat?"

"No man can think on an empty stomach."

Rain slammed against the cab windows. The
night was dark. As dark as it gets in Manhattan.
Neon and halogen streetlights pierced the shadows. Tom slouched down low in the backseat,
shoveling chow mein in with a pair of wooden
chopsticks. What the hell was he doing, staking
out Marla's building, anyway?

This was stupid. If she hadn't thrown him out,
he and Anton could have put their plan into action and whoever was after Marla would be
thinking that he, Tom, was gone. Then he'd get
them as they emerged—like the cockroaches in
his apartment. Instead he was in a cab eating

chow mein, and Marla was in there. Surely Anton would spend the night. Small consolation, but Anton could at least dial 911.

"This is great. Your cousin cooks Chinese?"

"My cousin's husband. He is from southern China. We are a very cosmopolitan family," Rama said, and took two more bites. "There is now someone emerging from your woman's doorway. See under the awning there?" From their vantage point in the shadows across the street, Tom could see the entrance to Marla's building very well.

"She's not my woman. I just watch over her. That's her hairdresser. Damn, I was hoping he'd spend the night."

"She is having her hair done at eleven P.M.?"

"It's a long story. He's all right." Tom leaned toward the window and watched Anton wave for a taxi.

Instead of a cab, a shiny black sedan pulled over to the curb next to Anton. Tom felt a chill of recognition as B.B. Ray got out of the passenger side and approached Anton. What the hell?

A heavyset man emerged from the back of the car, put his hand on Anton's arm, and all but shoved him into the backseat.

"Oh, this cannot be good. Those gangsters are stealing your woman's hairdresser!"

Before the heavyset man got back into the car, he stepped back and opened the trunk. The headlights from a passing car illuminated the interior of the trunk, and Tom stared in horror as the man re-arranged what looked very much like . . . a body.

"Holy mother of a sainted cow, those men have kidnapped your woman, sir!"

Tom, by now, sat bolt upright, his skin crawling with nerves. "Follow them!" he shouted.

Rama had already started the car. He hit the gas and plastered Tom against the backseat. Tom buckled up.

God, what if Anton was in on this? He felt sick thinking of how he had as much as handed Marla to Anton. Why had he trusted him? Anton could be working with Rita, even B.B. They could all be in on it, collecting her policy and dividing it three ways. Maybe even four ways . . . hotheaded Paris, too.

"Don't worry, sir, we will be glue upon those wicked kidnappers' behinds."

"Tom. It's Tom Riley. Stay with it, Rama."

"Thomas Riley, was I not telling you about the auspiciousness of our meeting? I knew immediately when you stepped into my cab that something was of a fateful nature. Hold on, Thomas." Rama took a quick curve.

Tom grabbed the door jam handle and hung in there. "Look, Rama, they're stopping at that newsstand. This is my chance. I'll jump out and try and get close. Keep the engine running."

Rama started throwing items in the backseat. "Here. Take my topcoat. What kind of a foolish man goes out without his topcoat in this weather? Take my umbrella and these Ray.Bans. Then you will be the invisible incognitable man."

"Thanks. Tom struggled into everything as he flew out the door. He put the umbrella up and pulled his baseball cap low over his face. Approaching the newsstand, he could hear the crusty old man behind the counter grumble about the rain. The other voice he heard was B.B.'s. Tom turned aside and pretended to read the tabloids.

"I'm sick of this crappy weather. I'm gonna haveta put the tarps over my papers again. That wind keeps pushing it over my way." The old man's gravelly voice was still clear enough for Tom to hear.

"Vinnie, when you gonna retire? You're gettin' to old for this," B.B. said.

The heavyset man from the back joined them. "B.B., get your damn paper and get back in the car. Vinnie, howya doin'?"

"Don't rush me. I got time," B.B. stalled.

The man grabbed him by the arm and swung him around. Tom slipped out of the stand and behind the racks into the shadows, sensing trouble. He strained to hear their voices.

"No, you are definitely outta time. Now, we're tired of runnin' all your errands. Listen, fool, you screwed up. We gave you an extra month, and your plan got nowhere. Mr. Scamandi wants his money. We are gonna make sure he gets it. Understand?

"First we're going to your mom's place with that dummy 'delivery' in the trunk, which will get us in the door. Mr. S. wants us to check out the books and be sure you ain't holdin' out on us. Then we're gettin' rid of your boyfriend, Anton. We'll drop him at his place. Then we're gonna take care of that dame you've been havin' so much trouble with."

Tom found a tiny crack in the frame and took a long look at the bozo. He could see B.B. turn pale.

"Okay, Jocko, okay." B.B. sounded scared. Real scared.

The bozo took B.B.'s cheeks and squeezed them. "It's in our hands now. You just collect the dough from Mommy when it arrives." Bozo Jocko made a quick step over to Vinnie, reached in his pocket, and peeled off a hundred-dollar bill from a big wad.

"Here's for my friend's paper, old man. You ain't heard nuthin', as usual. Right, Vin?"

"Right, Jocko." Old Vinnie grabbed the hundred in his bony hands and grinned.

Rama's headlights were off, and Tom had to feel his way back through the pouring rain. This time he got in front beside Rama, who was already pulling out.

"Wait a second. We've got it wrong." Tom felt the relief flood through him as he spoke. "That wasn't her in the trunk. It was a dummy. But the guy said something bad. Let's get back to Marla's place as fast as we can. Her life may depend on it!"

Tom grabbed the dash and swung a seat belt over himself just as Rama went into another amazing U-turn, shoved in a cassette tape, and started singing along to what sounded to Tom like a Puccini opera, in Italian, as he sped down the rainy streets, keeping time on the steering wheel. So it was B.B. all along. Mommy's dough—that had to be B.B.'s gambling debts again. Was Anton really involved? And Rita? Tom rubbed his eyes and let out a groan. Something was just so wrong about all of this. Take care of that dame B.B. had had so much trouble with? Please don't let that be Marla.

The most wrong, though, was him being out here instead of with her. How could he have left Marla alone?

"Do not worry, Thomas Riley, we will get there and save your woman."

"How could I have left her alone, Rama?"

"It's like I said, Thomas. In matters of love, it is always the man making the mistakes. We men are burdened with our testicles. This is a problem."

"You are so right, Rama. This is a problem."

* * *

The Indian food wasn't sitting well in her stomach. Marla rooted through the cupboard for some ginger root among all the vitamin and herb bottles. There, a brand-new one sat in the back. She grabbed it.

Actually nothing was sitting well: not the food, not Tom Riley, and not her current situation. She slammed the cupboard door hard. No herbal remedy was going to fix this.

Anton hadn't helped at all, talking about Riley like he was some sort of vacation destination: "Under that mildly irritating exterior lies a truly good man, Marla. A man you can count on. A man to get stranded on a tropical island with."

Sure, last time they were on a tropical island he'd gotten knocked out by a coconut. Marla gave up trying to peel the seal off the ginger root bottle with her fingernails and took a paring knife out of the knife block next to her. What were they thinking with these safety seals these days?

Of course, right before that she'd been ready to let Riley make mad passionate love to her on the beach. She winced at the memory. A wave of heated embarrassment curled over her, and it made her feel more nauseated. She got one edge of the plastic up and started hacking at the tiny rip. Damn this thing!

Why had she thrown herself at her insurance agent? Was she that pathetic, that lonely? Or was

Tom Riley, with his intense brown eyes and his amazing kisses, getting to her? With one good thrust, the paring knife tore through the seal of the herb bottle and stuck straight into her hand. Shock and pain pierced her like . . . a knife. She carefully extracted the tip out of her flesh and flung the offending instrument on the floor. Blood ran down her wrist, and she dove for paper towels.

Applying pressure to her wound helped stanch the blood loss, but her blood *pressure* was rising higher and higher. She grabbed the ginger root bottle with her good hand and threw it with all her might across the room. It made contact with several champagne glasses, knocking one over and breaking another. Shit.

Marla let out a primal scream. Then she stomped across the floor to get her coat for a trip to the emergency room. The bleeding had soaked through her paper towel batch, but felt like it was slowing. She wrapped a small kitchen towel around her hand.

Someone started pounding on the door.

Why hadn't Carl buzzed? She stayed very quiet and went to look through the peek hole.

Riley. He was the last person she wanted to see. She didn't want him to see her all stabbed up from opening a stupid bottle of herbs. She didn't want him to see her temper-tantrum-in-the-kitchen mess. She didn't want to hear his theory about it being yet another plot. Marla slowly backed away from the ever-increasing noise at the door and went toward the back exit of her apartment. The one Riley didn't even know about. It was far enough down the hall where she could slink around the corner and take the west elevators.

"Marla! Marla, are you all right? I'm not going away until you answer me," she heard Riley yell at the door.

Here she was, sneaking out of her own apartment. That man was always causing her problems. She cracked open the door and slunk out into the hall. Just before she made the dash for the elevator, she saw Thomas Riley kick down the door of her apartment. What the hell was he doing? She stopped and doubled back.

"Oh my God . . . Marla. Rama, we're too late. Search the place. Maybe she's still alive." Tom ran toward the pile of blood-soaked paper towels on the kitchen counter. Then he saw the knife, spattered with red blood, lying on the pale wood floor.

He put both hands on the counter, bowed his head, and let the horrible images scream in his mind. He wanted to tear something apart. He had to pull himself together and search the apartment for her . . . for her . . . He couldn't even think it.

"Are you completely out of your mind, Riley?" The voice came from behind him. He turned. Relief flooded through him and caught in his throat. All he could do was go to her and take her in his arms.

"God, Marla, I thought you were dead." He ran his hand through her hair and pressed her against his chest. For a second he felt her rapid heartbeat. Good heart, still beating. Then she shoved him away.

"Why are you and your friend ransacking my apartment, Riley? Is this part of your master plan? What possible explanation can you have for doing this?"

"Marla, you're in terrible danger. We have to get you out of here."

"That was exactly what I had in mind. I'm on my way to the emergency room to get my hand stitched up. But first I'm going to call the cops and tell them my house was broken into by a crazy insurance man and . . . who the hell is that, Riley?"

"Your woman is alive, Thomas Riley! This is very good. What is that wonderful curry I smell?" Rama walked past them into the kitchen and opened up the refrigerator. "Mmmm. Taj Mahal lamb curry is fairly passable. May I?"

"Sure, help yourself," Tom answered.

"*Riley!*" Marla yelled. "That's it. You just stay right here. I can't deal with this anymore. You and your friend stay here and eat take-out food. I'm going to the emergency room."

"No, please wait." Tom reached out to her, but she was already stepping through the shards of wood that hung where her front door had once stood. "Marla, stop. Listen to me." Tom was ten feet away. He saw the elevator button light up where she had touched it.

As if in a nightmare, Tom saw the elevator doors open, and the face of a man. Before he could get to her, Marla had stepped into the elevator. The doors closed in his face. He beat them with his arms and fists, shouting, but she was gone. He heard the sound of a muffled scream descending downward.

"Rama! He's got her. We have to take the stairs."

Rama was suddenly behind him as he ripped the stairway door open, taking the stairs two at a time.

"Thomas Riley, we are on the twelfth floor." Rama was close on his heels and barely winded. Tom had no time to think about that. Only reaching Marla. Adrenaline surged through him, propelling him forward. He careened off the walls and grazed the corners.

He'd never make it before the elevator got there. He focused on catching up with them as fast as possible. Carl. He'd be there. He'd stop them. If he let his mind go anywhere else, he would go crazy.

In a blur, the opening to the lobby finally appeared. Throwing the heavy door wide open, he ran toward the elevator. There stood Marla, adjusting her coat. Inside the elevator was a crumpled, semiconscious man. The guy groaned and his body slid farther down the wall.

Tom decided it looked like the jerk might rouse himself, so he stepped in and right-hooked him in the jaw. His head slumped down on his chest, out cold.

"Holy women's liberation, Thomas Riley. Your woman has saved herself." Rama stood beside Marla as they stared at the scene before them. Tom was still gasping for air. His lungs burned from the effort of running down the stairs. Marla came over to him. Despite her kung-foo victory, she looked scared.

He caught his breath, put his arms around her, and pulled her close into his chest. She let him.

"Marla, I've been so stupid. I shouldn't have left you alone."

"Women who live alone learn how to protect themselves," she said quietly. His arms felt safe. She felt Tom take a deep breath.

"Marla, I don't exactly know what's going on. B.B. was headed for the agency with a bunch of mobsters. Something about the books and Rita's money. It was all to pay his gambling debts. I'm not sure who all is involved yet."

"The guy in the elevator was just after my money, Tom. I don't even know if it's related." She held the front of his shirt tightly and looked into his eyes. His warm chocolate brown eyes. Riley had tried to save her. Whatever this was all about,

Tom Riley cared about her, and not just because he was getting a bonus.

"All I do know is that we have to get you out of this city," Tom said "Until I figure out the truth."

From the corner behind them came muffled sounds. Marla tensed. Riley motioned to Rama to move next to Marla.

She watched Tom approach the sounds, then move behind the front desk. She heard Riley gasp, then bend down and drag Carl out from behind the partition. Carl had duct tape over his mouth and was hogtied with rope. Riley gave the tape a tug.

"Oowww. Miss Meyers, I'm so sorry. He got me with a blackjack. He must have tied me up when I was out. Are you hurt? Your hand is bleeding!" Carl wiggled out of the ropes as Tom loosened them.

"No, Carl, the creep didn't hurt me. I took self-defense at the Y. You'll find your man in the elevator. My hand . . . I cut on a kitchen knife. We better call the police, Tom."

"And get you to the emergency room. This could all take hours. We can't leave Carl here alone with the thug. Can you hold on until the cops get here?"

"Sure," Marla said. Somehow that wasn't quite right, because the room started weaving, and her knees shook. She leaned on Rama.

"Thomas. Take your woman upstairs. I have

also skills in the martial arts. With Mr. Carl's help we two can hold the bad man until the police come."

Rama passed Marla over to Tom, then spoke in low tones to Carl. Marla couldn't make out what he said. She was just glad to have someone to hold on to.

"Get this guy out of the elevator, Carl. I'll take Marla up to her place," Tom said.

Marla watched in a haze as the other two dragged the guy out of the elevator. Carl gave him a thump with his foot.

"I owed him one," he said, looking sheepishly up at the others.

"Rama," Tom called, "I owe you for cab fare. Can I reach you tomorrow? Leave your number with Carl."

"This ride is on the house, Thomas. But please call me tomorrow and tell me Miss Marla is all right." Rama gave a small nod toward Marla, then continued to drag the thug.

"Thank you for everything, Rama. I'll be in touch," Tom replied.

She saw ropes and felt much better knowing Rama and Carl were going to tie the guy up. Then her knees buckled again. Tom swooped her up in his arms and carried her into the elevator. She just let go and leaned against him. He hit her floor button with his elbow.

"I'm not letting you out of my sight until we find a place to hide you. Marla, I . . . can't let anything happen to you. You . . . mean too much to me."

"Tom. I don't want you to lose your job over me."

"Shut up, Meyers. I don't give a shit about my job. I know I'm nobody, but I care about you, damn it."

Marla looked up at Tom's face and saw the fierceness of his emotions written there. It sent a wild tremor up her spine. She couldn't find any words. The silence hung heavy between them.

She let him carry her through the broken door and into her bedroom. He leaned down and pulled back a blanket, then gently placed her on the bed.

Then he lay down next to her. He pulled her close to his body and stroked her forehead with his hand. She wanted nothing more than his comfort at this moment. Not to think about how she felt, or what was going on in her life. Just comfort.

They had about fifteen minutes of peace. She could hear people stepping on the broken door fragments, but she stayed right where she was. Tom's muscles tensed a little, but they both heard the yell—"Police!"—and Tom answered back, "In here."

The police entered, and Marla and Tom sat up as a paramedic came over to look at her.

"I'm fine, just a little shaken up. I cut my hand myself."

The paramedic unwrapped it and turned her hand around. "It's not too bad, I've got some bandages we can use. Can you make it to the bathroom? We should clean it up."

She got up slowly. The three of them went into her bathroom and tended to her cut. In the other room she could hear the police taking pictures and talking. She even heard some hammering.

"She's in mild shock. After we're done, put her to bed and keep her warm," the paramedic directed Tom.

Tom nodded and watched as he finished up her hand.

One officer came to the bathroom. "Want to tell us what happened?"

The next hour was tedious, and her hand hurt from being disturbed. The police finally understood Tom had broken the door down looking for her. Marla noticed Tom didn't share his theories and just stayed with the immediate facts.

Tom may have his gut feeling, but she did too. Weird as it was, something inside her knew that it was all too random. However, the possibility did exist that she was in danger. One way from an unknown, unproven source. The other way from a very proven source. A man.

She needed to get away and think.

And write. Her writing had suffered unending delays. Her editor had left a message on her machine yesterday with a note of hysteria in her voice. Poor Edith.

Somehow, she didn't know who to trust anymore. Marla felt sick to her stomach. Who was her friend, and who was her enemy? Suddenly she missed her father.

The police and medics finally left. She managed to get her clothes off and into some pajamas. Tom waited outside the closet like a watchdog. She was bone-tired, but too frightened to sleep. She climbed in bed and tucked the covers around her.

Tom knocked on the door. "Can I get you anything?"

"No, I'm fine, Tom. Thank you for . . . everything." There was silence from the other side of the door. She closed her eyes for a minute, but the image of her mugger leaped into her head. "Tom!" she called out, louder than she intended.

The door swung open and he stood in the doorway.

"Do you think . . . would you mind sleeping in here?"

He came and sat down in her purple velvet bedroom chair, next to the bedside table. "I'll stay right next to you. Close your eyes and rest."

"Is the front door still a hole?" she asked.

"No. The cops put up some boards. I'm sorry about the door. I was worried about you."

Emotion choked her, and a couple of tears slid down her cheek onto the satin pillowcase.

Then he was beside her. She laid her head on his shoulder and pressed up against his warmth.

"Have you decided where to go?" he asked quietly.

"I think I'll fly home to my dad's place in Indiana."

"That sounds good. Let's book your flight now so you can leave in the morning." Tom reached for the phone, and together they made the arrangements for a flight out to Dayton, Ohio. There she would rent a car and drive to the farm near Centerville. It was too late to call her dad; she'd have to reach him tomorrow.

Sometime in the hours that followed, she shivered in her half sleep and felt Tom pull the covers around her shoulders and bring her closer to him.

Tom Riley.

Tom Riley. She opened her eyes and looked at him. His eyes were closed, but she could tell he was only resting lightly. His face looked tense in the shadow cast by the bedside lamp.

What was she going to do about this? She sighed and rolled over on her side, facing away from him. She could only deal with one problem at a time. He responded to her movement and positioned himself behind her. Close as spoons in the drawer, she relaxed into his warmth and drifted into sleep again.

"Call me as soon as you land. Leave a message at your place. I'm going to see to the door and clean up." Tom leaned in as he spoke to her. His baseball cap bill tapped the rim of her rain hat. Marla knew how to make herself unrecognizable pretty damn well. He looked into her bright blue eyes and couldn't help himself. He turned his hat backward, went the four inches farther, and kissed her. His body ached for wanting her. How could he put her on a plane and out of his sight?

Her lips were the softest he'd ever kissed. He touched them with his fingertips. She was still there, eyes wide open. What did he want from her? Obviously something she wasn't capable of giving. She was running away from more than danger; she was running from him.

"Don't worry, I'll be fine." The noise of an airplane taking off interrupted her. She awkwardly brushed a stray strand of hair from her face. "I've made this trip before. My dad'll be waiting." Her voice was businesslike. "Tom, what's going to happen now?"

"I've got some investigating to do. I'll give you the word when it's safe to come back. I'll talk to

Rita and have her put you on vacation status. I'm sure you have a week off coming."

"More than that. I haven't taken a vacation for at least three years. I guess we should have thought of that one before, Riley. We could've had me take a few weeks off out of our thirty days from hell."

"True. Sometimes we get so focused on some tiny aspect of life we forget about alternatives." Tom stood up as they called out the rows for the flight. "There's your plane."

"Be careful, Tom."

"You have my office number and my apartment. I'll hear from you." It was a statement, not a question. He hoped she understood that.

He picked up her carry-on and walked with her to the gate. She took her bag from his arm. For one second he thought she might speak, or maybe kiss him. Then she turned away. He watched as she walked down the boarding ramp and disappeared.

Chapter Thirteen

MEANWHILE, BACK AT THE FARM

She knew the way so well. West on 40 until she came to downtown, then a right on North Centerville Road, past the church.

The shade trees were bare, but the small buildings had fresh white paint on them. It looked like the locals had been sprucing up the town in anticipation of the coming months. Summer was high season for antiques, and Centerville was a destination for treasure hunters.

Marla smiled, remembering how she and her dad, a year after her mother died, packed up Mom's precious things: china, linens, family photos, strange knickknacks. Like the ceramic goose girl that always sat on the kitchen windowsill.

They were probably worth a fortune now, but they were her treasures, waiting for her like a promise. Waiting for the day she had a real home and a family to share them with.

The two of them had hid the boxes in the barn to keep Ivy Richardson from throwing them out. It had meant so much to Marla at the time. It meant her father understood at least that much— that he needed to protect her from Ivy's "make-over" of their lives. Thank God he'd finally divorced her.

Coming home had that feel, that smell. The air held that special scent for her, and she opened the car window to let it in. Past the town and out Centerville Road, the winter wheat rippled in the sun. Soybean fields were hinting at green. She crossed the railroad tracks. That was the sound that always told her home was near.

The pretty white farmhouse with dark green trim stood like a longtime friend waiting for her to come back. Her tires crunched on the gravel driveway. The row of poplar trees Dad had planted for a windbreak was about twenty feet tall now. They cast long shadows on the grassy field beside the house.

Had it been that long since she'd been here? Wasn't it just a year ago Christmas? Two years; that's right. It was after her visit Dad had called with the news he and Ivy were splitting up. She knew clearly that finally telling her father the truth about Ivy and her coldheartedness made her father leave Ivy. It wasn't revenge, it was just the truth, and it set them free.

There was her dad in his overalls, standing on the porch, hands in his pockets, grinning. She slammed the car into park and sprang out the door, running like a ten-year-old girl. A funny thing happened on the way to her daddy's arms: She started to cry.

"Oh, Daddy." Marla only had two words in her by the time she got to him.

"Honey, I missed you. It's all right. Whatever it is, we'll fix it together." Her father held her and wiped her face a little with his blue bandanna handkerchief. "We'll get your stuff later. Come on, punkin. I'll make you some stinky tea."

She choked on a laugh. He put his arm around her and walked her into the house. The screen door made that slow spring and quick slam behind them she'd heard all her life.

Marla sat at the kitchen table, hiccupping between sips. "Stinky tea" was chamomile with honey. It was their special joke. The cup, she noticed, was one of her mom's. Cream-colored with an orange, black, and yellow floral design. She looked around slowly and saw that her dad had taken down all of the kitchen things Ivy had brought with her and replaced them with Marla's mom's treasures.

Her dad sat in the painted chair with its green corduroy cushion. His arm stretched across the table to her. He pushed a strand of hair out of her face and tucked it behind her ear. She smiled a red-eyed sobby smile at him.

"I'm making pot roast."

"Since when do you cook like that?"

"Two years as a bachelor, I figured I better learn or starve. I got sick of frozen dinners."

"I'll make dessert. Got any chocolate sauce? You know, the kind in a can?"

"Yep."

"And vanilla ice cream? The square one you slice?"

"That too."

"Good. It's as good as made."

"Goofball." Her dad ruffled her hair. "At least it's just us now. I'm sorry it took me so long to figure it out about Ivy. It's like the days just went by for many years. Then, when you were here for Christmas, I just saw it all. Then you told me. I owe you a big apology, honey."

"Thanks, Dad. That means a lot to me." Marla reached out and patted his arm. "And thanks for putting Mom's stuff back out. It's beautiful."

"You let me know if you need to talk. Right now we have a pile of potatoes and carrots waiting to be peeled. Grab a knife, kid."

"Oh, I did that. See my hand?"

"What'd you do?" He turned her hand around in his.

"Vitamin bottle plastic coating."

"Don'tcha just hate those things? Seems a bit over the top. Okay, then, you still have a good right hand. We'll put a rubber glove on this one and keep it dry."

They marched to the kitchen and took their positions. Marla manned the peeler, her dad took the slice-up station. A breeze ruffled the cream-colored curtains at the kitchen window where they stood. Marla could smell the roast starting to "simmer up" as they used to say. Maybe everything would work out after all. For now, she wasn't even going to think about . . . Tom.

"Hurry up, slowpoke, we gotta get these in the pot," Marla said. She picked up the peeling pace and started the traditional race—peeler vs. chopper.

"Watch out, I'll be caught up with you in a minute flat," her dad responded to the challenge.

Tom was going to set a bug bomb off in his apartment. At least that would clear the creepy

crawlers out for a week. Oh, that's right. The
neighbors took a dim view of that toxic stuff seeping through the walls.

Not knowing what possessed him, Tom Riley
had decided to clean his apartment. So far a pile of
laundry three feet tall had grown on his stripped-
down single bed. Looked like a night of quarters
at the Laundromat.

He'd even borrowed a vacuum from his landlady and sucked up dust bunnies the size of
cocker spaniels from under the bureau. Now with
a scrub brush and bucket, he discovered that the
linoleum under his dull brown throw rug was actually red. Amazing. All this time he though it
was dirt-colored.

Tom decided he needed to think. He needed
space to think, and there was none to be found.
Plus it was time for his son to see that an adult
man was capable of cleaning a thirty-by-thirty
studio apartment. He got off his knees and rummaged in the kitchenette drawer for a hammer.
The corners of the linoleum were in need of a
tack-down.

Apparently the guy below him was not in the
mood for Tom's project.

"Hey, what the hell is that noise? It's two A.M.,
you asshole!" the voice of his underneath neigh-
bor yelled.

"Shut up! I'm fixing the floor. . . . There, I'm done. So shut up," Tom yelled back.

Shit. He'd lost track of time. Tom looked at the bed full of clothes. Nowhere to sleep. Besides, he wasn't tired.

Shoving the hammer back in the crammed drawer, he decided to take a midnight prowl. New York was the city that never slept anyway. Maybe he'd go to Jay's and get a beer.

Instead of Jay's, he hailed a cab and ended up at Marla's. He decided to see if his brother-in-law Jim had finished fixing the door. Good thing he had her code for the outside security lock. Carl was always asleep by now.

The original door was repaired nicely and re-hung. Jim was really a craftsman. Rosalee was lucky to have him. He put in the key Marla left with him, stepped in, and pushed the door closed behind him. Like an old habit from childhood, he headed for the kitchen and opened up the fridge.

Leftover Indian food. Interesting thought. Tom found a spoon and dug something out of a take-out carton onto a plate with some rice, then popped it in the microwave. A pleasant curry fragrance drifted up. He grabbed the plate and sat down at the counter. He'd even found a cream soda in Marla's fridge. Imagine that. Must be for her chili dog kind of moments.

Her apartment reminded him of an older person's place. It had a kind of thirties genteelness: all shades of beige and soft vintage green, wrought-iron pieces, with floral accents. Everything toned down. Elegant. He picked up his plate and wandered around, eating.

Her stereo equipment was top-of-the-line, that's for sure. Wafer-thin speakers blended into their surroundings, all the components housed in an antique armoire. Her collection of CDs was impressive: Ella Fitzgerald, Diane Shur, all the old big bands, and some classical stuff. There it was, Cleo Laine; her favorite. Tom set his plate on the floor and messed with the disk and buttons until a smooth-sounding vocal came through.

There. A little distraction to keep him from thinking. He had to quit thinking about Marla. He stepped back on his plate and it cracked in half. Damn.

Scooping up whatever was left of the food, he headed to the kitchen trash and dumped the whole mess in.

Maybe he'd just get some sleep. At least her bed wasn't stacked with dirty laundry. He'd just get a blanket and sack out on top. She had a bookcase full of Mike Mason books, he noticed. That made him all twitchy again. She loved mysteries, jazz; like, hey, if she wasn't one of the *beautiful* people, the Manhattan elite, they'd have enough in common to make a go of it.

As it was, he'd already made as much of a fool of himself as he was going to. It was her call now. He'd finish his job and get back to his former dull life.

Tom stood by the bed and stripped off his shirt and T-shirt.

He sat down on the side to get his shoes off, but suddenly Tom got that funny, hairs-on-the-back-of-his-neck prickling feeling. No sooner had his hairs risen, than an earsplitting shriek emitted from someone . . . in the bed.

"Wha . . . ?" Tom spun around and in the semi-darkness saw someone clutching bedcovers right beside him. With a dark mask over the face, it was hard to tell what the hell was going on. He grabbed the covers and yanked them.

Another shriek and the mask was torn away to reveal a very disheveled Anton. Tom started laughing as Anton pulled earplugs out of his ears.

"What the hell are you doing here?" Tom choked out.

"Well, back atcha, big boy. I'm housesitting. What are *you* doing?" Anton gathered the covers around his black-and-white-striped silk pajamas.

"Shit, I don't know. I came to see if the door was

fixed. Didn't you hear me in the kitchen? Geez, I turned on the stereo, even."

Anton held out his earplugs to explain his not hearing.

"My place is a mess. I think I came seeking a clean bed to sleep in." Tom sat in the small, upholstered chair next to the nightstand.

"Oh, and Marla's bed sounded good. Boy, you've got it bad. Go fix me a drink, Tom. My nerves are all jangled. You'll find the liquor cabinet to the left of the dining table. Low deco-looking thing. It lifts up. Brandy or something. Care to join me?"

"Don't even think about getting me drunk, Anton. No amount of liquor would ever make me find you attractive." Tom's deep laugh filled the room.

"Very funny, Riley, you're half naked. If someone showed up in this apartment, you'd have a tough time explaining this."

Tom went silent. "Damn. You're right." He grabbed his T-shirt and headed for the kitchen.

Tom found the brandy and a couple other things. He decided to surprise Anton.

As he gathered items and poured his concoction into a cocktail shaker, Tom recalled the previous night and Anton getting in the car with the mobster and B.B. He thought it all through carefully as he plopped ice cubes into two short glasses. Better stay on top of things. He poured a generous drink for Anton. For himself he made it look like more with extra ice.

Tom brought the drinks in. "Here you go, Anton, I used to be a bartender in my youth. This here's called Between the Sheets."

"My, my, aren't we the good humor man." Anton took the drink and sampled some. "Mmm, this is delish."

Tom restationed himself on the chair. "So, Anton, explain to me again exactly what you're doing here."

Anton propped himself up against the upholstered headboard and took another sip. "You'll have to teach me how to make this."

"I want to hear your explanations," Tom pressed. "Let's not get into a fight, Anton. It's late, we're both tired."

"All right already! Well, Marla called me from Indiana. She told me everything that happened. She asked me to check on the place because she was getting nervous about her stuff, what with the door broken and all. I came over and met your brother-in-law Jim. My, isn't he handsome?"

Tom rolled his eyes and motioned with his glass for Anton to continue.

"Of course, when I got here," Anton went on, "Carl was keeping his eye on things, and, well, the door was boarded up before. So . . . I just decided to stay and keep Jim company. Then I got tired and, well, I keep overnight stuff here for when-ever Marla and I have slumber parties. She has a great tub. That's it."

Tom looked at him hard. "Why did you get in the car with B.B. and his friend last night?"

"God, it was starting to rain, and I had cash-mere on. I must have been out of my mind, though. They took forever to get me home. We stopped at a newsstand, and then at the agency. B.B. had a mannequin to put in the fashion room. I was really regretting my choice by then. I tell you, Tom, it was positively weird the way that dope B.B. forgot his keys and had to borrow mine.

"Used your keys?" Tom repeated. "That's what they wanted with you. Anton, they waited for you to come out of this apartment. For the last twenty-four hours I've been thinking you might be in on this, Anton. I trusted you, and that really bugged the shit out of me."

Anton stared at Tom, then took a big gulp of his drink. "That hurts, Tom."

Tom stood up and paced the room. "What a sap I've been. Here I thought I had it all figured out. I followed you. When they stopped at the news-stand I heard them talking. Did Marla tell you any of this?"

"She left a few details out, I guess. Except for the fact that she had to leave town because she was in danger. I couldn't believe you'd actually convinced her."

"Well, one guy said something about taking care of that dame B.B. was having so much trouble with. Do you think he meant Marla? Do you think the guy in the elevator was sent by them?"

"I shouldn't have given B.B. my keys. I should have stopped them." Anton looked very agitated.

"What could you have done? They would have stuffed you in the trunk with the dress dummy," Tom reassured him. "Okay, buddy, we have some work to do. You and I are going to have a chat with Rita tomorrow. This all revolves around B.B.'s gambling debts as far as I can tell. I don't think Paris is involved, but she's so whacked it's hard to say."

"I'll do whatever I can to help Marla. You know that." Anton yawned.

Setting his drink down, Tom surveyed the situation. "Anton, since you're already tucked in, I'll just take a quick shower and sleep on the couch." He got up and headed toward the bathroom.

"Just don't scare the life out of me again." Anton snuggled back under the covers.

"Right. And no shower peeking."

"Oh, all right. Spoilsport. Tom?"

"What."

"Do you think just the two of us can really head off the mob?"

"Yes, we can. We have to. Otherwise, we'll never get her back."

"We'll talk about that tomorrow," Anton said sleepily. "I have a few insights for you. For one thing, you should wear more olive green. It brings out your brown eyes. Good night, Riley."

Anton sounded confident. About what, Tom wasn't really sure. He'd think it through in the morning.

Tom and Anton stood in front of Rita like they were at the principal's office in grade school.

"It's just a damn good thing the shows are over for Marla, you two, otherwise she'd be missing six runways a day. I think I can reschedule a few things. I'll have to replace her for the Lauren layout. I'm sure Paris will do it." Rita tapped on the pages of her appointment book nervously, erasing and scribbling names in slots.

"Rita, your son is in trouble," Anton said quietly. He turned around and shut the door to the office behind them.

"Oh God, what now?"

"I overheard a conversation between B.B. and a very shady-looking guy. Then B.B. took the guy here because he insisted on looking over your books," Tom explained. "I'm not sure how it all adds up, but B.B.'s got himself in some kind of jam. He may be behind Marla's accidents. He may be planning to embezzle the insurance settlement."

"B.B. would never hurt anyone." Rita sat up straight and pushed her hair back with a shaking hand.

"His life was on the line. His gambling debts are out of hand. You're right about one thing: B.B. couldn't hurt anyone. But he could hire it done. We're going to have to get the truth from him."

Rita bent her head into her hands and leaned against her desktop. "What kind of proof do you have?"

"Mostly the conversation I heard. I can't really sort it all out, but you can make him tell us the truth. It's important. Marla's safety may depend on it."

Rita looked up, and Tom saw the pain in her eyes. He felt real bad for her. It couldn't be easy hearing this. He just had to know the truth of it all.

"Tom's in love with her." Anton positioned his hand as if he were telling Rita a secret that Tom couldn't hear.

"Anton, for Christ's sake."

"Do tell." Rita tried to brighten up a little. "Does she know?"

Tom shifted his stance and crossed his arms. "I don't believe the feeling is mutual. Which has nothing to do with this discussion."

"Marla Meyers has no idea what she wants. What she needs is a good man like you, Tom. I've seen this many times. If she continues on this way, she will forget to get married, forget to have kids, and end up alone." Rita slapped her desk. "Believe me, with all his flaws, I'm glad I had my son."

"It's all preordained anyway. Her rising Aries is in his sun sign. Of course, that's what makes them both so stubborn too," Anton rambled on. "Did you know they met on a blue moon?"

"Back to your son, Rita." Tom jumped to change the subject. "I'm glad to know you aren't aware of all this. It was hard to picture your involvement. Marla thinks very highly of you. Now, we're going to have to work together. I have an idea, but it will take all of us."

"Anything, Tom. I love Marla like a daughter. I love my son too, but I can't let this continue."

Tom sat across from Rita, and the three of them huddled like football players, as Anton explained a minute later when Tom removed Anton's hand from his butt and threatened to kick his ass.

"Boys, boys. Not now. Okay, we meet at one on Friday at Vito's Restaurant. I'll deliver B.B. into your hands. I'll give you twenty minutes, then come back in. Don't forget, it's the room to the right of the kitchen. It's a private dining room."

Rita paused. "But promise me you won't hurt him?"

"I promise," Tom said through gritted teeth. He'd like to nail that weak bugger for all the trouble he'd caused Marla and for a certain coconut. "Let's go, Anton. We need backup. We've got to find my new friend Rama and get into a couple of suits."

"Fun! I know just the one. I have a tweed English-looking thing with back detailing and everything." Anton kind of bounced out the door. Tom rolled his eyes at Rita and followed the bouncing hairdresser.

Chapter Fourteen

MIKE MASON MEETS THE MOB

The Smith Corona kicked on and hummed. What an old song that was. Marla rolled two layers of paper into place and tapped on the keys. There was something so . . . hands-on about her old typewriter.

How many short stories had she rolled off of here? She used to put carbon paper between two sheets in the old days. Now the double sheets were just to get a better impression out of the old keys. Her fingertips, stained from changing the ribbon, left ink smudges on the edge of the paper.

So O'Shay was close to the truth. That put him in the path of a killer with a habit of dropping red

roses. My research had turned up an old Holly-
wood scandal. Delores DelMarco's first husband,
an English actor named Trevor Thompson, had
turned up dead. She'd been put on trial for his
murder.

Rumor had it she'd been having an affair with
her attorney. When it came time to go to court, he
had refused to defend her. She was acquitted for
lack of evidence, but a year later, she killed herself.
That attorney was Randall Crantz.

So why would a crime committed fifty years
ago come back to haunt old Randall? And what
did that nosy reporter know that he didn't?

Then what? How was she going to work out of
this scene? She'd walked the fields, scrubbed both
bathrooms, cleaned and mopped the kitchen. All
this had resulted in two paragraphs in the last two
days. She thought maybe warming up her old
typewriter would inspire her, but laptop or
Corona, the keyboard seemed to stop after five
lines.

Why hadn't Riley called? She'd tried his office
and his apartment. She'd left a message at her
place. He was supposed to call her. Marla slid out
of the old wooden schoolteacher chair and
flopped down on her childhood bed. The white
chenille cover gave her fingertips something to
do. She stared at the wall and rubbed the bed-

cover bumps mindlessly. The ceiling fan whirred above her.

"Marla, are you up there writing?" Her dad's voice carried up the stairs.

"I'm up here." Sure as hell not writing.

"Take a break and eat lunch. I made sandwiches."

"Uuhhhhhhhh," she moaned.

"I made peanut butter cookies."

Her favorite. "Okay, okay." So that's what smelled so good. She rolled off the bed and trudged down the stairs.

"You've been busy this morning."

"Yep. What's that? Baloney? Yum." Marla peeled a round thick slice out of the package, rolled it in a tube, and ate it.

Her dad just watched. "Lemonade?"

"Sure." She picked up the pitcher and poured a large jelly glass full of plain, cool lemonade. "Anybody call, Dad?"

"Nope."

"I think I'll wash the windows today."

"I s'pose I should wait until you repaint the chicken coop and wallpaper the parlor, but how about you call him instead? This is the twenty-first century, after all." Her dad took that casual stance with his thumbs hooked in his belt loops and his baseball cap tipped back.

She copied him, grabbing the loops on her jeans

and leaning back against the counter. "Since when do you suggest your daughter go chasing after some man?"

"Since she turned twenty-eight and hasn't bothered to get married. I don't believe a phone call constitutes chasing after him. Most of our problems in this family came from the lack of communication. Since I finally rid myself of one roadblock to happiness, I don't intend to set any more in the way. I suggest you do the same." He didn't change his posture, just stared at her.

"For pity's sake, Dad . . ." Marla started to protest, but all of that was true. Basically it was silly to sit around and wonder what was up back in Manhattan. She might as well call and see what progress Tom had made. She gulped down her lemonade, grabbed the sandwich her dad had made for her, and headed for the kitchen wall phone. "Fine. But I already tried yesterday, if you must know. I'll just try again. Did you put mustard on this?"

"Yep." Her dad quietly left the room.

She took her black leather planner out of her bag, which stayed in the kitchen these days. First, she tried Tom's office. Amazingly enough, he had no answering machine. Then she tried his apartment. Nothing.

He was probably still sleeping, knowing Riley.

Now that she wasn't there to get him up in the morning, he'd gone back to his old ways. Undoubtedly. Well, there. She'd tried. Now she'd go ahead and do those windows after lunch. She'd also set up her mom's old sewing machine upstairs in the spare room. Maybe she'd mosey into Centerville and get a pattern and some fabric. Maybe make some new curtains for her room.

Marla stuffed the rest of her baloney sandwich in her mouth and chewed.

As promised, Rita and B.B. were doing lunch in the private dining room of Vito's. B.B. was stuffing antipasto in his face and washing it down with red wine. Rita looked around nervously. Tom caught her eye. She leaned over to B.B. and excused herself, then rose, grabbed her purse, and stepped out the opening of the room.

Tom signaled to Rama, who slipped the headwaiter a fifty. Anton was like Tom's shadow, only instead of a plain dark suit, he'd dressed in a pale gray pinstriped double-breasted suit with a black shirt and white tie. Oh, and the gray felt fedora. He was taking this gangster thing as far as he could. Tom would have laughed if he wasn't hellbent on B.B.

As the three of them stepped into the dining room, B.B. looked up. First surprise, then some-

thing like terror washed over his face, closely followed by some kind of attitude. Rama slid the
pocket doors of the room closed behind them.

"What's this? My birthday's already over. You
missed it by a week. Geez, guys." B.B. remained
seated.

"Unless you want to celebrate your next twenty
in jail, you better tell us everything we want to
know. Confession time, B.B. Or should I call you
Bertie?"

"I ain't done nuthin'. You guys are screwy." B.B.
started to rise from his chair. Anton and Rama,
flanking him on both sides, each pushed a shoulder, and B.B. sat back down in his seat with a
thud.

Tom leaned into B.B.'s face, his hands braced on
the table. "You hurt someone I care about. I'm
gonna keep real calm, here, while you tell me all
about it."

"I never touched her."

"No, but your hired idiots did. You rigged her
shoe so she'd fall down. You hired someone to trip
her on the runway. You hired someone to coat that
angel wing costume with chemicals. And you
hired someone to cut that coconut down, which,
by the way, hit me instead, so I owe you one." Tom
bent in farther with every accusation he made. He
was inches away from B.B's face now.

B.B. pulled at his tie nervously. "You're nuts. I

did no such thing. I don't know what yer talkin' about."

"Don't you? You're up to your eyeballs in gambling debts, and you set her up. You figured a few accidents would get her to take out the policy, then sent in your guys to take out her face, so your mom's agency would collect the three million, which you would then steal."

Tom continued. "Did I miss anything? Oh, yeah. Since you failed, the mob decided to take over." Tom grabbed B.B.'s collar and kept talking. "The other night some mugger tried to kill her."

Just then Rita slid through the doors and shut them back up. "Is that all true, B.B.?" she asked, standing at the end of the table staring at him.

"There's only one part true. I got debts. Mr. S. is gonna have me killed if I don't come up with a hundred thousand bucks. I don't know nuthin' about messing Marla up."

Tom tightened his grip on B.B.'s collar. "Mess her up? How about I mess you up, and we'll see where that gets us?"

"Tom! You promised not to hurt him." Tom let go of B.B., but stood right next to him. Rita took a step his direction. "B.B. If you don't tell Tom the truth, I'll cut you off without a dime for a phone call. I should have been a tougher mom, but I was always working. I guess I let you get away with murder because I felt guilty about not being there.

Well, I've *been there* for the last ten years with you, and I'm not going to let you get away with it this time."

"Shut up, Mom. You don't know what you're talking about."

Anton took one step over and slapped B.B. flat on the face. It was a nice, crisp slap, and left a red handprint. B.B. was so shocked he didn't move except to put his hand up to his cheek.

Anton was a fine shade of red that went well with his suit. "Don't you talk to your mother like that, you insensitive, clueless *lout*."

Rama pointed at B.B.'s nose. "You have been dishing out some very bad karma, Mr. B.B., and you will reap what you have sown, now. Your only hope is to throw yourself on the merciful court."

"And you're lookin' at your judge and jury, B.B.," Tom said.

B.B. looked down in silence. Rama poked him in the side.

"The truth will be setting you free, Alberto."

"The truth. Everyone's always worried about poor Marla. I went for her in a big way, and she just tossed me aside like dirty socks for that worm Derek Stiles. I knew he'd hurt her. I wasn't good enough for her. She should have listened to me. She should have loved me instead." B.B.'s voice broke a little. "But I'd never hurt her, ever. You've got the wrong guy."

Rita heaved a huge sigh of relief.

Tom felt like a bomb exploded in his head. He took two steps backward and sat down hard in a chair. "What about Jocko saying they were going to take care of that dame you were having so much trouble with?"

"That was my ex-wife, Kay. She pawned a piece of jewelry that belonged to me. She wouldn't give me the ticket. I was gonna sell it. Jocko and I went to see her that night to get it back. It was valuable!"

"Ex-wife," Tom repeated.

"That witch you married for six months is still in the picture? You've got more problems than gambling if you have to go to her for jewelry to sell," Rita said.

"What about your gambling debts?"

"That part is true. I've been takin' advances off my salary. The boys wanted to check the books to see if I was lyin' about how much I took. I told 'em I could only do so much at a time."

Rita put her hands on her hips. "I've given this a great deal of thought in the last few days. Here's my offer, B.B. First, I'll pay off your debt. Something you don't know is that you have a trust fund. I just haven't been willing to tell you about it because deep down I knew you'd blow it. Looks like we'll be putting half of it toward your health. That is, keeping your companions from putting cement overshoes on you and dropping you in a river. I still love you too much to see that happen."

She wiped at a stray tear, but went on. "Second, you are going to attend Gamblers Anonymous. I'll be taking you there myself. If you miss one meeting, or fall off the straight and narrow, I'll *will* cut you off without as much as a dime, just like I said."

"You would not." B.B. sat up like he was scared. "Besides, it takes more than that to make a phone call."

"From now on I hold the keys to every cent you need. How dare you compromise my agency by pulling funds out without my permission? An advance? Please. If you ever want to see your trust fund, you will do as you're told."

Tom got up and went over to Rita. He put his arm around her. "You're doing the right thing, Rita. Maybe your son has a good side that needs to be kicked out into the open. After all, he has a little of you in him too."

Rita hugged Tom. "Thanks. I needed that." She turned back to B.B. "This is the last mess I'll ever clean up for you, B.B. You contact your gambling friends and tell them you're ready to pay up."

The sliding doors parted as if by magic. A small old man in an outfit that just about matched Anton's stepped into the room. He carried a cane with a golden lion's head on top. B.B. leaped out of his chair. The two "escorts" that opened the doors closed them just as quietly.

"M-m-m-ister Scamandi." B.B. nodded his head politely.

Mr. Scamandi tipped his hat to Rita. "Siddown, Alberto." The old man gripped the lion's head and leaned on the cane for support. "No one walks around this town owin' me as much as you do for long."

Rama, Anton, and B.B. let out a mutual gasp that surprised even Tom. Rita grabbed the back of B.B.'s chair.

"Look, Mr. S.," Tom spoke up, "we've been working out a deal, here."

"I know. The whole room is bugged. I decided to take care of you myself, Alberto. And by the way, Mrs. Ray, we don't do no cement overshoes no more. Dead guys in the river is bad fer the environment, ya know. We have better ways now." Mr. S. wobbled a little when he pointed at B.B.

Rita looked like she was going to faint. Tom stepped over to her side.

"If you heard the deal, then why talk about killing him? Mrs. Ray is willing to pay B.B.'s debt."

"I came in here 'cause I can't stand a man who would jerk his own mother around. Don't get me wrong, I'm still takin' the money. You don't deserve that trust fund, Alberto. But we ain't ever gonna let you into our tables again. You're on the blacklist. Better do what your mama said, Alberto, or we'll be payin' you a little visit." Scamandi twisted up as he spoke and his spine cracked. "I'm gettin' too old for this."

Tom walked over to the old man and pulled out a chair for him. "What about the girl, Scamandi? Marla Meyers. Is B.B. telling the truth?"

Scamandi lowered himself into the chair. "Mr. Riley, you've been real amusing to watch. We keep tabs on B.B., here, and you've been gettin' in the way a lot. I hate ta tell ya, but yer girlfriend is just clumsy. If we wanted to help B.B. cash in on her policy, it wouldn'ta been much work for us, she's always trippin' on somethin'.

"We thought about it, don't get me wrong. Three million could get B.B., here, in pretty deep with us, and that's good for business. But hey, she's a dish. I kinda like her myself." Scamandi laughed.

Tom looked Anton and Rama, his new friends, in the eye. He should just choke this guy, Scamandi, to death and save the state some trouble. "You got insurance, Mr. S.?"

"Shaddup, Mr. Riley. We know where you live. By the way, you have cockroaches. Get that bastard landlord of yours to put in for pest control."

Tom felt a little ill. Maybe he should just stop while he was ahead. Hearing the words that

Marla was safe was enough for him anyway. A strange lightness came over him. Like, a brickload came off his chest. Could he really have been so wrong about everything? The shoe, the cake, the wings, the coconut? And what about the guy in the elevator? Just a strange coincidence?

Tom was filled with relief, confusion, unsettledness—it was going to take him a long time to think it all out.

"Now, Mrs. Ray, it's Friday, and you ain't had lunch. The chef made a good sole today. We'll go over your boy's life and have some lunch on the house. If that's okay with you. Maybe I'll cut off a little of his . . . debt if I like your ideas."

"I'm willing to have lunch and talk it over," Rita agreed.

"Anyone else?" Mr. S. gestured to Tom and the others.

"Um, I think we'll be going and let you all discuss things," Anton squeaked. He scooted around to the door like lightning, followed by Rama and his smooth, calm strides.

Tom opened the doors, only to find a burly waiter on the other side. He stepped out of the way. "Rita, you'll be all right?" Tom asked.

Rita nodded. "I'll call you later."

Tom followed his two friends out the door. The classic Italian restaurant was packed, and the scent of marinara sauce and Italian sausage made his stomach growl. But no way in hell was he dining with Scamandi and his fishes.

"Oh my God, we did it," Anton said. "We even got out alive. Lunch is on me, boys, I know a great place two blocks over." They all burst out the front door of Vito's.

"Just watch where you're taking us, Anton, I don't want any more action today. Right?" Tom said.

"Oh, you goose." Anton smacked him on the shoulder hard enough to unbalance Tom.

"Hey, not bad!" Tom laughed. "But seriously, now. I've got to think this through. It's hard to believe I've been so off base about everything. At least it looks like she's not in danger."

"Thomas Riley, I could weep with joy. We have been successful in finding no danger for your woman's life." Rama's eyes teared up and he wiped them on his sleeve.

"That's it, boys. We're going to a rib joint I know and down some brewskies. I've had enough sensitivity for today." Tom strode ahead of them.

"Thomas, I do not eat cattle, you know, but I will join you for some fish. This American food is so barbaric. If each of you would sacrifice some of your cattle consumption, you would be doing the planet a great favor." Rama lengthened his stride and moved ahead. He had the longest legs Tom had seen on a guy.

"All right, I'll have chicken. But what if my Aunt Tillie came back as a chicken?" Tom talked as he kept the pace up.

"We will have a long philosophical discussion about this thing while we drink back some *brewskies*," Rama answered.

"My uncle thinks he's a chicken already," Anton said as he caught up.

"You two are completely nuts." Tom led on. "But I need you both to lay all this out on the table. That, and I'm starved."

They slid into a dark booth and ordered quickly. The help was fast in this place. A pitcher of beer and three glasses were on the table in one minute. Tom poured his and sat back. Anton served himself and Rama.

"So. We've got Marla and her broken shoe tripping on my stairs. We've got the flying bride and cake thing. We've got wings that gave her an allergy attack, a falling coconut that got me instead, and a guy in an elevator."

"Don't forget her hurting her own hand," Anton added. "I hate to say it, Thomas, but it looks like we've all been wrong. Except for the guy in the elevator. That was not her doing, and it was bad. But random bad things do happen, particularly in the big city."

"That's true." Tom paused and thought about Marla. How she'd kept trying to tell him that the motive just wasn't there. "She's going to kill me for this. And it will be justifiable homicide," Tom said aloud.

Both his friends took a simultaneous sip of their beer, stared intently at him, and nodded their heads in agreement.

"But you were saving her from the bad elevator man," Rama suggested.

"She saved herself. I just turned it into episode five and made her leave town over it."

It was Anton's turn at philosophy in the round. "Tom, getting mugged is a terrible thing. Marla needed a break. Sending her away was a good thing. Besides, we were operating under the conspiracy theory at that point." He gave Tom's arm a pat. "Don't be so hard on yourself, buddy. Besides, she didn't object to leaving. So she must have felt the need to get out of the city."

"She ran away from me." Tom was getting more depressed by the minute. His relief at finding out B.B. wasn't after her was lost in a sea of fog. He couldn't seem to shake the feeling she was still in danger. Maybe it had become a habit.

"Thomas, you have done enough beer crying now. You must know you are creating your own reality here, and this indulgence of the self-pitying characteristics is not going to manifest the results you desire."

"Totally right, Rama," Anton added. "Just snap

out of it, Tom. I'd slap you myself, but you'd hit me back hard."

"You got that right," Tom said sullenly.

"Look, your head is getting in the way of everything. I've known Marla forever, and I've never seen her so confused about a man in my life."

"And that's good?"

"Actually, confusion is a very high state," Rama explained. "It is the point at which the old ways come into conflict with the new desires and must be set straight in order for life to progress to the next level."

"Good Lord, my man, you're on a plane above the average bear, aren't you? Well said!" Anton clapped.

"Anyone care to translate?" Tom asked from his ever-so-unenlightened confused state.

"Oh, wake up. She wants you. She just doesn't know what to do with that information." Anton started his preaching gestures.

"If you are wondering what steps to be taking at the present, Thomas, I would say to release all hold on your former life. Create a vacuum to allow the new life to flow into. Do you understand?"

"Vacuum?" Not a bad idea. Tom lifted his gaze from the rim of his beer and looked at his two oddball companions. "Okay, boys, let's get this lunch finished. We're going to vacuum."

"I am not sure Mr. Riley has fully grasped the meaning of our concept," Rama said to Anton.

"One never knows. But it might have the same effect, you see?" Anton said back.

"You two had the cod, right?" Tom ignored their chatter and focused on his reincarnated barbequed chicken.

Chapter Fifteen

SPRING CLEANING

Three full rolls of quarters, and every piece of clothing Tom owned was washed and dried, along with his sheets and bedspread. Gee, who knew they were actually green?

After he'd washed it all, Tom weeded through every single pair of bell-bottoms and rust-colored polyester leisure suits from 1969 his dad left him.

He then deposited everything but the absolutely basic clothes in the Goodwill drop that some brilliant person had placed in the Laundromat.

Rama, who was fast becoming his personal taxi, volunteered to help. It was kind of fun teaching Rama blackjack as they waited through the multiple loads of washing and drying. The last few hands Rama beat him fair and square, collecting the leftover quarters from Tom's reserve roll. Good thing everything got dry in one pass.

It was a light trip back to his apartment, and Rama gave him many blessings for releasing the past by setting old things free to find new homes with others. He even let Rama come up to his place with an armful of folded clothes.

"Thomas, your place is sparkle plenty."

"I vacuumed."

Rama laid clothes on the dresser, which had recently been unearthed in the room. "Are you going to call your beautiful woman and tell her the good news about our problems being over?"

"I am going to call her, but she's not really my woman, Rama." Tom set down his own stack and looked around. Even clean, it was a bleak studio he took to keep his expenses low and his child support high. Picturing Marla here was a joke.

"I know what you are thinking, Thomas. Do not forget there is more to offer Miss Meyers than outward appearances. You have a genuine spiritual love for this woman."

"Yeah, and debts, and a ten-year-old son. . . . Well, actually, he's an asset. Rama, I'm just going to have to face facts, here. Miss Meyers can have any man she wants, and I don't think I'm even in the running. It's best if I get back to my life and forget about her." The more Tom thought about it, the worse it felt.

He'd call Doris. That would cheer him up. Good joke. But hanging with Max tonight would. He usually spent the night on the couch at her place Fridays so he could make breakfast for Max and just hang out as much as possible. Doris was happy to have her evenings free. He just needed to get back on track.

"Rama, it's getting late. Can you give me a lift over to my son's place? It's a ways out of town— Queens, you know? About thirty minutes."

"Yes, Thomas. I know the way. We should both be getting to our families before dinner. Don't forget about what I said."

"I'm gonna take a little thinking break. I'll be sure and get hold of Miss Meyers and tell her the coast is clear." Tom broke off the conversation and stuffed a few things in a bag to take with him.

"The coast is clear. It is just like the private eye movies, and we have solved the case. Except there was no case. I am extremely pleased with us," Rama rambled as they left the apartment.

"So am I, pal. Thanks for everything," Tom said.

Max made a flying leap into Tom's arms. He had on his "X-Men-Wolverine" costume from Halloween. Man, that boy was getting big.

"Yippee, Dad! Where's Marla?"

"Hey, buddy! She's visiting her dad's farm in Indiana."

"Wow, cool, can we go?"

"Nope, we have a date with a pizza, and I believe it's time to renew our ongoing Scrabble-thon. Don't you?"

"Mom wants to talk to you."

Tom set Max down and shut the front door behind him. What now?

"Okay, my man, you go in your room and find our game while I talk to Mom in the kitchen. I'll give you the high sign when the coast is clear," Tom said.

Doris came around the corner of the kitchen all dolled up. She had on a red dress and shoes. "Tom, I tried calling, but you haven't been in the office. You know, I should be able to reach you," she launched in.

"I guess leaving a message with my landlady isn't a very good option. You're right. I'll get an answering machine or something. I'm sorry. Was anything wrong?"

"No, I . . . well, there's something I need to discuss with you. Can we sit?" Doris gestured to the table and pulled out a chair for herself.

Tom sat across from her. "Things okay at school? I didn't miss any program or anything, did I?"

"No, no. It's about me. And Howard. You know he works for Holiday Cruise Lines?"

"No, I didn't know that." He listened very carefully. His stomach was starting to twist up.

"Well, it's like this. Howard's been promoted to the line's executive staff. He's going to be on board the Emerald Line most of the time. He offered me a job running the ship's spa. I'd oversee the whole thing: nails, hair, and treatments.

"It's a great job and pays about three times my current salary. It's a real opportunity." Her voice cracked. Laying her head on the table, she broke into sobs. "Also . . . he wants to . . . marry me," she hiccupped out between crying.

Tom put his hand on her arm. "That's great, Doris. I'm fine with this. We both knew one of us would eventually remarry. I'm glad you found someone."

"Tom . . ." Doris raised her head. "I can't take Max on the cruise ship with me. You know I love him, but I feel I could make our lives better if I go for this chance."

"Are you asking me to take him?"

"You're just as good a parent as I am. He adores you. I just think he'd be better off with you while I pursue my career. I'll be gone two to three weeks a month. I know this is a huge deal. I know it means all kinds of changes."

Tom ran his fingers through his hair while the shock waved through him. "Doris, don't even think twice about it. I'll be happy to take Max full-time. We can work out anything you like."

"I was thinking you could take this place. Your studio in the city is too small, and his school is here. It would be less disruptive." Doris grabbed a paper napkin out of a ceramic lady and wiped her eyes.

"That's fine. Your mortgage is actually lower than mine. When is this all happening?"

"Max is ten years old now. It'll be great for him to be with you more." Doris waved the napkin around and started crying again.

Tom took her hand. "I know this is hard on you, but you're right. This is a great opportunity for you. You could put money away for Max's educa-tion, really get your life together. Also have a chance to spend some time with that new hus-band of yours. Max seems to like him." Could Doris really mean it? Tom felt his heart pound.

"Yes, Max likes Howard. He's a swell guy. I'm very happy. The truth is, though, we both know Max loves you best." Doris looked him straight in the eye. "It's okay. You two just have a special re-lationship. I'm okay with that. It makes it a little easier."

"Have you told him yet?"

"We've gone over some of it: my job offer, Howard. I wanted to be sure about your feelings before I went on from there." Doris stood up. "Let's you and I talk to him together now. I have about an hour. I'm gonna spend tonight at Howard's place."

"That's fine." Tom phoned in the pizza order and went to get Max. He felt a kind of happy shock. Pictures of what their life would look like started forming. He looked around the little house. Doris had done a nice job in a kind of Sears meets rococo way. Maybe she'd let him take down a few gold cherubs. Most importantly, Max felt comfortable here, and his school was close. So much to think about. Maybe that whole vacuum thing worked. Tom went on into Max's little room.

The phone was ringing. She could hear it from her perch in the barn loft. There was no way she'd make it in time. Dad was even farther out; he'd walked to the mailbox. Marla felt like she had in high school. Would he call? Would he ask her to the dance? Did she want to go to the dance with Tom Riley? He was one amazing dancer.

That was the real question. Marla flopped back down on the straw-stuffed mattress her dad had made for her years ago. Her secret place. She'd written stories up here since she was a little girl. The high barn doors were open, so the sky looked huge. A few stars popped out in the streaked colors of light between sunset and darkness.

She and Dad had looked at the farm account

books this morning. It startled her to realize she had paid the mortgage off sometime last year. Even the equipment loans were paid off. The farm was supporting itself without any debts in the shadows. She was pleased and surprised. Shocked, even. There had been a few very bad years with ruined crops. But things were going well now.

She was also lost. A fog of confusion muddled her up inside. She closed her eyes and tried to picture her life. What now? And Riley. Two weeks, for heaven's sake. She'd known him two weeks. What did they have in common? Chili dogs? Jazz? Hot and sour soup? Mike Mason?

It confused her why she couldn't stop thinking about him. A particular memory kept haunting her. Even that was foggy. A kiss in her closet. The first real kiss he'd given her. Then there was Chinese food. Somehow she had those two things all mixed together. Every time she thought of Chinese food, she got . . . hot. Every time she thought of his arms around her, his lips moving up her neck, and his amazing kisses, she got hungry.

Oh, for pity's sake. Marla got up and dusted the back of her jeans off. She'd just call him and find out about B.B. and the *danger*. That would at least give her some information. She wasn't normally an indecisive woman.

Climbing down the loft ladder, Marla spotted the mama cat she'd been trying to find.

"Aha! Taffy, you can't keep hiding those kittens. They're too big to drag around much longer." She kept her voice soft and approached the cat and her wiggling kittens slowly. Taffy purred and rolled on her back. Marla scratched her behind the ears.

One adventurous, extremely fuzzy orange and white kitten toddled over to her. Marla scooped it up and soothed it until it relaxed in her hand. A little girl. She stared into its cute, furry face.

"You long-haired beauty, I think I'll keep you. Stay with your mom another week, then we'll start feeding you squished cat food and evaporated milk. Okay?"

The kitten meowed and started purring loudly. Marla set it back down with Taffy and headed for the house. She'd call tonight, then tomorrow get some writing done early in the morning like she used to.

Her dad got to the back door at the same time she did. He wiped his hands on his pocket bandanna and stared at her head. "You've got straw in your hair."

She felt for it and pulled out a few stray sticks.

Dad pulled out another one. "It's Friday night. Want to go to the picture show?" he said.

She put her arm around his waist and walked in with him. "Sure. Will they let me in with straw in my hair?"

"Yep, but I'd clean up a bit if I were you. I heard Raef Nielsen was in town. He got a divorce from Heather, you know."

"Well, aren't you just the town gossip. Am I now only fit for Heather's cast-offs?"

"Seems to me he mooned after you before he married her."

"That was ten years ago." A strange feeling crept into Marla's chest. She was twenty-eight now. It came as a small shock.

"Oh, you don't think he'd be interested in a beautiful, intelligent girl like yourself?"

Well, at least she could look good.

"I'll wash my face." Marla headed toward the little downstairs bathroom. "What's playing at the Centerville Cinema these days?" she called back.

"*Music Man*. It's Classic Musical Movie Revival Month." Her dad came over and leaned on the doorframe. "You loved that movie when you were little."

"Great. Spinster librarian falls for traveling con man."

"To music," he added with a wry smile. "Let's go. Show starts at eight."

This phone thing was getting irritating. He really needed to tell her the coast was clear. Tom put his feet up on Doris's ottoman. She'd made a pretty wise move selling their original house and buying this little cottage. It was in good shape.

Max was a trouper. He'd finally gotten settled down to sleep after all the discussions, all the pizza, two games of Scrabble, and a hundred questions.

Tom had tried one more call to Indiana, but no answer.

Maybe he'd write her. Rita or Anton would have the Indiana address. Wait, she had a life policy with Granite! He jumped up and went over to the desk. Doris had a computer; they'd bought it together for Max last fall.

It took him a good half hour to remember how to get on-line and get to Granite's agent site. Then he had to remember his password: *Ramsey Lewis*.

There it was. 290 Palmer Road, Centerville, Indiana. Curious, Tom scrolled through Marla's life insurance policy. It was a million-dollar policy with her dad as the beneficiary. The original application was included, and from the date it looked like she took it out about eight years ago.

Her health screen was excellent. Well, that was obvious, she had a fabulous body and ate all those green things. Tom had a memory of running his hand down her side, over the curve of her hip, while they were on the beach together.

It listed her occupation as writer. Must have been her premodeling days. So many kids came to the big city on that artistic quest for fame.

Tom reached in the desk drawer and shuffled for a piece of stationery that didn't have flowers all over it. Failing at that, he grabbed a piece of printer paper.

Dear Marla,

The danger is over. Actually it never existed. I was wrong. You can return to Manhattan at any time.

He tore that one up. What a weird thing it was for him to write a letter to someone he cared about. Nothing came through in the words. Not to mention she was on the first vacation she'd been on in years. Maybe he should just try calling again tomorrow. He'd tell her about Max and encourage her to stay there anyway.

Tom paced. It was time for some big changes. No more sloppy ways, no more late nights. He thought of that movie *Mr. Mom.* He sure didn't want to be the dad who ironed cheese sandwiches for his kid. He'd set up some new routines for himself.

Where Marla Meyers fit in with all of this was difficult to say. She was the most attractive, intelligent woman he'd met in years. Hell, maybe in his whole life. Somehow he just couldn't picture Marla settling down with him and Max in this little bungalow. Would she even want to date him when she returned to Manhattan? It all sounded

like a tabloid headline: SUPERMODEL SLUMMING
WITH ORDINARY INSURANCE AGENT.

But in many ways, Tom didn't feel ordinary
anymore. His world had been turned crazy upside down in the last weeks. It felt more real, more
alive than before.

Tomorrow he'd take Max and go see his family.
Grandma Riley would be glad to see them.

Raef was as handsome as ever, even with a
touch of graying hair. Marla spotted him across
the room and he gave her the big Raef smile she
remembered so well. He came straight over to her
as she stood in the concession line.

"Marla, you look exactly the same. Do you remember me?"

"Yes, Raef, it's only been ten years."

"Are you coming to the reunion in June?"

"Oh, wow, I completely forgot. I'm not kidding.
My dad told me they sent a card, but I've been so
busy, I didn't reply. Ten years. Where did it go,
Raef?" Marla moved to the saltshaker and liber-
ally sprinkled her buttered popcorn.

"Hey, I don't know about you, but I spent mine
married until last month. You remember Heather
and I got married right out of high school?"

"I remember."

"It's not easy going to my reunion newly divorced." Raef stuck his hands in his pockets and

looked down. His boyish good looks were still there, she noticed. He stole a glance at her, apparently to see what her reaction was.

She was having one too, but it had more to do with her own situation: not as hard as going to your ten-year high school reunion *never* married.

"What've you been up to? Still writing? I remember you won all those short story contests back in high school. I heard you moved to New York."

"Yes, I live in Manhattan." So much for the famous cover model thing. "Well, Raef, my dad's waiting. It was nice to see you."

"Can I give you a call? I'm here in town for the rest of the month on family business."

There was no escape. Her country hospitality went on autopilot. Actually, she'd been hoping to feel a spark of interest for Raef, football captain pretty boy of the school. At the moment she was more interested in her luscious bucket of popcorn. "Sure. Nice seeing you." She strung out some more platitudes and headed for her seat.

"Raef say hello?" her dad asked.

"Shhhhh, the movie's starting." She made a face at him and scrunched down in her seat, shoving popcorn in her mouth. Geez Louise.

The next morning after breakfast, Marla tried Tom's office, then his apartment. Where the hell was Tom Riley keeping himself? Marla sat back and started thinking. Her mind went places like dark alleys and mobster's trunks. What if his plan to straighten out this mess with B.B. went bad on him? Her skin started tingling and a huge fear rose up inside her. Losing Tom Riley actually mattered to her.

On a panicked impulse, she picked up the phone, dialed information, and asked for Doris Riley. The operator connected her through. Surely Doris would know if anything had happened to Tom.

"Hello?"

"Max, is that you?" Marla was taken aback by Max answering. She sure didn't want to alarm him.

"Yeah, it's me. Hi, Marla!"

"Is your mom home?"

"Nope."

Now what? Marla paused.

"My dad's here; he's in the garage. He's gonna live here now!"

Marla went dead in the water trying to get her bearings. Tom was living there? Oh my God, he's gone back to Doris!

"Shall I get him for ya?" Max asked.

"No, I'll get back with him. Have fun with your dad, okay?"

"Okay. 'Bye."

Well, he was alive, all right. Alive and well and

living with Doris. From everything she and Tom had talked about in the last few weeks, she didn't see this one coming. Not that he'd said anything bad about Doris. It just hadn't seemed like he was mourning over the divorce. And Doris had talked about a new beau.

Maybe it was for Max's sake. Marla stumbled over to the couch and curled up on one end with her old red and white quilt. She felt suddenly cold. Her chest hurt. Sadness, like an ocean wave, engulfed her.

Hours later she heard her dad come in from his work and wash up for lunch. She felt him sit down at the other end of the sofa.

"Not feeling good?" he asked.

"Miserable." Marla sniffed and picked up her mound of tear-drenched tissues.

"Isn't it about time you tell me what's up?"

"It's a guy. I think he went back to his wife. I shouldn't be upset, really, we didn't spend much time together."

Her dad made a long face. "He's married?"

"No . . . no. Divorced. He has a son. Really, I should be happy for him. He was unhappy being separated from his son." Marla gathered herself, threw a tissue in the trash basket, and straightened her flannel shirt.

"Well, hell. I have a book to write. I might as well get to it."

"Are you in love with him?"

Marla folded the quilt into thirds. "It's only been a few weeks. I'm not sure how to answer that, but I . . . feel—something. That's a new one for me."

"I'll tell you a little secret. I only knew your mom for a week before I decided to marry her. Sometimes you just know. She kissed me on the porch of her parents' house and that was it. It curled the hairs of my mustache."

"You had a mustache? Dad. How weird." She sat back down. "But things were so much simpler back then. And basically you're telling me you had the hots for Mom."

"I suppose, but that's how everything gets started in the romance department. That's still pretty simple." He slapped his knees and rose off the couch. "It's a risky business, but you gotta take a chance sometimes."

"Hmph," Marla replied. She knew it was true, though. If she lost Tom, she'd regret it. Maybe forever.

"Let's make tomato soup and I'll grill a couple of cheese sandwiches. Then you can write on full fuel."

"Comfort food. Well, I guess that works. I could always just eat myself out of the blues."

"Sounds like a Mike Mason title to me. *The Mallomar Murders.*"

"*Sundaes Kind of Mystery,*" she countered.

"*Dead Man's Root Beer Float?*"

"Eeuuww. Let's not."

The phone rang and Marla bolted across the house into the kitchen to grab it. "Hello?" She tried to catch her breath and act casual.

"That's you, breathlessly beautiful Marla."

It was Raef. "Oh, Raef. Did you get that reunion information for me?"

"Sure, gorgeous, but I called to take you out to dinner tonight. We can look at it over a glass of wine. How about it?"

"Tonight?" Marla paused.

"They have a special date-night dinner at Ché Marie tonight," Raef added.

Dinner. Life pretty much sucked right now anyway; she might as well sit in a nice restaurant and have a steak with an old school chum rather than cry her eyes out at home. She wasn't one for wallowing in self-pity anyhow. "All right, Raef. I'll meet you at Ché Marie about seven. How's that?"

"Super. It's the best place in town these days."

"I'll see you there." She hung up the phone.

"A date?" Her dad strolled in.

"As if you didn't hear every word. I'm going to have dinner with Raef tonight. He's got some information about our ten-year reunion. I forgot all about it. Besides, there's no use me sitting around crying in my tomato soup all day."

"That's true. No use crying in your soup."

Her dad was the master of saying volumes with just a few words.

Chapter Sixteen

THE LADY
IN RED

After lunch Marla told her dad she was going to try and get some work done and headed for her laptop upstairs. She'd given up on the old Smith Corona typewriter for now. She was on a roll with her story and her thoughts came faster than the keys could manage.

Plus it was pretty slow moving paragraphs around with scissors and tape.

There was something very therapeutic about entering into her made-up Mike Mason world, where all the mysteries got solved right down to the last flower. She always used one signature flower in each story, somehow woven into the plot. You'd think that one thing would give her readers the tip-off that M. B. Kerlin was a woman. She'd decided to use her mother's maiden name, Kerlin, way back when. As a tribute to her memory.

"Listen, O'Shay, we're going to have to join forces. I've got something you want, and you've got something I want. Surely you're anxious to get your story written?" I laid it out on the table for the guy.

"You've got me all wrong, Mason. I'm trying to help someone. Tell me what you've got." O'Shay lit a cigarette nervously. Not an endearing trait.

"Okay. See, Randall Crantz was having an affair with Delores DelMarco, his client. Kinda unethical, ain't it? Well, that wasn't the half of it." I waved the smoke away and coughed. Hated that stuff. "When Delores went on trial for the murder of her husband, Trevor Thompson, Randall took a powder. Now, you figure maybe he didn't want the fact he was sleeping with Delores to go public, but I think it was more than that. I think he murdered Trevor himself. Something went terribly wrong with the whole setup. He was supposed to get the girl in the end, but that never happened. She cracked up during the trial, and even though they acquitted her of the crime, after a year in the nuthouse, she killed herself."

"So what's the connection to Randall's death?"

O'Shay took another drag and played it calm. I kept my guard up. I just wasn't sure about this guy.

"I'm gettin' to that." I pulled my collar up. Sitting at an outside bistro in the winter was a bitch. "Here's the deal. Delores DelMarco had a kid in secret, before Trevor was killed. She never told anyone, and she gave it to her mother to raise. In a minute I'll tell you why I think she did that. After Delores's death, the grandmother died, and the kid ended up in foster homes."

"Where'd you get your information?"

"In the offices of Randall Crantz. He kept a file on the child. Kept tabs on her until she was eighteen and she vanished. See, that whole bit with the rose, that was from a movie Delores made in 1951. Shadows of the Night."

"I've seen it."

"Oh, you're a film buff, are you?" I watched his eyes shift away from me.

"Maybe." He flicked his cigarette down on the sidewalk and twisted it with his shoe.

"So here's the rap. I think Delores's kid came back for revenge. Her name is Rose, by the way, a very odd twist there. She's using the old film bit where the crazy woman scares the murderer off a balcony. The red rose with the black ribbon. Same one. She probably looks so much like the mother that old Randall was scared shitless and backed *right up into that elevator shaft. She probably stalked him for years waiting for the right moment."*

O'Shay went ghost-pale on me. Something was hitting home. I went on. "There's just one more thing."

"What's that?"

"What Rose didn't know is that Randall Crantz was her own father. She was his child, not Trevor's. And that's why Delores gave the child away. So you see, without knowing it, Rose just killed her own father."

O'Shay got up so fast the metal café chair he was sitting on clattered to the street. I stood up. He ran crazy into the street, almost getting himself killed. Boy, I sure hit the nerve that time. I had a pretty good idea why, but it'd take me an hour in public records to confirm my suspicions.

I set O'Shay's chair upright and headed for City Hall. At least I could warm up in there.

"Marla Beth, It's six o'clock," her dad called up the stairs. She dragged herself out of Mike Mason's world and back into her own. Flawed as it was. Damn! just when he was about to find out O'Shay's secret.

She freshened herself up and put on a pair of clean white jeans and a white sweater with beading on the shoulders. It was actually one of her mom's. She hadn't packed too many clothes, and besides, vintage was cool.

Most of her suitcase space had been filled up with shoes. She pulled on a great pair of Gianni Milanesi beige half boots. She'd have to try and keep out of the mud on her way to the car.

Her hair was all tangled up in a scrunchy and needed major work to get tame. Maybe she'd cut it all off. To her that meant she would be through with modeling.

She had some big decisions to make. Sadness swept through her again, and she ended up crying while she yanked the knots out of her hair. Marla threw a cold washcloth over her face and reapplied her makeup. Time to go cheer up.

It was unusually warm for February, she told Raef, among a few dozen other weather-related comments. It really was, though. Ché Marie's had opened the café windows to cool the place off. The breeze felt good.

"So tell me about your love life, Marla. Let's cut the weather report." Raef smiled and handed her a roll. He had always gotten to the point quickly.

Marla laughed. "Pretty dismal at the moment. There was this guy, he was assigned by his company to watch me, but—"

"You had a bodyguard? Had you been getting threats?"

"No, no, he was from my insurance company. He came up with this great theory that someone was after me. I kept having all these accidents— you remember what a klutz I was in high school? Well, here's the list: I fell down his office stairs, fell in a cake at a fashion show, had some allergic reaction to a costume, then he gets hit by a coconut he thinks was meant for me. I mean, you can't help but figure someone must be behind all that."

Marla laughed, then she looked up at Raef. "But last week a guy mugged me in the elevator, and then I wasn't sure if maybe he was right. So I came home."

"You were mugged? Did he hurt you?" Raef's genuine concern felt good. Maybe talking about it with someone she had no emotional ties to would help.

"I think I hurt him. I took self-defense the first year I moved to New York. That was the first time I'd had to use it. It really shook me up." Marla took a bite of her scampi and the taste flooded her with memories of her time on the island with Tom. She took a moment and washed down the emotion with a sip of chardonnay. Not a very good wine.

"Marla, I'm so sorry. Did they get the guy?"

"Yes, that insurance guy and his friend rushed in at the last minute. Boy, that really fueled the theory that someone was after me, though. It has been extremely strange, and I can't yet say his plot theory isn't true. It's very complicated. I've been waiting to hear."

"Forgive me, but we started out with your love life. I take it the insurance hero was interested in you?" Raef pressed on. Obviously fishing for her availability.

"I don't know how to answer that. There was an attraction, but it seems he's gone back to his ex-wife. They have a son, and he is very devoted to . . ." Marla stopped talking and tried to head off the tears with a gulp of water. It went down the wrong way. She choked, covered her mouth with her white linen napkin, and gasped for air.

"Are you choking?" Raef started out of his chair. She put up her hand to stop him and knocked her water glass over straight into his lap. He jumped back, knocked over his chair, and started laughing. By then she'd hacked herself red-faced, gotten the water out of her lungs, and let some air in. She was even laughing underneath the napkin.

"Well, I think we've proven one part of the theory, anyhow." Raef mopped at his crotch and sat back down. "You do have that clumsy thing down pat. But with a body like yours, who cares, right?"

Marla stopped laughing. Always with Raef it was how pretty she was. He had no idea who she was or if she liked jazz or chili dogs or handmade ice-cream sandwiches coated in chocolate, washed down with a Coke. "I'm so sorry, Raef. Let's finish our dinner and call it a night. Shall we?"

"Sure, sugar." Raef didn't seem fazed at all.

She gazed out the open window to the familiar town. They were at street level and she could see the shop lights going off as the town was closed up for the night. Streetlights illuminated Centerville's Main Street. A flicker of color caught her eye and she saw the shadowy figure of a woman cross the street right beside the Ché Marie facade, behind Marla's table. Then the woman slipped behind one of the old maple trees lining the side streets. Lady in Red, just like her book. How funny.

Ivy Richardson pulled her thin red car coat up around her ears to keep the chill out. She walked fast. She hadn't seen her, just hadn't. Marla was too self-absorbed to look up from her latest conquest and notice an old woman outside in the cold.

Marla. Back to visit her daddy and tell him more lies. Ivy almost ran the last block to her car. She'd forgotten all about her errand when she'd seen Marla drive by an hour ago. She'd followed her. There she was, with some man, eating in the best place in town.

Here she was, with nothing. Living in the same old run-down farmhouse she'd grown up in, with the ghost of her own dead mother still haunting the place. If Marla thought she was mean, Marla should have met that woman. Oh yes, that woman would have none of Marla Meyers's sass. She would have just backhanded her across her pretty little mouth for telling lies.

Ivy put her hand up to her own mouth, remembering. She threw open the door of the old Ford station wagon and crawled inside. She started up the engine and threw it into drive. The heater didn't work, and the ride home was long. All the way to Richmond.

She slammed her hand on the steering wheel. She wanted her life back. Her warm house. No ghosts in that house. Well, just the one, Walt's first wife. Always hanging around Marla. Marla and her ghost mother had taken it all away from her.

She'd heard everything Marla had told that man. How she'd had all those accidents. How she wasn't sure if someone hadn't planned them all. How she got mugged.

Ivy's mind turned like a Ferris wheel at the county fair. She turned it this way, and that way. That girl was gonna tell Walt more lies and she'd never get him back.

If somebody was after Marla and then some-

Chapter Seventeen

INDIANA TWO-STEP

Tom toweled himself off, dressed quickly, and ran through the day in his head. Max was officially on spring break from school now, which at least gave Tom some time to pull his act together. His mom and sisters had poured on the advice and the seafood paella, their Saturday night standard with the leftover fish from Friday thrown in. The whole family seemed excited about Tom and Max.

First thing, though, he was going to track down Marla, if he had to call the Centerville sheriff to do it. Then he'd take his brother-in-law over to his old place, pack up his meager belongings, and close up the roach-Ritz apartment for good. Geez, he'd cleaned it for nothing.

No, that wasn't true. It was as much as ready to rent. His landlord would be thrilled. Plus he'd created that vacuum Rama and Anton had talked about.

He loved Manhattan, but he could live out of the city. He'd liked living in the 'burbs before. It made him feel like planting a geranium or something. This little house was going to be great.

Doris had called this morning bright and early to wake him up to remind him what Max liked for breakfast, as if he didn't know that already. He'd listened patiently, though. This was a rough transition for her.

Max bounded up out of bed like only a ten-year-old can do.

"Hey, buddy, let's stuff down some pancakes and get my junk moved over here."

"Yeah!" Max cheered. "I'll make some bacon."

"I don't know, man, all that hot grease and stuff. Better let me."

"Hey, Dad, get with the times." Max went in the kitchen and pulled a box out of the fridge. "Microwave bacon, dude."

"Like, wow. Okay, then, I'll whip up some pancake mix, you nuke the bacon, and we'll pour a couple of orange juices. I've gotta make a phone call while I'm mixing. Throw me a couple of eggs."

"Marla called yesterday."

"What?" Tom whacked his head coming up

from a lower cupboard with a mixing bowl. Yesterday? Leave it to a ten-year-old to forget to mention that. How did she get this number? Marla must be getting frantic, to track him down here at Doris's house. "What did she say?"

"She said she'd get back to you. I told her you were living here now!" Max tossed an egg at Tom, which he barely managed to catch. The next one cracked in his hand up against the first. He slid it into the bowl.

Tom was sure Max didn't go into too much explanation. This could be misinterpreted on her part. "Hang on, Max, I'm gonna make my call and finish this in a minute."

He wiped the egg off his hands and pulled a chair up to the kitchen phone. Fumbling for the scrap of paper he had tucked behind it, he finally managed to pull it out and dial the long-distance number.

"Meyers."

"Mr. Meyers? This is Tom Riley. Is Marla at home?"

"Tom Riley from New York? *This* is Walt Meyers, Marla's dad. Before I get Marla on the phone, you and I should have a talk. Are you the one with a ten-year-old son and who recently went back to his ex-wife?"

"That's not exactly the story. My son left out a few details when Marla talked to him, sir."

"That's good, because I think my daughter is in love with you. She's been mooning around for days."

Tom was speechless. Talk about direct. Marla's dad went ahead and filled Tom in on his theories. Tom finally managed to explain the arrangement he and Doris had made. Guess he and old Mr. Meyers where getting to know each other real quick.

"I'd suggest you get together with her as soon as possible. You're welcome to come down here. The boy too," Walt said in an encouraging tone.

"Thank you, sir. I don't know if you're right about Marla's feelings for me, but I'll think that over."

"I'll get her."

There was no way her dad had this pegged right. Marla must be tired, stressed, confused. Something. Tom tapped on the wall phone with his fingers to keep from leaping out of his skin.

"Tom?"

"Hi. I'm so glad we finally got connected." Tom felt awkward. "There's a lot I need to tell you."

"I'm glad too. I was worried about you. Did you manage to get things with B.B. straightened out?"

"Yes." He swallowed his pride and started in. "You were right, Marla. B.B. wasn't after you. Nobody was. All of the things that happened to you were just accidents. My friend at the lab even told me today that the stuff on the feathers was an insect repellent they sometimes use when they're storing costumes like that. The guy in the elevator, well, it's hard to believe, but it was just a coincidence."

"Honestly, Tom, I tried to tell you. But when I got mugged it did kind of look like it all fit together."

That was as much I-told-you-so as he was getting? No screams, no stabbing remarks? Tom was amazed. Although the voice he was getting from Marla wasn't the one Walt predicted. It might be better to hear her yell than be distant. Then he remembered what she must be thinking. "When are you planning on coming back to New York?" he asked.

"I assume you're saying it's completely safe?"

"Yes, you're in no danger. Listen, Marla, I have some personal stuff to tell you." This was really stupid, trying to feel his way through this on the phone. "You talked to Max?"

At the mention of his name, Max abandon his microwave bacon and hoisted himself up on the counter next to Tom. Two big ten-year-old eyes stared at his every twitch.

"Yes. He told me about you living there. That's great, Tom." Marla's voice sounded strained.

"Well, I think he forgot to mention that his mom

is getting married and has a new job on a cruise line." Tom thought about how to word this part. "Max is going to stay with me now. We decided I'd take her house." He heard Marla laugh a short little laugh. It almost sounded . . . happy.

"Oh brother, I sure jumped to some conclusions. I thought you and Doris got back together. I'm glad you're going to take Max. That's great."

Tom paused, all kinds of thoughts rumbling around in his brain. Or was it his heart? At any rate, none of them was making it to his mouth. He thought about Rama and Anton. He better start creating his new reality pretty fast, here, or he'd lose it forever.

"Miss Meyers, don't forget I'm still responsible for keeping you and that face of yours safe. I'm afraid I'm going to have to insist on seeing my job through. And don't forget, my company will fire me if anything should happen to you." Tom said all that in his best fake-serious business voice. Max snickered at him.

"I thought that was only when I'm on the job," Marla answered dryly. But there was a hint of something in her voice. A tiny, sparkling hint.

He went on. "Oh no, it's the full thirty days, no matter where you are."

"I'm having a fine time out here and I've no intention of coming back to New York anytime soon, so you'll just have to imagine me staying out of trouble."

"What if you fall in the pigpen or something?"

"We don't have a pigpen."

"What if the cow kicks you?"

"Riley, forget it. I'm not coming back. I'll keep in touch with you. I'll call you every three days."

"I guess that will have to do for now. At least you're in good hands with your family." Tom was working hard on keeping his voice even. He focused on Max's unblinking stare. "Well, then, I'll be hearing from you." In, like, twenty-four hours he'd be hearing, and that was going to be when he walked in her door. He'd made up his mind. He hoped she could too.

"Thanks for getting things fixed up there, Riley. I'll call." And with that she hung up the phone.

Max jumped down from the counter. "I think she likes you, Dad."

"I think she does too. How'd you like to go visit a farm in Indiana?"

"Cool! Can I ride a horse?"

"All I know is they have no pigs." Tom poured milk into his pancake mix bowl and got it all stirred up. "We've got a big day ahead of us, pal. We're going to have to get all my stuff moved. I'll get airplane tickets for tomorrow. Better call your mom too."

Max started jumping all over the kitchen. "Yipeee! We're gonna fly in an airplane! We're gonna go to a farm! We're gonna go get Marla!"

"First things first. Let's eat!" Tom turned on the electric skillet. If there was even a drop of a chance that Marla Meyers might be "mooning" over him, he'd be a complete idiot not to pursue her to the ends of the earth. Or even to a farm in Centerville, Indiana.

The next morning she got up earlier than the rooster and hit the naked page. She was going to throw herself into working so she didn't have a minute to think about why she'd let Tom Riley go on the phone. Just like that. She said she'd call every three days. It seemed like a good idea at the moment. Now she'd rather it was every three hours.

Well, now. This would give her time to think. To sort out her feelings for Tom. She was going to take this very, very slowly.

By seven she had written almost two chapters and was nearing the end of the book.

I never liked it when nice people got hurt. Jake O'Shay was a nice guy and it turned out badly for him. It was so clear to me now how, every step I took in the case, O'Shay was ahead of me.

I watched O'Shay take Rose in his arms and

*look deep into her sweet blue. Eyes like those, you
just wanted them to be innocent. "I'll wait for
you. I love you, Rose," he told her.*

*At least the judge only gave her two years in
Washington State Mental Hospital. You can't
call it murder when she never touched Crantz.
Just scared him to death. Ghosts. I shivered.
O'Shay kissed his wife good-bye.*

*I walked out of the courtroom office and into
the Seattle rain. The idea of a wife crossed my
mind. Someone to dry out my overcoat and make
me a warm supper. Maybe I'd go over to the Dog-
house Café and have Kelly make me a bowl of
chili. I loved her chili.*

Boy, this was turning into a romance novel,
Marla thought. Oh well, it was about time for
Mike Mason to get a little action.

"Hey, Marla," her dad called up the stairs. "I'm
sorry to break into your writing, but I need a
hand."

"Hang on, Dad." She slipped her tennis shoes
back on and came down. "What's up?"

"That dang junction on the south irrigation
ditch is stuck open. I need you to hold the thing
up while I screw it back together."

"Sure." They walked together out of the house
and toward the back end of the field. "Who called
so early?" Marla asked.

"Oh, some salesman. Figured to catch a farmer early, I guess. We're gonna flood the soybeans if we don't get this closed off. Glad you're here."

"Me too, Dad." Marla smiled. Without all the troubles between her and her stepmom, the farm felt like home again. The way it used to when her mom was alive.

A deep, ancient memory stirred in her, of walking beside her dad like this, her child-sized legs working hard to keep up with his long strides. Of him slowing down for her, finally lifting her up on his shoulders, and singing "Sugar in the Mornin'" while they walked, in his deep baritone voice.

"I love you, Dad," she said quietly.

"I love you too, honey." He looked at her and smiled. They kept on toward the south ditch.

"Now, you just hold that section up a little and I'll slip this bolt in and tighten it back up. You're gonna have to stretch out, there."

Marla checked out the situation and figured there was no way but the snake way. That was down on her belly in the dirt. She scrunched down and grabbed the metal contraption, holding it back into its hinge. The brown water splashed against her arms.

"Okay . . ." Her dad leaned in and jimmied the bolt in place, then took a pair of pliers and a crimp bolt out of his overalls pocket. He was on his knees getting them tightened up when the bank gave way a little.

"Whoa!" He caught the partition, but still went in the water sideways. Marla let go just as a big, muddy splash hit her straight in the face. She sputtered and scrambled up. Her dad stood chest-high in the ditch, laughing at her.

"Oh, *very* funny." She shook herself like a dog.

"Hey, now, don't tell me you haven't paid good money to get mud on your face back in New York City." Her dad found a hold and hoisted himself out of the water, with Marla grabbing his arm on the way up.

"Here." He took out his blue bandanna and wiped at her face. Unfortunately, the bandanna was soaked too. He wrung it out and started over. "There, you can see, at least." He put a hand around her shoulder and gave her a squeeze. "That's my girl."

They walked back to the house with the unexpected February sun warming her shoulders. Her hair started to dry a little. She twisted it into a rope and stuck it in the back of her sweatshirt. Dad's shoes made that squeaky sound wet shoes made. What a pair.

"I suppose I should tell you that Tom Riley is on his way to Indiana."

She stopped dead in her tracks. "What? Was

that who called so early? Why, Walt Meyers, you fibber."

"Did not; he *is* some kinda salesman. He sells insurance. I just thought I better tell you so you'll hose off or something. They caught an early flight, but it'll be hours before they get here."

"They?"

"I invited him to bring his son."

"Oh, you *invited* them, did you?"

"Oh, now, Marla Beth Meyers, you're in love with him. I'm not going to get any peace at all until you get this worked out. Besides, I want to meet both of them. Now, can we get back to the house before I freeze?"

Marla shuffled her muddy Keds in the dust as they walked. "For heaven's sake, Pop. I just don't know. I look a terrible mess. It's a damn good thing you decided to 'fess up."

"Watch your mouth, young lady." Walt chuckled to himself as they got back to the porch.

"I've got nothing to wear. I'm gonna clean up and drive into town. I'll get Jeannie to open the shop up early and pick me out a dress."

"Sounds good. I'll put on a meat loaf for dinner."

"Okay, I get upstairs, you take downstairs. You have to sweep out the house before they get here."

"Deal."

She ran up the stairs and stripped her wet

muddy clothes off to jump into the shower. It would only take her two hours to clean up, get into town and back. Then she could help her dad with supper. Maybe she'd bake a pie.

Marla was shivering, waiting for the water to warm up. She stopped and looked at her mud-streaked face in the bathroom mirror. A very big smile climbed up out of her heart and broke out all over her face. He was on his way. She danced naked around the aqua chenille bath mat and finally jumped in the shower. In her finest off-key singing voice, she sang her new favorite song, "Moonglow."

She drove too fast in her blue Ford Escort rental. A beat-up old white station wagon was behind her for most of the short drive to Centerville, but she lost it as she turned onto a side street. It was just nine, so Jeannie was probably inside setting up her register. If she banged on the door, she'd let her in. Jeannie understood a fashion emergency.

"Why, Marla Meyers! Come in, honey. What'd you do, forget to pack all your beautiful New York clothes?"

"Of course I did! Someone special's coming over and I need a nice dress. Besides, I like your clothes way better than all that high-fashion craziness. You know I always have."

Marla and Jeannie were already flipping

through the rack, with Jeannie gathering every bit of information possible out of Marla as to the man and the occasion. Marla had three things flung over her arm in ten minutes. Jeannie came up with two more, and Marla was in the dressing room in fifteen. She came out in another fifteen wearing her best choice.

"How about this one?" It was a red-knit, almost cashmere two-piece dress that clung to all her curves but still had room for comfortable movement.

"Nope. You said his son was coming too. Try the blue. It brings out your eyes."

She tried the blue. A pale blue sweater the exact shade of her eyes. Jeannie was right. It was a very simple shape. A classic low-cut sweater that just skimmed her shoulders. Not too daring, but just enough. Jeannie matched it with a pleated skirt the same color that went quite long. It had a nice flow. With navy flats, this could be good.

"Fabulous," Jeannie declared. Marla changed back into her jeans and T-shirt and her brown suede hippie jacket she'd stored at her dad's place all this time. It had fringe.

"Just run along, now, I'll send you a bill to Walt's house. I know you're in a hurry. 'Bye, hon, you come back in before you leave, okay?"

"I sure will, Jeannie. Thanks so much." Marla

walked out with her pink box and headed to her car. She stopped for a minute and shielded her eyes against the morning sun. That same white station wagon was parked right behind her.

An old, frightened feeling swept over her as Ivy Richardson came out of the station wagon and walked toward her.

"Why, Marla. How nice to see you."

"Ivy."

Ivy came up close to her and took hold of her hand, giving it a gentle pat. "I was hoping I might run into you. I thought we might have a little chat, just the two of us. Kind of set things straight, you know?"

Maybe clearing the air would be good. Marla remembered Anton's words about settling up the past so she could move on. She looked down at Ivy, with her gray-streaked hair pulled tight into a scraggly ponytail. She looked so much older than even two years ago. "That would be nice, Ivy. I'll be in town for the rest of this week. We could have a cup of coffee at the Corral."

"I'm going to visit my sister in Dayton tomorrow. Do you think we might have our little chat right now? My place isn't too far from here. I have something of your mother's I'd like to give you."

"You do?"

"Yes, somehow I ended up with her wedding

dress. I imagine you'd like that, wouldn't you?" Ivy's voice was dead calm. She stared into Marla's face with an unnerving steadiness.

Her mother's wedding dress. Marla fought to keep her emotions, and her tongue, under control. It was quite a gesture for Ivy to surrender such a precious item. "That would be very nice. Yes, I will come now. How about I follow you?"

"That's lovely. I'll make tea. You just follow me. It's south of town, you know, my family's old place."

"Yes, I know the place." Marla walked to her car and waved to Ivy. Ivy opened her driver's-side door and paused for a minute. Marla started her car and watched Ivy pull out a red car coat and slip it on, then slide in the white wagon and turn the ignition. They pulled out together.

Marla's heart was pounding. She wasn't a child anymore. Ivy couldn't hurt her now.

Chapter Eighteen

MY HEART STOOD STILL

Walt Meyers stood on the front porch and saw a red sedan coming down the driveway. A rental car. But not Marla's blue Ford Escort. He looked at his watch. Two-thirty. The car parked by the house and the driver's-side door opened. A good-looking dark-haired man stepped out of the car. It must be Tom. Walt walked out to meet him. Tom Riley was not going to like what he had to say.

"Tom Riley? Walt Meyers."

"Nice to meet you in person, sir." They shook hands.

"Is your son in the car?"

"No, he decided to give me a head start. I left him with his aunt and uncle."

"That's good. That's good. Come inside, Tom."

Marla's dad opened the screen door and let Tom inside. Tom sensed something was off. Maybe Walt Meyers wasn't so glad to see him.

A police officer sat at the kitchen table. Tom's heart twisted like a knife.

"Oh God, Walt, what is it? Where's Marla?"

"She's missing, son. She went off this morning about nine o'clock."

"How could this happen?" Tom strode into the kitchen and straight to the officer. "Tell me everything."

The policeman looked at Walt, who nodded. "Mr. Riley, is it? We know she went to a local dress shop and left there about nine-thirty. The owner of the shop wasn't in, but a clerk said there was a bill to Marla made out with the time stamped on it.

Tom went over to the kitchen counter, pressed his head against a cupboard, and slammed his fists on the white kitchen tile. All day he'd been haunted with the feeling that Marla still wasn't safe. He'd brushed it aside over and over again as just a habit from worrying about her for days on end, just his overactive imagination. How could she possibly be in any danger at home in Indiana?

"What've you got?" he asked gravely.

"We contacted the man she went out with Saturday night. Raef Nielsen. He's completely in the clear," the officer replied.

"She went out on a date?" Tom's insides went completely bad on him.

"Just dinner with an old school friend, Tom. We'll talk about it later," said Walt.

Just then the phone rang. Walt made a quick move, but the officer held up his hand for him to slow down. He turned on some equipment. On the second ring, Walt grabbed the receiver. The phone went on speaker and the tape began to record everything. Tom held his breath.

"Meyers."

"Walt? This is Jeannie. I am just beside myself. I'm so sorry I wasn't here when you needed me. I went into Dayton for some supplies."

"Jeannie." Walt stopped her and got right to the point. "Try and remember anything you can about Marla's visit. It was about nine o'clock. You weren't open yet."

"Yes, yes. She knocked on the window and I opened up. She stayed about a half hour, Walt. She's a quick shopper. Walt? I don't know if it's important, but I saw her talking to Ivy out in the street. They talked a few minutes, then they both got in separate cars and drove off. I didn't think much about it until I heard what happened. Maybe Ivy knows something. That's all I can think of."

"Thanks, Jeannie. You call us again if anything comes to mind." Walt ran his hand through his thin white hair and set the receiver back on the hook.

"Stan, we better get out to Ivy's house. She's got no phone out there. It's her folks' old place, you know," Walt said to the officer. "Tom, Ivy's my ex-wife."

"We're waiting on the county guys to show, Walt. I have to stay close to town for about an hour and Reggie's stuck doing the radio."

Tom paced the length of the kitchen nervously. "An hour's too long. Walt, you know the way. We just need to ask her some questions. Let's go now."

"Okay. I've got a cell phone, Stan, we'll call in if we run into any kind of real trouble. We'll take my truck. She knows it and it won't scare her off to see me coming. She's been pretty reclusive since we split up. Folks have talked."

"Tell me about it on the way." Tom strode toward the door.

Tom saw the dim lights of Ivy Richardson's place about fifty yards from the road. The windows were heavy with dirt, and curtains prevented any clear view of the interior.

He felt it, though. There was a bad air and it filled his head and his lungs and made him crazy. He grabbed the dashboard as they ran over the ruts in the road. The truck came to an abrupt stop a dozen yards away from the house. Walt shut off the lights.

"Walt, I know this is gonna sound like I'm nuts, but I have a bad feeling. I'm going in slow. You stay right here. You can use your cell phone to call Stan for help if I yell." Walt nodded. Tom got out of the truck quietly.

The sun had moved behind a hill and left Ivy's house in blue shadows. There was light enough for Tom to see what bad shape the place was in: shutters broken, paint peeling. He moved to a side window and found himself a thick log to stand on. Hidden in an overgrown laurel shrub, he looked in. There was Ivy, sitting at a table, talking to someone just as nice as you please. He couldn't hear the words, but she seemed calm. He watched her pour what looked like tea from a dull white teapot.

He had to shift himself to see who she was with. There she was. It was Marla in the other chair. He saw the back of her long, beautiful blonde hair. She was nodding.

Now, wouldn't this just take the cake? Here he came all the way from New York, to come busting in on Marla having a tea party with her stepmom. Probably making up and having a heart-to-heart.

He sat on the log. His adrenaline was so high his heart was rapid-fire. He took a deep breath and let it out. There was only one thing wrong.

His guts. His damn guts were still twisting in the wind, telling him something was bad. That Marla needed him.

He picked up the log and repositioned it for a better look. He'd just give this thing one last shot before he made a fool of himself yet one more time.

He got as close as possible to the windowpane and glanced in. Yes, Marla was still there, still moving her head. Ivy was still chatting. He watched Marla's head shake no this time. And there, at the end of her long hair, he saw her hands behind her back, tied with rope. She was twisting that rope as hard as she could.

Tom moved fast. The front door was locked. He broke it down in one shoulder slam. Ivy turned and with a surprisingly fast response time, threw the teapot straight at him, but her seventy-year-old pitch wasn't strong enough. It clattered on the floor, spilling its contents.

"Now look what you've done. I'll get blamed for that, you know, I'll get beat, and it's all your fault," Ivy screamed at him. Tom went straight for Marla. Her blue eyes were wide and angry. A piece of duct tape covered her mouth. She had on a wedding dress. Her feet were tied too.

Without hesitation, Tom picked Marla carefully up out of the chair, pulling her so high her tied hands cleared the chair's back. He turned and carried the tied and taped Marla out the broken door in seconds, kicking the broken teapot out of his way. As he strode out to the truck, he heard Ivy's voice screaming about the spilled tea and how she was going to get blamed.

Walt held the passenger door open for Marla and Tom set her inside the cab.

"I called in. They'll be here soon," Walt said. He was working on Marla's hand ropes.

"Marla, I'm so sorry, but I'm gonna have to rip this tape off of your mouth," Tom warned her, then grabbed a corner and gave it a quick yank. She screamed loud.

"Let me loose. I'm gonna go kill me an old woman," Marla screamed.

"Marla, your dad called the police. They'll take care of Ivy." Tom tried to soothe her. "Is that a wedding dress you have on?"

She let out another gut-wrenching scream.

"Now, Marla, let's be reasonable. You'll hurt her." Tom was laughing that kind of crazy, relieved laughter and ripping at her leg ropes. "Hold still, now. I've almost got it."

She burst free and jumped out of the truck so fast she pushed past him before he had a chance to think. She was hell-bent for Ivy's front door. That was one mad woman.

"Marla, now, Marla!" Tom ran after her. "She's nuts. She's in her own private hell. Sweetheart, please stop." He beat her to the door and blocked it with his body.

"Get out of my way, Tom Riley."

"No, I can't let you do it, Marla. It's bad karma."

She looked straight in his eyes, then laughed. "Bad karma! That's your friend Rama talking. Or Anton. All right. I promise." Tom relaxed his stance and took a step toward her. She crouched like a linebacker and made a rush for the door. He countered. She stopped.

"Marla! You'll ruin that pretty dress. And you're going to need it when you marry me." Tom stayed ready. She looked down at herself, then back up at him. Straightening up to her full height, she smoothed the satin front of the gown out and smiled.

Just then a squad car rolled up the driveway.

Tom took three steps and caught her in his arms. She let him.

"What the hell are you doing in Indiana, Tom Riley?"

"Just doing my job, ma'am."

"You're just plain crazy, Riley."

"I love you, Marla. I'm crazy in love with you."

She tried to say something, but he covered her mouth with a kiss that showed her he meant what he said. He was in love with Marla Meyers.

Chapter Nineteen

ISN'T IT ROMANTIC?

Tom glanced up as Marla descended the stairway. She looked like a dream. A pale blue dream with light pink lips. Her hair was tied back with a white scarf. He noticed the light pink fingernails. He noticed the long, smooth, tan legs under the flowing pleated skirt. A Bahama tan. He noticed how the sweater curved around her full breasts.

Tom cleared his throat. Marla smiled and walked right past him into the kitchen.

Tom got up and followed her, having regained his composure—sort of.

"I'm starved. Did you fix me one?" she said to no one in particular.

"Right here, Marla, we put extra catsup on it. Your dad said you liked extra catsup, like me." Max pointed at the plate. Tom watched Max drink down his second glass of lemonade. That boy sure had been hungry and thirsty after their long drive from the Dayton airport. It was incredibly kind of his family to help out with the cost and flying Max down in person.

A warm fire burned in a small kitchen wood-stove. Walt was shuffling a deck of cards. Max had cleared his plate off the table and awaited the deal. They looked like two old-timers settling in for a good stretch of poker. But it was gin rummy, Tom heard. Walt better be ready. Max was one lucky gin player. A soft radio was playing something with a country twang.

Marla sat at the red-speckled laminated kitchen table with its chrome edges and looked like the picture of a fifties housewife. Tom went to get himself a glass of water on that "wife" thought.

It had been two years since his divorce. Two long years of canned soup and dry baloney. Of an empty bed and no one to drink coffee with on Sunday morning.

He had all but proposed to Marla the other night out at Ivy Richardson's place. She just hadn't answered him. It was now Thursday.

They'd all needed time to sort out the wild

events of the past few weeks. He'd needed time to go get Max and bring him back.

He'd need a two-week vacation to recover from the adrenaline rush this dame had taken him on. And the ride wasn't over yet.

She picked up her meat loaf sandwich and took a huge bite. A blob of catsup stuck on the side of her mouth. Her dad made some gesture at her and she grabbed a napkin while she chewed, wiping her mouth at the same time. Yep, he had it bad for Marla Meyers.

Walt saved the day with some chitchat. "Glad you could spend some time with us, Tom." Walt had a strange sparkle in his eye. Uh-oh, what was the old fox up to now?

"Just doing my job, sir," Tom answered, staring at Marla from his position against the kitchen counter.

"Well, thanks for helping my daughter. She's always been a handful. Use to ride a horse bareback all over the county."

"Wow, you did? Do you guys have a horse?" Max said as he looked up from his cards.

"Yep. I'll let you feed her tonight. Daisy Mae's pretty old, but I'm sure she wouldn't mind a trot. We'll see to giving you a ride," Walt answered.

"Dad, did you hear that? I get to ride a real horse on a real farm."

"Those pony rides in Central Park were Max's favorite till he got a little big for them. He's been trying to get the mounted policemen to give him a ride all this year," Tom explained to Walt.

"I was horse crazy when I was ten too, Max. I read all these horse stories like *Black Beauty* and *Misty of Chincoteague*. I used to pretend I was in a horse race," Marla said to Max.

"I like to read too," Max answered, rearranging his hand and discarding a card.

Walt picked up the discard. "When she wasn't on a horse, she was reading a book or writing her stories up in the barn. Guess that's how she got to be a famous writer. She's on her tenth Mike Mason now. Did you know?"

Tom's whole body did electroshock. His water glass slipped right out of his hand and crashed onto the black-and-white-checked floor. Holy Mother of God. He uttered a long *"Uhhhhhhhhhhh,"* like all the air was let out of him.

Max's eyes were big as lollipops. He all but threw his cards in the air. "Dad, that's your favorite! Dad! M. B. Kerlin is Marla!"

Marla had frozen midbite. She had lettuce sticking out of her mouth, both elbows on the table, and a meat loaf sandwich poised before her face.

Walt held his cards very still in front of him. Then he slowly pushed his reading glasses up his nose a little, discarded a queen, and a huge-ass grin broke out all over his face. Walt looked like he was going to expire from holding in his laughter. "Yep, Marla Beth Kerlin. Kerlin was her mother's maiden name." Finally he wheezed out an endless whooping laugh.

Max caught the wave and the two of them, Walt and Max, had tears streaming down their cheeks, slapping the table, unable to control themselves.

Marla rose and got the broom and dustpan and a towel. After sopping up the water, she quietly swept up the glass. Tom watched her, speechless. As soon as she poured the shards in the trash, he grabbed her, broom and all.

"Tell me the truth. Are you the author of Mike Mason mysteries?"

"Oh, for pity's sake. Don't you think a woman could have written him?"

He pulled her into him, hugging her around her glorious shapely waist. Her broom handle smacked him in the head.

"Ouch. My God, you have got to be the most amazing woman on the planet. I've already asked you once. I'm asking again. Will you marry me?"

"Yeah, Marla, marry us!" Max jumped out of his chair and cheered.

"Max, you and me better make a new plan." Walt wiped his eyes and cheek with his fresh bandanna and got up from his chair. "Let's leave these two lovebirds to talk. We'll go into town and catch a movie and a hamburger."

"That sounds just swell, Walt." Max paused. "But wait a sec." Max picked up his cards, drew one out, and set it on the table. "Gin. I win. Let me know how it turns out, okay, Dad?" Walt and Max made a hasty exit, with hats and coats flying. Tom heard the screen door smack shut. A very nice sound.

He still had Marla in his arms. Now he had her alone. He ran his lips up her long, graceful neck and across the top of her mouth. He breathed in her splendor. Holding her hands in his, he put his nose on her nose.

"Marla, I know I'm nobody, but I'm yours. I'm completely in love with you. All I have to offer you is a tacky bungalow and a great ten-year-old son. My income will buy us hamburgers from McDonald's and clothes from Wal-Mart. I'm like an out-of-date computer, but if we put a few more memory chips in and the right software, I can be upgraded."

"Shut up and kiss me, Riley." Marla dropped the broom and pan on the floor and pressed her entire body against him. Her leg wound around his and she moved her hips in a slow motion that made every part of him come alive like he'd been in the Ice Age and this was the big, big thaw. He groaned and put his hand up to cover her breast.

The sweater she was almost wearing let the sweet round flesh spill out. He slid down the fabric and took her into his mouth. He ran his other hand up her leg and right up against her panties. She was dripping wet. A sound came out of her mouth, right next to his ear, that made him insane. He slid his fingers between the silky material and her soft, sweet flesh. His thumb pressed into her most sensitive spot. He ran his tongue over her nipple. His fingers slid into her. She arched back and cried out.

His tongue slid up her neck and found her lips. Into her mouth, the heat was so intense between them that he thought he would explode. He slowly withdrew his hands, kissing her mouth wet with desire, and picked her up in his arms. She was a panting, hungry, wild creature nestled against him, mouthing his neck. He made it up the stairs, and she pointed to a door with her foot.

He kicked the door closed behind them. He laid her down on the pale yellow sheets. He wanted to rip her clothes off, but instead he slowly peeled off her sweater, unhooked her lacy bra, and slid the pleated skirt off of her, panties and all. When she was completely undone, he stopped and looked at her. She was wild-haired and wild-eyed, and a sweet smile spread over her wet, swollen lips.

She sat up slowly and pulled him closer. Her fingers fumbled with his jeans button a little, then slid the zipper open. Her eyes rested on his bulging, throbbing silk shorts. Her hands rested on them for a moment, then she tore down his underwear.

Those and his pants fell around his ankles and he danced out of them, kicking his loafers off. She grabbed the two ends of his shirttail and gave a mighty yank, ripping his shirt completely off. This time he'd come prepared, and he pulled his miles of condoms out of the pants pocket on the floor.

At long last, he lowered himself onto her. He just let every part of her touch every part of him and savored her body for as long as he possibly could, then he pushed himself into her sweetness. She welcomed him with everything she had.

Her eyelashes brushed open against the pillow. She and Tom were woven together, close as a breath. She didn't move, but sank into the feeling of his body next to hers. His breathing was quiet and steady. She felt . . . happy.

She closed her eyes again and drifted into visions. Visions of their lovemaking; so amazing, so tender. Had she ever really made love before this?

Tom Riley was a most gifted and talented man. His kisses were enough to send her body into ecstasy again and again.

She tried to picture their life together. The time they spent with Max in the museum. What their days and nights would look like in Manhattan. All she got was a fog. How would they fit their lives together? So much to consider.

Instead she tried to picture a wedding. Suddenly a vision of Anton in a pink chiffon bridesmaid's dress reared up before her. The bet!

She drew in her breath sharply. Tom opened his eyes. Then he kissed her softly on her closest cheek and across her mouth. Shifting, he wrapped his arms around her and pulled her up next to him.

"We've done it now," he spoke softly. "I'll never be able to look at you again without knowing what heaven is like." He propped them both up a little and looked around the room.

"There's a doll over there with teeth and she's looking at us."

"She's an antique. Too old to bite you. This is the room I grew up in."

"And you grew up so nicely." He ran his hands over her belly.

"I have to tell you that we have just lost a bet."

"What's that?" Tom played with a curl under her ear.

"Anton. He bet me a photo shoot with a famous friend of his I'd end up in bed with you before the thirty days were up. And now look, we've spoiled it."

"You're going to tell him?"

"It's no use trying to hide it; he always knows exactly what I've been up to."

"What was his end of it?"

"Never mind. I'll tell you later. We better get ourselves together. It's awfully quiet in the house."

"I'll go down first."

A few minutes later Marla was still dressing while Tom walked downstairs, then came back up.

"The truck is still gone." He moved in and took her up against him, kissing her, moving his lips over her temples and eyelids. He brushed back her hair with his fingertips.

"I'd say we had a good three hours." She pressed into him.

"I seem to recall proposing to you."

"You did. In the kitchen, and once at a crazy woman's house." Marla ran her hands up inside his torn shirt. His back was hard and muscled.

She heard a car crackling up the gravel driveway. Pulling her sweater into place, she went to the window.

"Oh dear. It's Raef."

Tom came beside her and looked. "Hmm, a Porsche. A red Carrera convertible, even. Was this the school chum date?"

"I'll go down."

"Yes, I guess so," Tom said.

Marla walked down the stairs. She heard Tom coming down after her. This was swell.

Raef got out of his Porsche wearing a Ralph Lauren polo shirt and tan khakis. A bouquet of red roses and baby's breath in one hand, a large box of Godiva chocolates in the other. He marched up the porch steps like a man with a mission.

Marla opened the screen door and stood holding it open. "Raef. What brings you out?"

"You, Marla. I couldn't stop thinking about you after I saw you in town." He came onto the porch. "I heard about Ivy, and I wanted to be sure you were all right. I care about you. I know it's been ten years, but I need to know if there's a chance for us."

Behind her, Tom cleared his throat. She turned to see him leaning casually up against the doorjamb. His shirt, which had no buttons left, hung open. His gorgeous chest was exposed. He was magnificent, and sexy, and . . .

She turned back to Raef. "I'm sorry you came all the way out here, Raef, but I'm getting married," she said. It sounded very good to her.

Raef's face fell into a frown. "Well, Marla, I wish you well." He smiled a half-smile and went back down the steps to his car.

"Oh, Raef, just a minute." Marla ran after him.

Tom watched her say a few words, then kiss Raef on the cheek. She came back up the stairs, and Tom met her on the porch. "What was that last bit?"

"I couldn't let him leave without knowing I used to have a crush on him in high school. Better to send them away with some ego intact. He gave me the chocolates for telling him that." She waved the box like a victorious prizewinner. He wrapped her up and spun her around, then stopped and kissed her.

"Did I hear you tell Mr. Roses you were getting married? Was that a yes, then?"

"That?" Marla brought the box of chocolates back around, opened it up, and casually looked the selection over. Setting them on an end table, she bit into something dark and chewy, and talked with her mouth full. "It was the first thing I thought of to get rid of him. I hate red roses." Marla looked in his eyes and lied with a smile.

She'd known since she saw Tom breaking down Ivy's door to save her that she was going to marry him. Besides that, any man who would fly to Indiana to find her was obviously in love. Then there was his kiss. It curled her toes.

"I'll try and remember that."

"Other than that"—she swallowed her chocolate—"I guess I will marry you."

"So then, that would make me, what? The luckiest guy on the planet?" He kissed her again, chocolate-filled and all.

"No, that would be me fulfilling my cosmic destiny, if you ask Anton." She kissed him back. "I love you, Tom. Tom?"

"Mmmm?

"The movie gets out at nine-thirty. We have two more hours."

He took her hand and led her back in the house, back upstairs, and back into his arms.

Chapter Twenty

A SUNDAY
KIND OF LOVE

On July Fourth, Marla married Tom in a beautiful garden she and her father and Tom had created in the back of the house in Indiana.

Marla had decided to wear her grandmother's wedding dress after all. Her mom's had been through a few too many scuffles. She found Grandma's in a trunk in her father's attic. Her mother had saved it perfectly, wrapped in tissue and a cotton sheet.

Grandma was a daring young woman who married her beau before he went off to World War II. Her dress was antique satin, cut on a bias, with a sweetheart neckline. It swirled around Marla's body every step she took.

Her hair was pinned with gardenias, and she carried three more in a 1930s spray bouquet. She felt her heart beating wildly under her satin gown. At least she knew Paris wasn't going to step on her train this time, because she didn't have one. A golden net snood took its place. Besides, bridesmaids go first in real weddings.

Marla saw that Paris was actually grinning at her from under the gazebo. She'd made her wear a rose-pink tea-length reproduction of a 1930s dress. Beside her, red-eyed, mopping his tears with a pink chiffon handkerchief, was Anton in a perfectly divine linen suit with cream and white linen Italian loafers to match. He sported a finely woven straw fedora to top it off. She let out a little squeak of relief. He may have insisted on being a bridesmaid, but at least he wasn't in pink chiffon drag. Decent of him.

Next came Tom's youngest sister, Kathleen, in the same pretty rose-colored floaty silk as Paris. The girls all carried summer flower bouquets and wore big matching picture hats.

Marla felt the butterflies in her stomach take flight as she made eye contact with Tom, standing next to the minister.

He was handsome and tan, and his linen suit made him look like he'd stepped out of a picture of gentlemen in the 1930s. Beside him, pulling at the collar of his button-up white oxford shirt and clutching the ring pillow, was Max in his kid-sized linen trousers. He stared at her like she was a princess when she got close enough to kiss his cheek. He didn't even rub it off. She was honored. Tom's brothers-in-law stood up with him. Jim was his best man.

It was a long walk down to Tom. Just once she hit a ripple in the runner and took a lurching, stumbling step. The crowd gasped. Tom's eye-brows shot up; Anton gasped and put a fist to his mouth. Her dad caught her arm and straightened her back up.

"Steady-up, sweetheart, here's the groom." Her dad gave her a little squeeze, then handed her to Tom. The minister smiled as they stepped forward.

A breeze picked up the organza swathed around the gazebo and sent a scatter of white blossoms around them. For a moment, she felt as if her mother had touched her cheek. As if she were standing beside her.

And with this ring, they were wed. Tom kissed his bride. She did love those kisses.

"Save a big kiss for me, Rittley!" Paris yelled. She pushed her way through the mingling well-wishers, grabbed Tom's entire body, and gave him a huge lipstick-smacking face plant.

"Holy cow, Paris, leave some for the bride," he

managed. "And it's *Riley*, as in *Mrs.* Riley. Got that?"

"I thought you'd go by her name, you archaic Neanderthal male." Paris took a pose as the camera flashed, then shrugged. "Oh well, Marla honey, you're in for it now. He'll have you barefoot and pregnant before you know it."

"I'm hoping." Marla winked, then gave Paris a hug.

The wedding dinner was laid out on long tables in a U shape, under a white-and-green-striped awning. Tom's mother, all his aunts, his sisters, and all their husbands and kids had come to the wedding. For an only child like Marla, seeing the big, noisy, happy family was fascinating.

Rita sat with Marla's dad and Max. Marla elbowed Tom when she saw the unmistakable signs of Rita flirting with Walt Meyers. Tom whispered a wild idea in her ear and she rolled her eyes at the thought of Rita living on a farm in her Chanel suits. Max crawled under the white-covered table and came out on the other side next to Tom's sister Rosalee's oldest boy. The two of them promptly disappeared under the table again.

Tom's best man, Jim, clinked his glass with a spoon and stood for a toast.

"A couple days ago, Tom and I staked out the foundation for the house he and Marla are going to build, right over there." He pointed a hundred yards away near a full-grown cottonwood tree. "We're going to miss Tom back in New York, but from the size of the outline, he and Marla will be able to put us all up for an extended stay in a year or so."

"Augh!" Tom groaned. Marla hooked her arm in Tom's and patted his hand.

"Anyway, I know I speak for all of us when I wish Tom and Marla all happiness in love and marriage. *Saludi!*"

The others raised their champagne glasses and echoed Jim's words.

Marla spotted Max and his cousins over by the cake, stealing frosting bits with their little fingers. One little girl with dark curls and a beautiful frothy yellow dress had cake all over her face. Marla giggled and pointed her out to Tom.

The sun pinked up the edge of the sky, and a purple-shadowed darkness fell around them. Stars started popping out. Her dad made some secret sign to Max. They disappeared, and within ten minutes a whistling sound was followed by a truly awesome fireworks display. The excitement went on for a full half hour.

When the grand finale filled the Indiana night sky, the wedding guests oohed and ahhed. Marla slipped away into her old bedroom to change her clothes. Paris tagged along. Flopping herself on the bed, Paris slipped her rose suede strappy shoes off and wiggled her toes.

"Ahhhh. Marla, I'm so happy for you I could spit."

Marla slipped the thick satin straps of her gown off. "Thanks, hon. We've had so much fun. I know you understand me quitting."

"If I had a film offer from a book I'd written, I'd quit too. I can't believe you kept all that a secret for so long. Oh, by the way, speaking of mysteries"— Paris swung her shoes around by one finger— "it was me who broke your black shoe."

Marla twisted around to look at her friend. "Paris, why didn't you tell me?"

"Oh, Riley was being such an ass, and I had triple-PMS, but the reason I was asking for the damn things is I was riddled with guilt and was going to buy you a new pair to replace them. I'm so sorry you tripped. I thought they would hold together anyway. There was only one little stress point."

"You owe me a pair of my favorite shoes, you terrible thing."

"I'll send you some Manolos to make up for it, since you'll be wearing Kmart sneakers now." Paris slid herself off the bed and rearranged herself in Marla's vanity mirror. "What has Mr. Riley decided to do for a living down here in Podunk?"

"Well, for one thing he's going to team-write a couple of mysteries with me. His plots are great. He has a wonderful imagination. Believe it or not, he's decided to take up farming. He's got some great ideas for growing all-organic produce. You know, that's so funny, because the first time I walked into his office the only thing that was out of place was this amazing plant he had managed to grow in the dingiest office corner ever. I guess he has a green thumb and he didn't even know it."

"It'll be just like *Green Acres*. You can wear your diamonds to milk the cow." Paris pulled her hat down low and sulked.

"I know you're jealous, but we'll see each other again. E-mail me every day." Marla finished buttoning her peach linen dress.

"On a computer?"

"Yes, on a computer. Will you get up to speed, dear?" Paris was so technologically resistant. Marla perched a pretty straw picture hat on her head and took a step toward Paris. She put her arm around Paris's waist. "Come on, sweetie, I've got a bouquet with your name written all over it."

"As if." Paris sniffed. "Let's go. Anton, Rita, and I rented a swanky convertible to drive back to Richmond in. I'll have to drink four more glasses of champagne to sleep on those retched scratchy sheets tonight."

"You're so spoiled."

Walking downstairs with Paris, Marla felt all the excitement and emotion of the day bubble up inside. "So this is what this marriage thing feels like. Like getting on a train to a new country."

"Yeah, a bullet train going three hundred miles an hour into downtown Tokyo where no one speaks your language," Paris said.

"Don't be such a cynic, Paris. Trains are fun," Marla replied, then made a funny, surprised sound. "Or a horse-drawn carriage!" She looked out into the yard to see an old buggy with twinkling lights attached to the rims and the horse's reins.

Tom was on the porch waiting for her. "Ready to go, Mrs. Riley?"

"I just have to throw this here bouquet, Mr. Riley." Marla grabbed the sweet william tossing bouquet and waved it in the air, motioning Paris to get into position. She had to tap her foot a little, waiting for the photographers. Wasn't that just the story of her life?

With a highly directed pitch, she landed the bouquet directly in Paris's hands with a thud. Paris juggled it like a hot potato, held on, then posed for the photos.

Tom grabbed Marla and headed her toward the buggy.

"Thomas Riley, Mrs. Thomas, I am so pleased to be driving you both toward your destiny."

"Rama? You're driving this horse? Tom, did you put him up to this?"

"He volunteered to do horse duty, since he was here for the wedding," Tom answered as he gave her a lift into the buggy.

"Rama, have you ever driven a horse and buggy?" Marla leaned out.

"Not in this lifetime, but I have had a long talk with the horse and he has agreed to be driven."

"Oh, that's highly reassuring. Well, this time of night the semis aren't around much, and it's a holiday, so we might make it alive."

Tom put his arm around her. "Don't worry, Marla, I'm not gonna to let anything happen to you. On to the Centerville Hotel, Rama!"

Marla snuggled up against him. "I've never felt safer in my life."

"Be moving forward, there, horsey," Rama called. And for some reason, the horse did.

Epilogue

I married that dame.

Avon Romances—
the best in exceptional authors
and unforgettable novels!